THE
SECRET
HOTEL
IN
BERLIN

BOOKS BY CATHERINE HOKIN

CATHERINE HOKIN

THE
SECRET
HOTEL
IN
BERLIN

bookouture

Published by Bookouture in 2024

An imprint of Storyfire Ltd.
Carmelite House
50 Victoria Embankment
London EC4Y 0DZ

www.bookouture.com

ISBN: 978-1-83790-005-3
eBook ISBN: 978-1-83790-004-6

For my father

PROLOGUE

NOVEMBER 1942

There is a moment somewhere between the first warning siren and the first falling bomb when the earth turns silent and stops.

The air tightens. The ground braces. The sky holds its breath.

Only the planes keep moving.

What happens next is anyone's guess. Perhaps the bomb doors will open; perhaps death will rain down. Perhaps the planes will roar on over Berlin and away. Whatever the outcome, the initial response is the same. Bodies freeze. Brains go blank. Buildings shift on their foundations and become fragile.

People look up, shrink away, crouch down. No one speaks. Words won't help; words won't change anything. As the sky darkens and drones, the only thing certain is fear.

Fear of being caught out in the open as the heavens crack apart. Of being caught deep in a cellar when the lights fail and the oxygen runs out and the water starts rising. Of the streets overhead collapsing back into their bricks and the cellar becoming a tomb. Fear of being caught in the wrong place.

On a cold clear night in November 1942 – as wave after

wave of British Lancaster bombers thicken the skies to a shroud – Lili Rodenberg is very definitely in the wrong place.

She knows where she should be – there's no shortage of options for a woman of her social standing when an air raid threatens Berlin. The obvious choice would be tucked inside a shelter with her family, pretending to hold her nerve. Or bustling round her daughter's bedroom, collecting teddies and coats for the trip downstairs, pretending that the exploding shells are no more frightening than a firework display. Or, as the owner by marriage of the Edel Hotel and – according to the Führer whose opinion is law – its beating heart, where Lili ought to be is centre stage in the Edel. Standing in its palatial foyer or ballroom. Calming her guests. Promising them that, whatever the planes flying over their heads decide to do or not do, the champagne will remain ice-cold and free-flowing. Wherever she chooses to be, she's supposed to stay visible.

Visible is the last thing Lili is choosing to be.

Lili isn't in any of the public spaces she normally commands; she's in the Edel's rabbit warren of a basement. That's not a crime in itself. She could be checking that the hotel's luxurious bomb shelter is ready for use, like a careful owner should. Except she isn't. She's pressed into the shadows of the basement instead. She's waiting for a blacked-out van, or a black-clothed figure, to appear at the end of an access road which – or so she tells herself every time she stands there alone in the dark – hasn't yet come under surveillance. Lili tells herself a lot of things. Not to look up at the sky. Not to think about bombs, not to listen for gunfire. That, because nothing has gone wrong before, nothing will go wrong now. She's working very hard at not being afraid.

The seconds tick by. Lili tries not to count them and cut down what is already far too little time.

She blinks her straining eyes. She crosses and uncrosses her fingers. She offers silent prayers and promises to anyone who might be left to listen. She's about to give up and assume that the chain has failed before it reached her as it's failed before and tonight's delivery won't arrive. Until it does. Until there's the faintest crunch of tyres over gravel and the van is suddenly there and gone again, in a blink-and-miss-it moment.

Now Lili is at the doorway, leaning out as far as she dares, beckoning a crouching figure forward. Hoping that he – or, rarely, she – has the sense to stay close to the small garden's side wall and winter-stripped shrubbery. That they won't sprint through its centre in full view of the wide-windowed suites at the back of the hotel.

Luckily this refugee appears to be less broken than some of the lost souls Lili has previously shepherded. She – because tonight the figure is feminine and the hair slipping from under the dark cap is long – stays low and moves fast. When she reaches the doorway, she doesn't ask questions. She listens intently to all of Lili's whispered instructions, even though none of them are welcoming and they all begin with *don't*.

Don't speak. Don't move around when I get you in there. Don't put your shoes back on no matter how cold your feet get. Don't leave until I come for you; don't put all our lives at risk.

The woman runs along the corridor's dark twists as quiet as a mouse, as quiet as Lili. There is no more whispering. There is leading and following, and two women trusting to luck because – this far into a war that has turned even more monstrous than the one that went before it – what else is there left to trust to?

For the woman on the run, who has learned to prefer night over day, luck means that this stop won't be the final one on her journey.

For Lili, luck means that she will get this latest charge safely into a hiding place before the hotel decides to pour its guests downstairs to the shelter. It means that the hotel detective – who, despite his easy manner and ladled-on charm, is a Gestapo man to his bones – won't notice that Frau Rodenberg isn't where duty demands she should be. That she will get her charge safely out again tomorrow night and get the woman back on her way. And that this won't be the moment when Lili's link in the chain which moves desperate Jews from one cubbyhole to the next is the one that snaps. That one more life will be saved for at least one more night and nobody will be made to pay for Lili's part in this – or in any other – rescue.

It's a lot of luck to trust to. It's not the first time Lili has asked the fates to look kindly on her, and it's a long way from the last time she'll call on them. It's the thinnest of lifelines to put all her faith in.

And yet, so far and against all the odds, it's holding.

PART ONE

CHAPTER 1

MARCH 1929

'I'm not sure what you're doing here, to be honest. You're such a slip of a thing, and Berlin's a challenging place. It moves fast, it never stands still and it's very easy to get swept away. Tougher people than you have made a mess of things because they can't take the pace of it. But here you apparently are, so at least take my advice and be careful. Don't let the city swallow you up.'

Lili's landlady had looked at her new lodger and seen a timid country mouse. Lili had let her. She knew exactly why she'd come to Berlin: to shed her old skin and find a safer one. If being perceived as little and quiet and uncomfortable with questions kept those questions away, Lili would play the mouse as long as she needed to.

And a place that never stands still is exactly what I was hoping to find.

Lili hadn't said that of course. She also hadn't said, 'Don't worry about me – I'm no stranger to cities.' Or explained that Leipzig – where Lili had lived her whole life until she arrived at the Berlin boarding house which would be her new home – was also cosmopolitan and bustling. She'd thanked her landlady for the warning instead and promised to do as she asked and be careful. And she'd hoped very much that the woman's assessment of Berlin's whirling tempo was right.

Which it was. Leipzig is a sleepy little village compared to this.

Spittelmarkt – the area of Berlin which Lili had chosen as her new starting point – burst with an energy that would rival a monkey house. The streets heaved with cars and trams and buses, and with people whose busy lives apparently demanded that they outrun the traffic. Lili quickly realised that stopping to take her bearings would be a mistake. That asking for directions would require a megaphone. Even the crowds edging the pavements and waiting for the policeman to blow his trumpet and create a safe passage across the road surged up on their toes. Spittelmarkt was colourful and loud and chaotic.

And anonymous and thrilling and perfect.

Lili leaped forward with the rest as the cars squealed to a halt, steering herself towards a flower shop whose name was listed in the folder crammed into her bag. She let the crowd carry her and reached her goal without mishap, slipping under the shop's striped awning to take a closer look and planting her feet squarely against the oncoming tide. Luckily, given that she had no great desire to plunge into the crowds again, this shop was far more promising than the others she'd seen. This one ticked every box on her list.

The window displays were as exuberant at close quarters as they'd looked from a distance. There wasn't a spare inch of space on the shelves. Silver buckets jostled for room with brightly painted ceramic and glass vases. Every container was full to the brim with bunches of frilly yellow daffodils and scarlet tulips, with roses in every shade of pink from blush to deep crimson and great swathes of almond blossom. The window held the flowers' perfume at bay, but Lili knew from experience that it would be heady and sweet, its onslaught as vivid as the colours. She peered closer, pressing her face against the well-polished panes. From what she could see of the shop and the cool green and aqua tiles covering its walls, the interior had also been crafted with care. It would have been a haven of calm, if it hadn't been jammed solid with customers.

As Lili pushed the door open, the clamour spilled out, drowning the bell's soft chime. The order requests and the cries of, 'I'm coming,' and, 'Give me a minute and I'll get to you,' rising up from behind the besieged counter were relentless.

Which is perfect too.

As Lili had hoped, the shop wasn't only pretty to look at; business was thriving. Its location close to the U-Bahn station made it the ideal choice for the workers flowing in and out of the area who were in need of a bunch of flowers to say *I love you* or *I'm sorry* with more elegance than their clumsy words ever could.

Who will disappear just as quickly if no one sorts out this muddle.

Lili had been wondering how to introduce herself to the shop's owner and now she knew. She wriggled her way through the foot-tapping customers until she reached the counter's hinged opening. Then she slipped through that, deposited her hat and coat on a nearby stool, and grabbed a handful of the stems scattered across the marble top.

'Let me help you.'

Lili didn't wait for a response from the frazzled woman trying to hold back the throng. She added the last blooms to an almost finished bunch and tied a pink ribbon round the bundle with a practised hand, taking orders from the next two people in line as she did so. She shook her head in a perfect imitation of her mother as a man requested a horribly clashing colour combination and guided him effortlessly towards a prettier choice. She plucked and prinked and wrapped until every bouquet leaving the shop looked as if it had cost twice its value. And when the last customer finally left, she pushed her thick honey-blond hair back into its bun, picked up a broom and began sweeping the fallen leaves and tissue-paper trimmings into a neat pile. Her mother had kept high standards: leaving an untidy floor at the end of the day was as unacceptable as adding orange flowers to a wedding arrangement.

The woman who had battled at Lili's side for the last hour sighed with relief.

'Well, whoever you are, you're a treasure and a godsend – the last hour of the day always seems to run away with me. I assume you've come about the assistant's position?' She nodded to a sign pinned on the door. 'It's yours obviously, and thank goodness for it. And I can't promise anything, but I'll put in a good word for you with the new owners, if any new owners ever appear. Money's tight out there, even for a business as solid as this one.'

And there it was: the third perfect moment of a perfect day, and the key to Lili's new life.

Work hard and be a good German. That's all that matters in the end. That's what will count when this nonsense is over.

Her father had clung hard to those rules his whole life. Now they were all Lili had to guide her, even if hard work and being the very best German he could be hadn't saved him.

And this isn't the time to be dwelling on that.

Lili pushed his voice out of her head. The tears her father's memory inevitably caused would turn her even younger than the eighteen years she could claim, and that wouldn't help her case. She put the broom down, wiped her hand on her skirt and stuck it out for the startled woman to shake.

'That's a really kind offer, so thank you. But I haven't come about the job. I've come to see the books.'

It was done.

There were still lawyers to consult and contracts to sign, but

– with a deposit that had made the owner's eyes shine and finally stop saying, 'But you're barely more than a child' – the flower shop was now firmly Lili's.

It was a heady moment, and a relief after visiting three other businesses who were struggling to get by and not what she wanted at all. She was glad the pavements had quietened a little when she stepped back outside – she needed a moment to stand still.

My new life starts here.

She stared at the shop, her heart bursting with wonder. *It's mine.* She patted the wood trim and the glass and glanced up at the sign: *Berlin Blooms.* That had a nice ring; that could stay. The aqua and green tiles could stay too, but the window displays, as pretty and eye-catching as they were, needed more drama. Lili's head instantly filled with centrepieces which would change with the seasons. A fountain of cherry blossom in April; a rainbow of roses in June. With bouquets fit for every purpose and wallet, wrapped in crisp tissue paper and trailing ribbons which matched the seasons – lemon for spring, orange for autumn, and crimson and gold for Christmas.

Mother would love it; she'd shine in there.

Lili caught her breath in a gulp as a vision of Marie laughing behind the counter rose up and wrong-footed her. Her mother had always had such a zest for life, but the illness that snatched her away far too soon had cared nothing for that.

I'll bring her back; I'll bring her here.

Lili blinked away her tears and slipped her hand into her bag where she kept the fading photograph of her mother tucked into an inside pocket. She'd find an artist who could copy it and capture Marie's beauty.

I'll put her painting behind the counter so she's always with me, cheering me on.

That thought brought the sun out again and lifted her

mood. This was a day for celebration after all, not one for letting sorrows – old or new – take hold of her.

'Storm! Storm! Storm!'

Lili whirled round as rough voices swelled in the distance. It was a mistake; it had to be. Her hearing was playing tricks on her. She'd been lost in Leipzig and grief for a moment or two, but that part of her life was over. That was, after all, what she'd come to Berlin to escape.

'I understand the impulse to leave Leipzig after what you've suffered, my dear, truly I do, especially as you've no family left here. And you certainly have ample resources if that's the route you choose. But give it some thought; that's all I ask. Don't just run – make some kind of a plan. Because they're everywhere, Lili. They're not some sickness confined to Leipzig. And there's no guarantee that things will go any better for our kind in Berlin.'

That was another voice Lili didn't want in her head: Herr Posner, her father's solicitor, and one of his oldest friends. He hadn't been happy at all when she'd sat in his office in the week after her father's death and declared that she was leaving, that she was going to take her inheritance and build a new life in Berlin. He'd told her that was shock talking, which it may have been, but he hadn't changed her mind.

Lili had, however, agreed to make a plan. She didn't want Herr Posner holding her future to ransom because he thought she was deluded by grief and incapable of making good choices. She'd proved to him how well she could balance a set of books. She'd let him make enquiries about flower businesses which might be available for sale in Berlin, and about respectable areas for a young woman on her own to live. And when he'd finally signed all the documents she needed to access her father's estate, she'd persuaded him – by threatening to walk round the city's less reputable pubs until she found someone to help her – to obtain a set of papers that gave her a new name. He'd done it in the end, but he'd still been trying to persuade her that new didn't always mean safety until the day that she left.

He may be right; there may be danger here too. But I'm not the same girl I was in Leipzig. I won't be afraid of them.

It was a brave hope, but it wasn't true.

All it took was a drumbeat and a flag. All it took was the first notes of that godforsaken song and suddenly Lili was frozen to the spot with fear, and Berlin and the present whirled away.

> 'Storm! Storm! Storm!
> Ring the bells from tower to tower!'

'Not again. You think they'd be tired of all the marching and the yelling by now. It never ends.'

Lili looked up from the bridal headpiece she was weaving as Else pushed the damp hair from her eyes. The older woman's face was as faded as her work apron; she was wilting quicker than the shop's flowers in the August heat.

She's tired; she's ready to stop working. She'd be glad to let me step in and run the business instead.

Lili had already told her father that Else was desperate to retire from her position as the flower shop's manager. She'd also told him that she was ready to be finished with school and start running the family business herself. She'd left him in no doubt about her views on the subject. Unfortunately, Benjamin – who'd indulged his daughter's every other whim since her mother had died of Spanish flu in 1919 – was proving unexpectedly stubborn over this one. Every time she brought the subject up, his response was the same.

'You're only seventeen and – despite how much time you've spent there and how much you think you know – you're not ready to take up your mother's mantle. I'll consider the matter in a year or two perhaps, but certainly not before.'

Benjamin had become a brick wall, impervious to Lili's ambitions, and her frustration had become a dead weight. Following in her mother's footsteps as a florist was all Lili had dreamed of since Marie had sat her little daughter on the counter top and taught her that flowers had their own language. It was all she thought about as she chewed her pencil in the schoolroom, longing for the moment when she would be released back to wrapping bouquets and delighting the customers with her clever choices. Imagining them telling their friends that Lili Krauss was a magician, just like her mother had been.

'Lili, are you listening? Can't you hear them? We need to close up and get going. I've no intention of getting caught up in their games.'

The thump of boots against cobbles and the roar of voices finally broke through. Lili stopped daydreaming about building a chain of shops under her brilliant management and turned towards the window. *Games* wasn't the right word. Nothing about the SA – or the brownshirts, as everyone called the latest bully boys running wild around Leipzig – was playful. Especially when it came to their hatred of the city's Jewish population.

> '*Ring the dead out of the grave!*
> *Germany, awake! Awake!*'

Lili shuddered as the lyrics stormed through the still air and in through the open door. That song was bad. The one which included the line 'Only when Jews bleed, are we liberated' made her feel sick.

She dropped the rosebud-studded coronet and crossed to the doorway. She could see the first line of marchers now, waving their flags with the broken cross symbol. The Sturmabteilung, or the SA as it was commonly known, behaved like an army, although it wasn't one, not officially anyway. Its members referred to themselves as *storm troopers* – an expression everyone now used as if it was perfectly normal. They called themselves the protectors of the National Socialists, a new political party which was apparently determined to turn Germany back into the great world power it had been before the war. Lili shuddered as the ugly voices grew louder. She was as patriotic as the next person, but she didn't understand the angry Germany these men wanted to build. They were thugs; they seemed more motivated by hatred than the desire to create anything good. And Else was right: being inside a shop which was known to be Jewish-owned and was directly on their parade route was not a safe place to be.

'Go out the back way, I'll lock up.' She brushed away Else's half-hearted protest. 'Father's supposed to be coming from the synagogue to walk me home. He'll know better than to go outside in the middle of this, but you know what he's like – he fusses; he won't want to break an arrangement. I'll go over there to him instead – it's not far. I'll slip in through the back door and wait inside with him until this horror show's marched past.'

It was a sensible plan, designed to keep everyone out of harm's way. Except Benjamin didn't know better and the mock-soldiers didn't march past and the sensible plan didn't work.

As Lili stepped out onto the pavement and locked the shop up, there he was. Walking down the steps, lost in thought, barely glancing at the hate-filled men streaming towards him and hurling insults at the synagogue and the good people who worshipped there.

He thinks he's protected. He thinks they won't hurt him.

Benjamin was as stubborn in that belief as he was in his determination to keep Lili in school.

'I did my duty. I fought in the war. I've proved that I'm a true German. All this nonsense has nothing to do with me.'

That was his other favourite refrain.

Benjamin held on to his years of service in the Great War as if they'd forged him a suit of armour. He never left the house without the red, gold and black ribbon of his veteran's insignia pinned to his lapel. Being a soldier made him walk tall; it defined him. His war stories were proud things, full of heroes and sacrifice. Unfortunately, the increasingly vocal and popular National Socialist Party didn't share that view. They'd started to accuse the Jewish troops who'd fought as bravely as anyone for the four long years the war lasted of being 'shirking soldiers'. Liars who'd put on a uniform to make themselves look loyal and then ducked out of the battles, or worked as spies and turncoats on behalf of the enemy. They'd started to blame the 'Jewish profiteers' who'd 'milked the war for their own ends' too.

Benjamin dismissed the hatred as nonsensical, as a crank's point of view. He refused to believe that the party's leader, Adolf Hitler, who he referred to as 'the little thug', could ever win over good hearts and minds. Or that that the NSP's virulent antisemitism would ever be tolerated in a country as decent as Germany. And he was proud to be Jewish, but he was prouder still to be German. He said that so often – despite the increasing provocation on the streets – the synagogue's normally mild-mannered rabbi had started to lose patience.

It was a principled position to take, and Lili was proud of her father for speaking up for the truth. Unfortunately, on the tenth of August 1928, neither principles nor the truth mattered.

Nobody could explain afterwards how the fighting began. Everybody knew that, when the SA were marching, fighting always followed. Perhaps it was the communists – riled up by the vicious and antagonistic songs they were meant to be riled up by – who started the violence. Perhaps it was Leipzig's ordinary citizens, sick of seeing their streets taken hostage and still under the illusion they could fight back. Or perhaps it was the SA members themselves – throwing a few punches inside their own ranks, knowing that those punches would spill out and provoke. Not that who started it mattered, in the end.

The marching columns broke formation; the synagogue steps disappeared. Lili stood paralysed as Benjamin lost his footing. As he was engulfed. She moved then. She ran towards him and she started to scream. It was too late. By the time the police decided that things had gone too far – or far enough – Benjamin was a crumpled shape on the ground. Bleeding. Not breathing. Gone.

And I didn't dare to be Jewish for one more minute after that.

Lili came back to the present as the drumbeats grew louder, as boots clashed against stone in an all too familiar rhythm and the marchers marched into view. They wore the same shirts; they carried the same flags and sang the same songs that had destroyed her life eight months earlier. But the columns were wider now and there were louder cheers from the pedestrians who'd stopped to watch. Who raised their arms as one in the National Socialists' attention-grabbing salute.

They're growing in number; they're getting stronger. They're not the flash in the pan Father swore they would be.

Lili took another step back and another as her body started to tremble. Berlin was supposed to be a fresh start, a place where nobody knew about her or her Jewish upbringing. Where she could be anyone she chose to be and couldn't come to harm. But what if she really had made a mistake? What if the Party had an even stronger hold here than they'd carved out in Leipzig? What if her newly drawn-up, and expensive, identification papers failed a more rigorous check than her landlady's cursory glance? Or if the SA really could sniff out Jews the way the vile *Der Stürmer* newspaper said its loyal members could? She fought for a steadying breath as her head began spinning.

I've been a fool; I've been stupid. What if I can't remake myself here? What if Herr Posner was right and nowhere is safe?

Suddenly the money she'd inherited from her father's house and businesses felt like a danger, something that could mark her out and point jealous fingers her way. Suddenly buying the shop – which at her age, and at a time when so many people were struggling to make ends meet would surely draw the wrong kind of attention – didn't feel like a step towards certainty. It felt like a very stupid thing to do. The pavement came rushing as her knees buckled.

'Woah there, are you all right? This isn't a good place to go fainting – you'll get yourself trampled on.'

The man holding her elbow, holding her up, looking down at her in concern, had the kindest brown eyes and a warm smile Lili wanted to believe in.

'It's not them, is it, who's frightened you?'

He nodded to the brownshirts who were now thundering past them.

'Honestly, I know they look and sound awful, but they're nothing to worry about. Berlin's always full of protests about one thing or another. This lot are just the latest ones shouting the loudest. They can't do you any harm.'

Lili's heart sank again. It might as well have been Benjamin talking. Her would-be rescuer was yet another man who couldn't face facts. Another man with too much trust in the world, who couldn't see that hatred of the Jews wasn't *one thing or another* to the National Socialists. It was the flame which warmed their blood.

They can't do you any harm, but they'd make a target out of me.

Everything about him, from his spotless black fedora to his highly polished brogues, signalled wealth and position. Lili stopped looking into his eyes. She didn't need kind smiles or knights whose armour kept them aloof from the world. She needed to build a life no one could touch.

The streets were filling up again, night-time revellers starting to stream out of the station to replace the home-going workers. Nobody was looking at the brownshirts; nobody was looking at her. *Don't let the city swallow you up* was the opposite of good advice.

'Can I get you a taxi? Or could I walk you somewhere?'

He was still talking, still radiating concern. Lili didn't answer him – she didn't have time to waste.

There would be friends one day, and people she could rely on, but not yet. Not until she'd found a safe place. She drew a deep breath, looked up again and met his eyes. She didn't let herself linger there.

'I'm fine. It's nothing. You've been very kind, but please don't bother yourself about me anymore.'

The crowds were thickening again, laughing and shouting, surging across the street, waiting to swallow her. Lili shook herself free of his arm and his protests and plunged in.

CHAPTER 2

MARCH 1990

We should turn Charlie's city notes into guidebooks and leave a copy in each hotel. That would be a different sort of tour for the guests.

Lucy got out of the taxi in Bernauerstraße, brushing the driver's concerns away as politely as she could when he asked her for the second time if she was sure she had the right place. She stared around her as he drove off, tucking her scarf tightly into the neck of her coat before the wind whipped it away. His confusion was hardly surprising.

The first point of call on her Berlin itinerary wasn't the Brandenburg Gate or Museum Island or the tourist-friendly hotel near the Tiergarten where her bag had been sent. Instead, it was a bleak stretch of concrete and sand with all the charm of a building site, which her boss had listed in his notes simply as, *Stop One: Berlin Wall.*

Another Charlie special.

The taxi driver might have been surprised at Lucy's choice of destination, but she wasn't. She was as used to learning her way around a city via its less obvious attractions as she was to walking for miles on the first day she spent in it. Charlie

Compton – the owner of the Compton Hotels chain which had been both her employer and the closest thing she'd had to a family for the last ten years – prided himself on being something of a maverick. When he had a new location in his sights, he didn't start with the building he wanted to buy; he started with the city that housed it. And that required his best managers – and in particular Lucy Stretton, who'd been sitting for a while at the top of that pack – to have very well-worn feet on the ground.

'I don't send my best people out location scouting to gather facts and figures. Any accountant can pull those together, and I'll have already scanned a summary before my staff get on the plane. I need my managers to get a proper feel for the city we're considering buying into. To think about how it's faring. To wander around and soak up the atmosphere and work out what makes it tick. Once they've done that, then they can go and get a feel for the actual hotel and ask themselves the final key questions: does its personality fit with the city, and does it fit with our chain?'

Lucy could still remember every word of the introduction Charlie had given her to his methods when she'd first joined the company at nineteen as a very junior employee. She'd thought it was an odd way of doing things then – she'd assumed that purchasing decisions were made solely on the basis of profit-and-loss sheets. That was certainly the case in the tiny corner of the hospitality business where she'd been learning her trade after school hadn't worked out the way it was meant to. She'd changed her mind within six months of starting her new job, when she'd seen for herself how well the method worked. Compton Hotels were – in the industry's words as well as Charlie's – always ahead of the curve. The chain had become a byword for discreet and distinctive luxury across Europe's key – and up-and-coming – cities. And up and coming was why Lucy was now wandering around the chilly streets of an about-to-be reunited Berlin.

How's the place faring?

It was a good question. It was also one that demanded a very different answer in March 1990 than if she had come at any other time in the city's post-war history. The Berlin Wall had fallen four months before Lucy's arrival, and the consequences of that collapse had been seismic.

Although maybe not as straightforward as the papers would have us believe.

Lucy had never been to Germany before, but once her latest assignment came in, she'd spent hours on her homework. Now she was in the city, what she'd learned about its latest incarnation felt a little one-sided.

The journalists who'd arrived in Berlin as the Wall came down, and were still combing the city for stories, were filing uniformly positive copy. Their reports spilled over with excitement at the city's forthcoming reunification, after almost fifty years spent being split between East and West and squaring up to each other on opposite sides of the Cold War. Lucy could understand why. A successful rejoining of the city's two parts was the easier story to sell; she presumed it was the one most people wanted to hear. But now she was in Berlin for herself, that relentlessly optimistic approach seemed a touch lazy.

The more time she spent wandering its streets, the more Lucy wondered if the gloss painted over the city's rejoined future had been too heavily applied, if the spin was too quick. The will to heal old divisions was undoubtedly there and spurring the politicians on to make quick decisions, but the Berlin Lucy had begun to uncover was a more complicated place than the newspapers made it out to be. Old scars remained highly visible and too often, or at least to her fresh eyes, the differences between the two sides were more vivid than the similarities. For every packed shopping centre decked out in neon and every smart café crammed with equally smart customers in the West, there was a row of homes with crumbling balconies, or an overgrown wasteland, or a factory with its doors padlocked shut in the East. It wasn't long before she stopped needing to check the map to tell her which side the streets had once belonged to.

So how is Berlin faring?

The further Lucy walked, the less sure she was of the right answer to that.

It's in transition; it's on the cusp. It's full of possibilities and pitfalls. It's exciting and it's confusing and I doubt it will ever be an easy place to define.

Whatever the right word to describe it was, she was hooked.

Lucy had stepped off the plane at Tegel Airport with her knowledge of Berlin wrapped round two fixed points: the Nazis and the Wall. It took her less than a day to realise that nothing about the city was that easily anchored. That history in Berlin was instead a shifting, rewritten, continuing process, with as many gaps as certainties in its telling.

The war was there – in the walls heavily pockmarked with bullet and shell holes and the cracked and peeling houses which looked as if they hadn't been touched since 1945. Other than that, the Third Reich had been completely erased, at least on the surface. There were no plaques to identify the buildings where the regime's nightmares had taken shape; she wasn't even sure that those buildings were still standing. There wasn't a definitive site for Hitler's bunker. The Lustgarten parade ground was a weed-tangled mess. And as for the Wall which had bisected the city since 1961 and had been used as a symbol of oppression by the West ever since? It too was quickly on the way to becoming a memory.

Bernauerstraße, Lucy's starting point for the day, hadn't yet – either by accident or by design – moved far past the events of

November 1989 when the Wall was first breached. The section in front of her was still firmly standing, in a long line of concrete slabs which ran down the centre of the street and a preserved section of the death strip which made Lucy shiver. But beyond that?

Two turns away from Bernauerstraße's empty guard tower and Lucy either couldn't see the Wall, or she couldn't imagine it as the solid and forbidding barrier it had previously been. What was left was disjointed and broken, punctured by gaps and crossing places, with diggers standing ready to finish the dismantling job which the celebrating citizens had begun. Some stretches of the death strip – which had once contained tank traps and dog runs and the ever-present threat of a bullet – were choked with weeds; others had been turned into playgrounds. History was already on the march and, although Berlin wasn't yet formally reunited, it was steadily burying its wounds.

And adding a new layer of secrets.

Everything Lucy had associated with the city was hidden beneath a hastily reassembled, if still thinly stretched, public face.

So maybe it's not a surprise I feel so in tune with it. Or so unsettled.

Long-buried emotions had started to bubble, and Lucy didn't need the distraction of that. She had to focus on the place and what it was going to be; that was, after all, what Charlie was paying her to do.

It's the old Berlin I'm meant to be marrying with the new, not the old and new Lucy.

Even with the pep talk, that wasn't easy.

She stood on Museum Island, staring at the shell marks, trying to imagine victorious Soviet armies swarming over the bridge which now contained tourists. She stood in Alexanderplatz, trying and failing to superimpose the Stalinist rallies which had once filled it onto the sprawling square, in the same way she'd struggled to fill the Lustgarten with Nazis. She watched the people, the men and women who looked as ordinary as she did, and couldn't put them into SS uniforms, or into the drab ones worn by the Stasi, the East's apparently almost as frightening secret police. Or imagine them stalking each other as part of the Cold War city's vast network of spies. Lucy couldn't make anything fit with the images she'd carried with her from England, but she couldn't stop looking.

What is it that I'm drawn to here? That it's a place which seems able to forgive all sins? Or that it's a place where it's easy to bury them?

Something about Berlin had definitely got under her skin and that skin was feeling too thin. Lucy stopped walking and gave herself a shake. She had neither the desire nor the time to get lost in her own history, even if she knew better than most that both routes – forgiveness and denial – held their attractions.

Even if I've never been able to work out which would bring me the most peace.

'Oh for goodness' sake, get a grip,' jumped out of her mouth before she could stop it, and turned puzzled heads. She hurried on, her cheeks scarlet, certain at least of one thing: the place had a strong pull. Berlin wasn't like any other city Charlie had sent her to. It wasn't Paris; it didn't come steeped in romance. It wasn't Rome. It wouldn't attract the kind of visitors who wanted to pay homage to a frozen past or tick famous sights off a list. But it would attract visitors in increasing numbers now that the whole city was open, Lucy was as certain as her boss about that.

This is a place to disappear into. To shed your past, or remake it. And whatever hotel we open here needs to be comfortable with that idea. It has to have lived its own stories.

Lucy stopped at a café in the shadow of the Brandenburg

Gate. She needed a moment to regroup, to put the present centre stage.

She pulled out her compact as she waited for her coffee and strudel and tidied the worst of the wind's tugs out of her wayward brown curls. Then she pulled out a folder containing a brief recap of the properties on offer. Post-Wall East Berlin was a fire sale, which was why Charlie's local contact had drawn up a list of hotels on the eastern side for the Compton chain to consider. Most of the luxurious pre-war hotels, like the Adlon and the Kaiserhof, no longer existed – bombing raids and the ferocity of the final battle for the city in 1945 had put paid to them. But a few old fixtures had survived relatively intact and were still limping along as government-run establishments. Hotels which might have lost their character in the years after the war – and even more so after the Wall was built and luxury went to the bottom of the Deutsche Demokratische Republik's priority list – but had retained the excellent bones Charlie insisted on. Lucy had a list of four of those whose ownership was in enough doubt to make them readily available.

Which means that I won't be the only one on the hunt for a good deal.

She glanced at her watch. According to her map, the closest recommendation was less than twenty minutes' walk away, which gave her time to get started on the second stage of her task and make at least one site visit before the light faded. She paid the bill, noting that – despite her reasonably fluent German – the waiter was eager to practise his English and, when she asked, he was very much in favour of the predicted influx of tourists. That augured well for the area. She was about to ask him if he'd heard of the Edel Hotel, but she checked herself. Whatever Charlie might already know about a property, he never provided anything to his managers beyond a street address. First impressions in his book were all about instinct.

Lucy walked along the Unter den Linden and Wilhelm-straße towards the hotel, imagining the approach as a guest might see it. The old Prussian palaces which had once housed the Third Reich's ministries were almost all gone and, like so much of the city, the area was in flux. There were open spaces where grass had crept back in and one or two buildings which looked too tired to be standing. But the location was good, within easy walking distance of the Brandenburg Gate and Museum Island and thick with the kind of history Compton's guests would enjoy. And as for Mohrenstraße itself…

Lucy slowed down and let herself take a moment to admire the huge windows and elegant lines of a long and very grand Belle Époque run of buildings. She took photographs of a set of what looked like art deco carvings above a delicate stone lintel and lingered for a moment by a strip of grass edged with neatly fenced flower beds in a small square partway down the street. There were daffodils nodding in those and cherry trees coming into bud. There was a sense that the area was ready for its next reincarnation. It was certainly a suitable fit for a Compton Hotel, and the property itself was definitely discreet.

She almost walked past the Edel's rather shabby glass-covered canopy. She only stopped because she caught sight of the name on a recessed doorway that was tucked like a secret hideaway between its taller neighbours. Her pulse instantly quickened at that. And then she stepped inside and it started to race.

There was neglect – Lucy couldn't deny it. The interior was brown and beige and worn out. The street-facing windows had lost their sparkle long ago. But there was far more space inside than she'd expected. And there was beauty too, in the curve of the double central staircase with its balcony overlooking the wide foyer, and the gentle dome of the ceiling floating above.

She needs someone to wake her up, that's all. She needs a little love.

Lucy walked further in, noting the details that cheap wall-paper and drab paint hadn't completely erased. A panel covered in brocaded silk paper on a side wall. A checkerboard flash of black and white marble tiles around the edge of a worn strip of lino. Tiny pink and green squares of glass set into the front windows and a set of branching candle sconces lining the stairs. A ballroom that could easily seat two hundred and a smaller room facing a courtyard garden that was perfect for afternoon tea and more intimate parties. There'd been glamour here once; there could be glamour here again. Charlie's voice was suddenly loud in her head.

'There's location and surveys and footfall. They're important. But there's also that moment when you stand at the heart of a building and let yourself breathe it in. When you feel its magic, and it speaks to you, and that's the most important moment of all.'

Lucy understood that – she'd felt magic in a building before. But not like this. There was something else in the Edel, something that ran deeper than any other hotel where she'd said, *Yes, this one fits.*

These stones know people. They know life. This place has lived through so much history, the past is soaked through its walls.

She closed her eyes and let that sense of time past and still present wrap itself around her. Felt her heart rate slow down, not speed up, as *there's a story here waiting to be uncovered; a story which might help me to face mine* slipped unbidden into her head.

Lucy opened her eyes and waited for her stomach to lurch, for her mind to start closing doors and say, *No, don't go there,* the way it always did. It didn't. Instead, she felt oddly at peace.

This is our next hotel.

She wouldn't be visiting any of the other sites on the list; she wouldn't have to defend that decision to Charlie.

There's magic here, and if I can feel it, so will the guests who come through its doors. In whatever way it speaks to them.

And Lucy knew that with absolute certainty, because the Edel was speaking to her.

CHAPTER 3

AUGUST 1933

The Edel was breathtaking.

No matter what mood Lili was in – and today was not a day of good moods – her spirits always lifted as she stepped into its hushed foyer. The hotel had captured her heart on her first visit and held it tight ever since.

Lili had come to a stop two steps in from the front door on that day and let out an extravagant, 'Oh,' which had delighted Marius. She was used to hotels – her flower business serviced a number of mid-range establishments across the city. From its reputation, she'd expected the Edel to be more gracious than those, to be in a different league. She'd expected to be impressed, but she hadn't expected to be dazzled.

The hotel managed to be both grand and personal at the same time. The swan-branched chandelier which dominated the foyer was dripping in crystals, but its bulbs were set to a flattering glow. The ceiling dome was so high, the reception area could have felt intimidating, but the nests of velvet armchairs carefully placed inside printed screens created an intimate feel. Every surface sparkled, but there wasn't the faintest hint of anything as pedestrian as polish – instead little porcelain bowls filled with potpourri filled the air with the warmth of cinnamon and vanilla. And every step Lili took further in revealed more magic.

The velvet- and tulle-swagged ballroom could have stepped out of a fairy tale. The palm court tea room was an oasis. The colour palette – which moved through every shade of green from mint to emerald, accentuated by mauve and cream – was deliberately tuned to be calming. The pages in their silver-and-plum uniforms moved as if they were on castors. Lili had never been anywhere which so effortlessly combined luxury with comfort. But that was only one side of the spell. The feeling of security which had instantly wrapped round her was the strongest part of the pull. To step inside the Edel was to step inside a cocoon.

Except the cocoon's well and truly split open today. How can I ever feel safe here again, now they've found their way in?

Lili's eyes filled with tears, but she brushed them sharply away. She didn't have time for tears or for regrets, although she was full of those.

I should never have got involved with him, or his hotel. I should have listened to my instincts and turned him away.

Marius and his beautiful hotel. What she wanted; what she couldn't have.

Lili stared at the book lying open on the desk, wishing she had the courage to grab a pen and score out the entry he'd written there. Wishing with all her head if not her heart that she could turn the clock back to the day three months earlier when Marius had overcome her defences in the flower market and rewrite the whole script...

'German Volk, we are stronger when we are one. German Volk, we are invincible when we are united. Germany will never be brought down by its enemies again.'

Was I the only one who heard the threats? The danger in 'Volk' and 'one' and 'united'? Was I the only one who heard what wasn't said?

Volk.

That was the Führer's word for the great myth he defined as 'true Germans'. It was a word designed to exclude; a word Lili didn't trust. Now she couldn't get it out of her head. Or the roars of approval and the sea of raised arms which had surged across the Lustgarten every time Hitler threw it out to the crowd as a rallying cry. And she couldn't deny – although she desperately wanted to – the power that rang through the new Chancellor's voice as he'd held his audience captive. Hitler's cadence-filled and perfectly timed way of speaking was as hypnotic as all the reports said.

'You don't have to agree with everything he believes in – obviously the way he's destroyed the Communist Party and any other opposition is appalling. And you definitely don't have to listen to everything he says because he does go on, but you can't argue with his ability to perform. He knows how to command an audience better than most actors.'

Lili had heard that said many times too, couched in a grudging admiration for the man's skills, and coming from mouths that should have known better.

None of the circle of friends Lili had carefully cultivated in the four years since she'd arrived in Berlin would class themselves as National Socialist supporters. That was a deliberate choice on her part. Lili had never stopped loathing or fearing the Party; she'd been horrified when it swept into power at the start of 1933, and she gave its members a wide berth.

Lili's friends were people she'd met over the last four years through her now expanded and highly successful flower shop, or through the cafés and restaurants it supplied. They were small business owners like her – wine merchants and grocers – or the writers and artists who ate in the dining rooms her flowers decorated. They were kind-hearted, generous people. But none of them were Jewish, which was a deliberate choice too.

The Lili who lived in Berlin was a careful construction. She'd reworked her past into a story that mixed loving parents who'd been taken too early with hard work and pluck and just enough sadness to stop anyone from probing too deeply. The story she presented was solidly middle-class and solidly German, and it had cut her off completely from her roots, placing her in a world which had no connections to Berlin's Jewish community. There was a loneliness inherent in the path she'd taken, and the familiarity she'd rejected, but Lili refused to let herself dwell on that. Her new life had done what it was intended to do: it had provided her with all the safety she'd craved in 1929. Her new friends reflected that need. Unfortunately, those friends were now all fascinated to varying degrees by Hitler.

Stop picking at it. He's in power, which is bad, but you don't need to get close to his people, and they've no reason to get close to you.

Lili pulled a spray of white roses from a nearby bucket in an attempt to distract herself. The flowers were just coming into bloom, their perfume was honey-tinged, their petals velvet against her skin. She instructed the delivery boy to add a dozen bunches to her order and moved on towards a display that was heady with lilacs. Selecting stock was her favourite job and one that – with all the demands running a successful business made on her days – she rarely got time to do. The Lindenstraße flower market was also her favourite place in Berlin: even at her loneliest, it never failed to lift her spirits.

So why won't it work its magic today?

The answer was simple: everything had been tainted by yesterday's May Day rally.

Lili shouldn't have been anywhere near that. She was always careful to avoid direct contact with the Party and its far too frequent parades and celebrations. If her friends let their curiosity get the better of them and chose to attend, Lili bowed out, insisting that politics was too dull to waste her time on. Unfortunately, there hadn't been time to say or do anything to avoid the May Day gathering. The crowd streaming towards the parade ground had swept Lili and her friends along with it the instant they accidentally turned the corner into its path. Trying to fight herself free would have attracted the wrong kind of attention.

There'd been ugly faces marching towards the Lustgarten that day. Men with mean eyes and clenched fists. There'd been ugly voices too, looking for trouble, complaining about the city's Jews, or rather the lack of them.

Lili had shrunk down inside herself, feeling sick, as the marchers swapped stories about the brawls they'd taken part in, the *defilers* they'd kicked to the ground and the shop windows they'd shattered. Her friends had heard the boasts too. They'd rolled their eyes and moved as far away from the laughing thugs as they could, but they hadn't protested or argued. No one argued with anything the NSP and their bully boys did.

Hitler had only officially been in charge since January, but his hold over the city, and the country, was unassailable. No opposition was allowed; all other political parties had been banned. And the antisemitism which Hitler had never hidden but too many people had thought they could curb had immediately reared its head. There were rumours that sanctions against Germany's Jewish population, particularly its lawyers and doctors, were imminent. There'd already been violence and a one-day boycott ordered against Jewish businesses. Lili's friends had rolled their eyes at that too, but no one had suggested taking a scrubbing brush to the stars which had spread like a rash across Berlin's storefronts. No one had pushed past the SA guards blockading the doorways and into the Jewish-run shops.

Including you.

Lili grabbed an armful of lilacs in the vain hope that their heavy scent would smother the voice pricking at her head.

You didn't go into any of the blockaded businesses either. You didn't raise your voice, not even in private. You didn't tell the SA that your shop should also be out of bounds.

Lili stopped dead.

The voice wouldn't quieten. The further she separated herself from her past – the further she tried to break the connection with the girl she'd once been – the louder it grew. There were days when she heard her father's heavy tones in it. There were moments when she was convinced it would take on a life of its own. When 'I'm Jewish' would spring out of her mouth to punctuate a pause in a café conversation or cut across the moment of silence at a rally as Hitler drew breath. When... When what? Her friends would step back? Her customers would melt away? When being a good German would slip down the scale and she would step outside the realms of the Führer's beloved *Volk*?

When I'd stop being a fraud? When I'd stop denying my family?

Benjamin might have put his German credentials first, but he'd always been firmly and proudly Jewish.

He wouldn't have understood me turning away.

Lili had spent a lot of sleepless nights wishing she'd been braver and stayed true to him. Wishing the sight of his broken body on the synagogue steps hadn't so utterly broken her.

'Excuse me, do we know each other? Have we met?'

It took Lili a moment to gather herself. To re-enter 1933 and the flower market. The man smiling at her across the lilacs looked familiar, but she couldn't fit his elegant good looks anywhere into her life. Before she could find a polite way to say as much, his face broke into a grin.

'It's you! The girl who fainted outside the flower shop and then disappeared quicker than Cinderella from the ball.'

His grin was infectious. It turned his slightly angular face boyish. And his description of her wild leap away from him back into the crowds thronging Spittelmarkt was so absurd, it made Lili laugh.

'That was four years ago. How on earth did you remember me?'

The smile was still there, but it wasn't a boy's. He was looking at her as if he couldn't look away.

'There's some faces you don't forget.'

She wasn't going to blush. Or – to be more accurate – she wasn't going to let him see her blush. Lili turned round and thrust her lilacs at the delivery boy. By the time she composed herself, her Spittelmarkt rescuer was standing in the same aisle, his hand stretched out towards her.

'Marius Rodenberg at your service. Hopefully for a little longer this time than the last.'

Rodenberg.

Lili knew the name, but it took a moment to slot it into place. She returned his handshake as her brain spiralled through all the lists she held there. That was it: the Rodenbergs were the owners of the Edel Hotel, one of the oldest and finest establishments in Berlin. And Marius, although he was only twenty-three and should have been years away from the job, had recently taken over the running of it from his father who was in poor health. Every food and wine supplier in Berlin had been buzzing with the news, hoping a change at the top would open the door to the businesses who'd always been held firmly outside Louis Rodenberg's tight, and equally as wealthy, circle.

Marius coughed as Lili was putting the pieces together and she realised she was staring at him, and still holding his hand. She dropped that quickly and managed to find her voice.

'And I'm Lili Falck. It's good to meet you again.'

Her new name rolled easily off her tongue now after so

many years of practice, although it didn't sit as comfortably as Krauss sat in her head.

'And I know the Edel, or by reputation anyway. It's very well thought of.'

Marius blinked at that and stared round at the high banks of flowers surrounding them as if he'd forgotten where he was. He suddenly looked completely out of place.

'Well it won't be if I don't get some help here. We've got a really important wedding tomorrow, and somehow the flower order got overlooked in all the fuss surrounding my father's retirement.'

He poked at the lilacs as if they were waiting to bite him and shook his head. 'I've no idea what I'm doing. I can't tell a rose from a tulip and those are the only two names I know.'

He paused then, and a look crept across his face which had far too much hope in it for Lili's liking.

'But you do, you must, or you wouldn't be loading that poor boy down with so many bunches. Are you in the business? Do you work in that shop where we met?'

Lili knew she should walk away, like she'd walked away from him before. She knew she should say no to his questions. She'd started to the second his eyes lit up. The Edel was known to her, but that was all – she'd never set foot inside it nor expected to. Its clients were drawn from Berlin's highest social ranks, including – or so she assumed – leading Party members. That wasn't a world Lili wanted to be associated with. Which was why she shook her head and tried to say goodbye. Unfortunately she hadn't reckoned with Marius's persistence. He didn't give her a chance to refuse or to go. He threw himself so over-dramatically on her mercy instead, all Lili could do in the end was laugh and tell herself that it was only one – potentially very lucrative – job and what harm could one job do?

Lili knew that Marius found her attractive; he was twinkling at her like a lighthouse. If he'd been someone from her own circle, she would have let herself find him attractive too. But his twinkling didn't worry her. She knew how to hold people at arm's length – she'd been doing that since her first day in Berlin. She assumed she could manage him for the time it took to find him a new supplier. So Lili gave up trying to say no. She asked, 'What do you know about the bride?' instead.

And walked straight out of my safe, quiet life.

One job. No being charmed by the Edel, or its owner, into taking more contracts and allowing more involvement. It had sounded so easy in the flower market. It had sounded like a sensible plan. It had barely lasted a day.

Marius had whisked Lili straight from Lindenstraße to the Edel so she could experience it for herself, and she was hooked from that moment. And then he'd woven the hotel's stories around her and she was lost. *Stand still and watch.* It had seemed an odd thing for him to say, but Lili had quickly understood why Marius had told her to do it. The Edel was far more than her beauty; her skills ran far deeper, and her magic began at the door. Lili had watched shoulders drop and faces smooth as visitors were ushered in. She'd watched the liveried doorman set the hotel's serene tone with his low voice and a welcome which was just on the right side of unhurried. And she'd listened to Marius's explanation and understood that the Edel was far more than a building offering a bed for the night.

'The outside world stays outside – that's our first and most important rule. Who you are or were out there doesn't make a difference to how you're treated in here. Hotels like the Edel – the *grand-dames* of the industry – exist as a place outside time. That's their point. It may all be running at full tilt below stairs – and, trust me, it usually is – but up here? Everything is calm; everything is possible. Nobody and nothing is judged.'

And there's the worm in the apple. There's the poison he can't, or won't, see.

Lili shook off the memories that were threatening to derail her. She stared at the two names written in Marius's hand in the appointment book and felt the apple collapse.

'There are two big gala dinners in the ballroom next week and a private lunch in one of the suites which would all benefit from your touch. As well as the usual floral arrangements for the foyer and dining areas. All the details are in the appointment book, but I'll be back tomorrow if there's anything you want to go through. Maybe we could do that over supper, just the two of us?'

Lili pushed the book – and any thought of intimate suppers – away. Marius's phone call the previous night to outline the hotel's upcoming events had been no different to half a dozen other calls. Which was what she couldn't reconcile. Why hadn't he warned her who was attending the lunch? Why had he assumed she would be comfortable providing the flowers?

Because they're simply guests to him, because this is where the men in charge come. And because he doesn't have to concern himself with who's at the top. He rules his world; they rule theirs – they all speak the same language.

She'd been ignoring that reality for almost three months and now here it was, literally in black and white in the pages of Marius's diary.

Lili hadn't intended to become so caught up in the Edel's affairs that she had carte blanche to go into Marius's office and consult his appointment book. She hadn't intended a lot of things. One job had, however, inevitably led to the offer of another, which was equally as tempting. Lili had stuck to her plan and said no. Marius had stuck to what was clearly his and refused to accept it. Then he'd offered her a financial deal which had not only allowed her to raise wages; it paid for extra staff in the shop. After that, she could hardly refuse to design displays for the foyer and the tea room, or bouquets for panic-stricken husbands who'd remembered to book an anniversary dinner but completely forgotten to purchase a gift. By August, Lili had two assistants employed solely to look after the Edel and she'd given up trying to refuse Marius.

Because I didn't want to. Or not till now.

She picked a browning petal off one of the dahlias in the vase on the desk and threw it in the bin. She wished she could throw the appointment book there too. It was never going to be just one job; it was never going to be manageable. She'd known that from the moment she looked back into Marius's brown eyes. But she'd let herself find reasons to be fooled. She hadn't had to deal directly with the wealthy clients who might try to dig into her credentials or offend her with theirs. Her professional life played itself out below stairs in the hotel's hidden areas, amid the bustle of the kitchens and the wine cellars and the laundry. She'd convinced herself that keeping her distance from the public face of the Edel wouldn't be a problem. And pretended that keeping her distance from Marius wasn't a problem either. Except Marius had been a problem from the start, although Lili had been firmly in denial about that too.

Marius was kind and funny and charming. And handsome enough with his tall frame and sweep of dark chocolate hair to send her pulse fluttering. The more time they spent together, the easier spending time together became, even with all the secrets she carried.

Lili had been careful with those. She'd told Marius the same story she'd told everyone else and skated as quickly as she could over it, but even those bare facts had been enough to create a bond. Marius's parents weren't dead, but they were a considerable distance away in Hamburg and more involved with their own lives than their son's. That lack of a parental safety net was one similarity, but they quickly found more. They both carried a level of responsibility for their own – and other people's –

livelihoods that most people in their early twenties didn't have to shoulder. They both knew what it was like to work too hard and to be lonely. Within a week or two, the touchpoints between them began to form a magnet.

But none of those touchpoints make us the same.

Lili jumped up from the desk without copying down the details of the following week's events, knowing full well that she wouldn't be providing the flowers for any of them. Or meeting Marius the next night. Knowing that she was as angry with herself as she was with him.

I was a fool to let myself get swept up in his smiles and his eyes and his constant attention. Scratch the surface and nothing about us is right for the other.

The problem was more than his wealth and his social position, although those were enough to make their burgeoning relationship impossible, even without Lili's past. The problem was the man those privileges had created.

As Lili had suspected at their first meeting – and he'd confirmed when he'd shared the Edel's philosophy with her – Marius walked far more easily through the world than she ever had. He treated everybody with the same level of courtesy, whatever their background or beliefs. And he didn't see danger. Lili had recognised that four years earlier when he'd dismissed the SA as not being a serious threat. She'd seen it in practice two days before. And she needed to focus on that blind spot now, so she could quieten the voice in her head which was full not with his flaws but his kindness.

'You need to teach your girlfriend better manners. It would be a shame if we had to do it for you.'

The words roared back through her, and the humiliation and the fear sewn through them.

That was another day which should have played out differently, although Lili had been more focused on how close the two of them were becoming, not how much she needed to walk away. Marius had taken her to Lichterfelde's new botanical gardens on an afternoon whose blue skies were postcard pretty. She'd worn her prettiest day dress – a belted emerald silk with puff sleeves and a white collar, which had brought out the green flecks in her hazel eyes. Marius had worn a pristine cream linen suit and turned as many heads as she had. The gardens too had been a delight, thick with the perfume of sweet peas and roses. She'd been laughing as she taught Marius the difference between a cosmos and a cornflower, smiling as his fingers twined themselves around hers, wondering if a kiss was finally coming as he pulled her close. She hadn't noticed the two SS men walking towards them; she'd paid no attention to their salute. She had ruined the day because she hadn't snapped instantly to attention.

No. That's not right. That's not how it happened.

Lili gathered up her bag and her notebook, her blood suddenly boiling. Marius had saluted the officers back without thinking – that was the problem. His arm had shot up and her jaw had dropped. And then she'd properly looked at the black uniforms and gone blank.

The SS were new to Berlin's streets, and they were still an unknown quantity. They were far more groomed than the SA; Lili had heard the word 'elite' whispered about them. Whatever they were, their uniform and their manner exuded menace. Or to her anyway. But Marius had apologised to them for what he called an *oversight*, and they'd stepped back when they heard his well-spoken voice. Then, as he'd done four years earlier, he'd brushed Lili's fears away and dismissed the SS men as over-dressed fools and the ones who needed a lesson in manners. The encounter had left him as untouched as it had terrified her.

Because he didn't see the threat – why would he? He's never lived in a world where you can lose your footing overnight. As kind and generous as he is, he's still one of them.

Lili knew some of that was neither true nor fair. Marius

wasn't a National Socialist. He had no interest in politics, and she was certain that, if he was ever faced with outright cruelty directed towards another human being, he wouldn't stand back or look away. But part of it was.

The part which had grown up secure in the Edel's enclosed sphere, mixing with royalty and power and wealth. The part which enabled him to dismiss men in uniform. Which had allowed him to write *Hitler and Goebbels: Private Lunch* in his appointment book and see it as simply another function.

The part which has to keep his life separate from mine.

Marius was a good man, but he wasn't, and he couldn't be, the man for her.

And, with all my secrets, I can't be the woman for him.

There was no point in wishing that wasn't true, although Lili knew if she let herself waver and see him again, she would wish very hard that it wasn't.

So I won't see him again.

That sounded simple enough.

She left the office and told Marius's secretary not to expect her back again. She walked out through the hotel's foyer and refused to be seduced by its glamour. She walked back to the flower shop thinking up ways to attract new clients to compensate for the loss of the Edel. Determined to do as she'd done four years earlier and keep Marius Rodenberg at far more than arm's length.

CHAPTER 4

SEPTEMBER 1935

'Today is a good day to be German. Today, our future is set in the stars and our country will rise strong and pure. Why? Because – thanks to our beloved Führer – from today, Jews are no longer citizens of Germany. From today, marriage between Jews and German citizens is forbidden, and marriages which have already taken place in violation of this law are no longer valid. Our blood is protected. Our country is made safe for the Volk.'

Lili switched the radio off.

Marius would be home soon. He was probably already on his way up to their private apartment from his last meeting downstairs in the hotel. She should be lighting the lamps, drawing the curtains, ordering dinner from the kitchens. She should be doing all the things she normally did to welcome him back from his day. Instead, she couldn't move; she couldn't think. She couldn't even cry, although she had so many reasons to cry. Until the baby turned and kicked inside her, and woke her out of her trance. Then the dam broke. Then the only thing in her head was, *Why on earth did I do it?*

'I won't fall in love with you, I can't. Don't let me.'

Her words had been as useless as dew on a lava flow. Her plan – to never see Marius again – had collapsed the moment he burst breathlessly into the shop, with his hair in chaos and his tie all askew. His resolve to be better had beaten her.

'What did I do to make you go? You have to tell me. I've been wracking my brains trying to work out what I did.' He didn't give her a chance to speak – he was too busy throwing apologies at her. 'Except it's not that, is it? It's what I didn't do. It's that awful encounter with the SS. I'm so sorry, Lili. I know I made a mess of that. I wanted to defend you, I really did. I hated what they said, and I should have told you that then. But I've never seen the point in tangling with men like them: all it does is fuel the fire.'

He finally drew breath. His face fell when her mouth set.

'I'm right, aren't I? I let you down. You think I'm a coward. Or clueless about the world outside the Edel.'

There was nothing Lili could say: he'd articulated everything she'd already decided about him too accurately to argue with. This time when he started speaking, his words poured out in such a jumble, she could hardly keep up.

'I can see why you'd think that, but it's not true. I'm not blind to the Party. I hate bullies. I hate cruelty. But the world I come from prides itself on taking care, on not finding fault. I've been taught to accommodate, to wait problems out. And I can see now why that's wrong. That maybe I've lost any sense of when I'm supposed to actually get angry and react. But I can change that; I can change anything you want. If you'll only come back to me, and the Edel.'

He clearly meant every word. Lili could see the strain in his tightly drawn face. And she'd missed him too, more than she'd let herself admit. The fortnight she'd spent avoiding him felt as if it had stretched into months. Which meant she'd hesitated rather than immediately sending him on his way. And he'd seen his chance and grabbed it.

'Help me, Lili. What is it I don't understand? Because there is something here, between us, isn't there? I haven't got that bit wrong?'

She'd nodded before she could stop herself. And wanted to weep as his face lit up.

'Then tell me what I'm missing. Tell me what really upset you. The only times I've seen you wrong-footed by anything, there's been uniforms involved. Did something happen to you? Can't you tell me what it was?'

That was the moment when I should have told him the truth, but I didn't.

Lili got up and began pacing as the baby kicked again, hoping the movement would ease its dancing.

If I'd been as honest as he deserved, if I'd told him I was Jewish, he would have stopped trying to win me. Not straight away perhaps. But once he had to tell his parents, once the Edel's public standing was threatened, he'd have done the right thing by his family and walked away.

And in that lay the answer to her silence. In the choice he would have made; in *walked away*. Their story would have ended the moment she told him the truth and – despite every plan she'd made, and despite what Marius deserved – she couldn't bear the thought of him leaving her.

So I was selfish and a coward. I kept silent and I kept him, and now we both have to pay.

Lili had told Marius more about her life in Leipzig than she'd told anybody else in Berlin. It was still a long way from the truth.

She told him about Marie's death, and how her father had raised her on his own until he died too. But she didn't tell him that one of her clearest childhood memories was of eating her mother's famous challah bread and how pillowy soft and sweet it was. Or how beautiful Marie had looked when she lit the Seder candles and her hair turned to gold in their glow. She told him how her father had got caught up in the horror of an SA mob and died of his injuries. But she didn't tell him that Benjamin had been killed on the steps of the synagogue where he was an elder. She told him that she'd hated Hitler and his party ever since and blamed them for her father's death. That she'd seen the diary entry and the thought of supplying flowers for the Führer had sickened her. She'd justified her omissions in the love that lit up his face, in the love that had already planted seeds in her heart. But she never mentioned the word Jewish.

I let him hold me instead. And promise me I never had to meet anyone I didn't want to meet. That the Edel would always be my safe haven, no matter who else came through its doors.

Living a safe life in the Edel, no matter what went on outside – it had been a beautiful dream, built by two people who'd been forced to grow up too fast, whose hearts desperately needed the refuge the other's heart offered. It was a dream that danced them through a speeded-up courtship which Marius refused to let his parents – who were horrified by Lili's lack of social status and wealth – object to. Into a wedding and a baby on the way.

Into a marriage that's now a crime.

The baby had settled, but Lili was tumbling, full of despair for Marius and fear for her child who would now be born caught between two worlds. Whose future she could no longer guarantee.

The noose was tightening around Germany's Jews. Everybody had known trouble was coming before Hitler set up the new legal framework designed to destroy them. So many professions – from medicine to the press to the stage – had already been purged and so many university courses' and school entry criteria restricted, that non-Jews no longer having contact with Jews had become the normality. And now that enforced invisibility had been turned into law. Hitler had split the country's population into German and other, and there was no going back. Not even at the Edel.

Lili sank into one of the apartment's thickly padded chairs, clutching its arms as the floor lurched beneath her. Marius had kept his promise to change. He still held tight to the Edel's mission to keep the outside world outside, but he was looking more closely at the outside now. He watched the changes creeping through the city, and he took as many small actions to soften injustice as he could. He'd ignored the growing pressure to pore through his staff's backgrounds and scrutinise their papers. He'd stuck firmly to the line that he built his teams on trust and merit, not on intrusion into their personal lives. It was a stance Lili had actively supported and was proud of. It felt as if she was using her position of safety to at least offer some help. Those efforts couldn't go on now. Not with these new laws. Not now that – according to the radio broadcast – the Party had drawn up a table defining what being Jewish meant, and how many degrees of *impurity* existed.

We can't keep on playing a system that's got tighter, not in Hitler's favourite hotel.

Lili closed her eyes; she forced herself to think of the baby and take deeper breaths. Hitler's favourite hotel. It was unthinkable, but it was true. One private lunch for the Führer and his closest advisors two years earlier had turned into a second, had turned into a weekly event. Nobody at the Edel had encouraged that development, Marius had simply done his job very well. Hitler loved the privacy and the personal touches the Edel excelled in. He treated the suite he used there as an extension of his nearby Chancellery, an honour which – according to Goebbels, the Reich's Minister of Public Enlightenment and Propaganda – the Führer bestowed on very few places.

Except it's not an honour; it's a nightmare.

Marius had promised her that she would decide who she met, that the Edel was as much her sanctuary as anyone else's.

He'd meant what he said, but, in the end, his promises were another impractical part of their dream.

Once Lili became Frau Rodenberg, once she became absorbed into the life of the hotel, there were no grounds on which to refuse a request, regardless of who made it. She couldn't dismantle the Edel's reputation for generosity and service to appease her own conscience. She didn't want to harm it in that or any other way.

Lili had fallen in love with the Edel almost as much as she'd fallen in love with its owner. She was fascinated by its workings, by the swan-like contrast between the calm upstairs and the frantic paddling below and the breadth of its extended family which ran from the lowliest bellboy to its forbidding maître d'. Within a few months of her marriage, she knew every inch of it, and – with her artistic flair and her head for business – she quickly became a valued asset to the team.

Marius sometimes pretended her devotion to the hotel made him jealous. It didn't; it made him proud. And the more he shared the weight of his work with her, the happier Lili became. So when the Führer complimented the foyer's flowers and requested a similar arrangement for his lunchtime table, how was Lili supposed to refuse? And when he asked to meet the magician with the green fingers, what was she supposed to do?

He wasn't what she expected. Lili didn't meet the great orator, or the actor. She didn't meet the writer whose vicious book, *Mein Kampf*, portrayed Jews as the personification of the devil, as the symbol of evil, as the contaminators of the world. Or the dictator who'd built a web of new prisons and filled them with anyone who stepped even an inch out of line. Instead, Lili met a man who kissed her hand with an old-fashioned bow and praised her floral skills. Who discussed the Edel's features with an architect's eye and asked her about her favourite music. A man who held the ministers he brought with him – Goebbels and SS Reichsführer Himmler and Reich Aviation Minister Göring – spellbound and vying for his attention. Lili met a human being not a monster, and that was worse.

And now I can't get free of him.

Hitler was a creature of habit. He insisted on the same suite when he was in residence; he always sat in the same chair with his back to the window. He always ordered the same menu: vegetable soup, liver dumplings with sauerkraut, apple cake with raisins and nuts. The only composer he permitted to be played in his presence was Wagner. And – although women were never included on his guest lists – he liked Lili to be there in the room at the start of his lunch parties, to greet his guests and pour the first drink.

The first time she'd acted as his hostess – because he'd asked her directly to do it and she couldn't refuse him to his face – Lili had gone straight to her private bathroom afterwards and been sick. His handshake carried the blows which had murdered her father; the fingers he touched hers with had wielded a pen to pour out hate.

The second time he requested her presence, Marius had offered to make excuses for her, to say she was indisposed. Lili longed to say yes, but she couldn't let him do it. Hitler's stamp of approval had sent the Edel's star soaring, but flying high was a precarious thing. There were other hotels in Berlin – the Kaiserhof and the Adlon chief among them – jockeying for the notoriously fickle Führer's patronage and dreading his displeasure and the black marks that would bring.

That thought, the realisation of how much was now more than ever at stake, pulled Lili back to her feet and into the bedroom. It sent her to the wardrobe and her suitcase and a frenzied attack on the dresses and jackets swinging from the rails.

Hitler's face darkened if his soup wasn't served at precisely the temperature at which he liked it to be served. He tapped his foot if she forgot to add sprigs of edelweiss to the suite's flower arrangements. Those mistakes, so far, could be corrected with an apology and a pretty smile. But if he discovered his favourite hostess was a Jew? Lili couldn't even begin to imagine the depths of his horror – or his vengeance – at that.

She was still throwing blouses and lingerie into the case, her ears filled with the Führer's voice raised in fury and threatening the livelihoods of everyone who worked at the hotel, when she heard the front door open. She ran into the sitting room as Marius finally appeared, ready to tell him that she had to go and to do that as fast as she could. But Marius looked rumpled, a word Lili hadn't associated with her elegant husband since the day he'd come running back to her. His collar was crooked, his hair jumbled out of its neat parting, and when he put his arms around her – as he always did the instant he came home – he hung too tightly on. Lili's courage failed her. She resorted to more solvable problems instead, anything to delay the moment when she had to plunge the knife in.

'What is it, my love? Who's worn you out? Are there problems with the wine contracts again?'

She loosened herself from his grip and stepped back as Marius shook his head.

'No, they're all sorted, thanks to you. André's certainly upset about something but I don't think it's to do with the hotel. Your intervention with the suppliers smoothed that hiccup out.'

That at least was a relief. André Lippert, the Edel's sommelier – who was more German than his professional name implied – was a stubborn and impossibly private man, but he knew more about wine than any of his peers in Berlin. And Lili was one of the few people whose opinions he would listen to. She was about to say how glad she was that one problem had been solved when a more frightening thought hit her.

'He's not been affected by these new laws, has he? He's so close-mouthed about his background. He's not...'

A chasm opened up, and she couldn't finish the question.

Marius flopped onto the sofa and pulled off his tie. 'No, he's not Jewish, if that's what you were about to say. Or at least I don't think he is. But others working here definitely are. And now I'm going to have to start asking all the personal questions we've managed to avoid asking up to now. And letting staff who've never been anything but loyal to us go.'

He grimaced. When he looked up, his eyes were dark smudges.

'I hate this. I hate that we have to ask perfectly good people to prove how *good* they are. I hate that we're being separated one from the other, when we're all German and none of the rest of it matters.'

Lili sat down beside him and took his hands.

I cannot lose him. I cannot let him go.

She refused to listen to *but you should.* She chose to put her faith, yet again, in his kind heart and *none of the rest of it matters.* To let their dream stay alive.

'You heard the announcement then? About Jews being stripped of their citizenship rights and...' She hesitated, but she had to hear from him how he felt. 'And the new rules about marriage?'

Marius nodded. 'I heard it this morning, from a journalist who was at the Reichstag when the changes were brought in. They're calling them the Nuremberg Laws, after the rally where the idea was concocted. Whatever they're called, they're cruel and they'll have far-reaching consequences. I've been down in the kitchen for the last two hours, dealing with frightened employees, making promises about their jobs I doubt I can keep.'

He closed his eyes for a moment. Lili forced herself to stay quiet until he was ready to start speaking again.

'And they're being used to cause trouble, which I assume was also what the Party intended. My contact said the mood everywhere is souring and snowballing. The denunciations have already started – people are revisiting old quarrels, pointing the finger at each other, accusing anyone they don't like of keeping secrets and hiding their backgrounds. And we've fallen foul of that, which doesn't surprise me.'

He was too busy rooting around in his jacket pocket to notice that Lili had turned white at the words *secrets* and *hiding*.

'I've never denied that we don't vet who works here particularly closely, although I don't make a song and dance about it. Now there's rumours spreading, from our competitors no doubt, insinuating that the Edel is using its *favoured status* to protect men and women who've no right to work here, or anywhere else. And that's not gossip we can afford.

He pulled out a piece of paper and held it towards her. She was so blind with fear, she could barely make out what it was.

'I don't normally like Father interfering. And I wish we didn't have to do this – it makes us sound as if we're standing in support of the new rules, which I certainly am not. But on this occasion, I think he's right, and we've got no choice. With all the paranoia these laws are going to create, we need to protect ourselves, and the Edel.'

Lili blinked hard and focused on the page he was holding out towards her. It was a draft of an advertisement, featuring the Edel's name in bold type. Marius gestured to the words below the main heading.

'This is going to run in tomorrow morning's editions. It's a statement from my father tracing the Rodenberg family back across three generations, proving that we're the *right kind* of citizens. Shutting up anyone who thinks they can create suspicion and muscle in on our success.'

The advert ran to two paragraphs, but Lili could only see one line.

'Why's my name included?'

Marius frowned. 'Because you're my wife and as important to the hotel as I am. Your heritage belongs to our story.'

I can't keep him. I can't be the one who destroys everything. That's not what love is. The only thing I have left to offer him is my protection.

'It's a lie. The past that I created for myself, that I told you, is a lie.'

She couldn't stop herself saying it, even though she knew every inch of what would come next.

The words were out. There could be no more pretending, no more hanging on to a flimsy dream. There would have to be a full confession of who she was. There would have to be a separation after that – a carefully managed one which wouldn't hurt Marius – and an ending to everything she held dear. What she was about to do to him, to herself and their child, was heartbreaking. But the price of silence and then discovery – because Lili was certain that there would be discovery, and she would save him and the Edel from that if it was the last decent thing she could do – was far worse.

Marius had finally registered her colourless face and shaking hands. He'd finally heard her. He stared from her face to the advert and back. He stopped explaining that she would need to give his father a bit more detail about her own family so that there were no gaps if anyone decided to be unpleasant and start asking questions.

'What are you talking about? What's a lie?'

Lili wished that she could freeze the moment and stop the avalanche of pain that was coming. She wished she'd never let things get this far. But she couldn't keep hiding from the truth, or trying to spare Marius from its consequences, even though the thought of hurting him tore ribbons through her soul.

The lie wasn't tucked away in her head; it wasn't lurking in the spaces of the story she'd told. It was there, laid out in the paper for everybody in Berlin and beyond to see. *The Roden-*

berg family, down to the present day and including my son who now stands at the Edel's helm and his new wife Lili, are true citizens of Germany. There wasn't a photograph at least – Lili was very careful to avoid being captured in them, and Louis was old-fashioned enough not to like his family's image appearing in the newspapers. But issuing denials often prompted deeper questions. The advert was as dangerous as a primed bomb.

She disentangled her hands from his. She prayed that the feel of them would always stay with her.

'And what's that? Lili, what's going on?'

He wasn't looking at her anymore. He was looking over her shoulder and through the open bedroom door.

'Why is there a suitcase on the floor? Why are your things in it?'

His skin was so pale it was hard to imagine it had ever held colour. His hands hung frozen between them. There was nothing to be done now but tell him a truth that was long overdue.

'I have something to tell you, Marius. I need you to listen to all of it before you say anything, and I need you to know from the start how much I love you and how truly sorry I am.'

She moved away from him as she began. Out of the reach of his arms. Out of the reach of his love. But she looked him straight in the eye.

CHAPTER 5

JUNE 1990

She's disappearing. I'm going to lose her again.

The thought made Lucy's stomach lurch. It brought the last glimpse of Emily's tiny face too bitterly back. And made her clutch at the small photograph even harder.

Ten years of constant handling had worn the picture brittle and blurred. The image was fading. The paper had thinned. The crease across the middle was a fold or two away from cracking. Lucy knew that she needed to stop stroking it, that she needed to take the photograph out of her purse and keep it somewhere safer. Except that was impossible: keeping the image close by was the only way to keep the dreams it carried alive.

She blinked hard, swallowed her tears and tried to make the day rational again.

It's understandable. It's the Edel's fault. I'm spending too much of my time here digging around in the past. It's no wonder that's starting to feel closer than the present.

There was a kind of logic there. Yes, there wasn't a day that went by without Lucy checking her precious photograph. But it was also fair to say that the past, and more particularly the Edel's history, had begun to obsess her.

In the two months it had taken Charlie to complete the paperwork and the purchase – a timescale Lucy only believed was possible when it happened – she'd fallen more and more under the hotel's spell. It was as full of layers as she'd hoped it would be; she'd already started to uncover them. A foray into the cellars had produced a treasure trove of boxes whose contents dated from the Edel's founding at the turn of the century until at least midway through the Second World War. No one appeared to have gone through them, or in the last few decades anyway; no one, until now, had attempted to put them in order. Searching meticulously through the dust-covered cartons had become the treat to balance the administration and supplier-chasing that filled Lucy's busy days.

She'd discovered floor plans and room designs with descriptions of furniture placements and faded colour swatches attached to them. She'd found hundreds of menus and elegantly engraved invitations to tea parties and balls. She'd found a stack of ledgers filled with purchase notes and detailed accounts which covered every item the hotel had required to keep functioning, from soap to a new grand piano. And from putting those together, she'd uncovered a vibrant, fashion-setting hotel and dozens of ideas to incorporate into the relaunch.

The Edel had been the first hotel in Berlin to serve Neapolitan ices. It had started the trend for tiny cakes served at afternoon tea dances, champagne sorbet palate cleansers at dinner, and confetti cascades from the ceiling at parties. According to the ledgers, the Edel's wine cellar had been the envy of every other grand hotel in the city and its New Year's Eve balls had been legendary affairs, with seven-course dinners and fireworks, and mimosa-fuelled breakfasts for the dancers who were still standing the next morning. Lucy had also salvaged enough photographs from the boxes to fill a dozen albums. Stiff family portraits, weddings and celebrations, great battalions of staff. Even though most of the people included weren't named, they formed a wonderful cast of characters.

Some of the items Lucy found were damp; others were fragile and faded. But they were all pieces of the jigsaw which made up the Edel, the details which would bring the hotel back to life. And it was impossible to meet those ghosts without feeling the weight of her own.

'Which was the challenge you set me on the first day I walked in here – you knew I brought my own secrets. You knew how long I'd been hiding from them.'

'Fräulein Stretton? Forgive me, I didn't mean to make you jump, or interrupt a private conversation...'

Lucy whirled round, stuffing the photograph back into her bag as she did so.

It was no wonder the man staring at her across the foyer looked puzzled: there was nobody else in the vicinity but her and she was nowhere near a telephone. For a moment, Lucy didn't know what to say. She prided herself on her professional poise, but now she'd been caught talking to herself; she had a horrible feeling that staring at Emily's picture had left her eyes red, and – for the first time in her professional life – she couldn't remember what was on today's calendar. Luckily – or unluckily, she didn't know him well enough yet to know which – her visitor spotted her confusion and sailed smoothly over it.

'I'm Adam Wendl, from RWA Associates, here to discuss your refurbishment plans? I think I may be a little early, which I assure you isn't a common German habit.'

His easy manner brought her manners back. And his smile made her wish she'd had time to check that her curls hadn't migrated towards frizz.

'It's a pleasure to meet you, Herr Wendl. You're not early at all, and you weren't interrupting anything. Apparently I have so many lists in my head, I've started talking to myself to keep them all straight. Perhaps I need to join the digital age and invest in a Dictaphone.'

She'd thought her recovery was neatly done, but the initial confusion had pushed her German out of her head, and made her speak not only in English but also far too quickly. Luckily Herr Wendl appeared to have understood what she'd said. He nodded as if he did anyway and switched languages.

'It's Adam, please. I know what you mean – this type of project does tend to lead to a lot of list-keeping. Hopefully I'll be able to help you to sort at least some of those out today.'

His English was fluent. His manner was confident. But he wasn't as at ease as he appeared to be. He kept glancing around at the foyer and up at the staircase, but not in the assessing way Lucy expected an architect would use to scrutinise a tired hotel's features.

He's not comfortable, and he's not appraising the hotel's condition or estimating the work that needs doing. He's hesitant. Something about being in here has made him nervous.

That didn't make any more sense than her talking to the hotel as if it was a friend, but Adam's left hand was tapping his thigh and his right – when Lucy finally shook it – was ever so slightly trembling. He also looked oddly familiar. His high cheekbones and hazel eyes and the shock of dark chocolate hair falling across his forehead reminded Lucy of a man she had seen very recently. First in a wedding picture, and then again wearing a uniform. She took a step back when she realised who that man was.

'Now it's my turn to say forgive me, but you look so like him, I have to ask.'

She realised that Adam's frown needed more of an explanation than simply blurting a name out.

'I'm sorry, that must have sounded rather strange. The thing is, I've been doing a lot of research into the Edel since I've been here, to help me decide how we best go forward into the relaunch. So much stuff has been left untouched in the basement, it's as good as an archive down there, or it will be when I get through the rest of the boxes. And it includes a lot of family photographs.'

She was talking too fast again, which wasn't her usual habit. She paused, giving him a moment to say, 'Ah yes, I know where this is going.'

He didn't say anything.

'Okay, well I don't know if you know this, but you're the double of Marius Rodenberg, the son of the man who founded the hotel. You're not related to him in some way, are you?'

Adam's lips disappeared. He looked as if he was about to deny it. Lucy really hoped that he was, that the resemblance was a coincidence. The hotel deal had gone through as quickly as it had because – according to the officials who'd dealt with the purchase – there was no one who could try and claim ownership of it. The last thing Lucy needed now was some long-lost family member swooping in to cause problems. Her heart sank when he took a deep breath instead and nodded.

'I am actually, yes. Marius Rodenberg was my grandfather, although I never knew him, or any of the Rodenberg family. And I didn't know about the connection or that the Edel existed until the Wall was brought down – this is actually the first time I've been inside it.'

No wonder he was appraising the place so furtively – he must have been trying to work out its value.

Now it was Adam who paused. Lucy's face had clearly given her away. She couldn't help that: she was already assembling legal arguments and working out who she might need to call. So the speed with which he tried to assure her that she didn't need to worry should have been helpful. It wasn't.

'I could have put that better, I think; I certainly hope I haven't raised a red flag. I want to be clear – and maybe I should have started with this – that I'm here because my firm will do an excellent job of the restoration, and that's all. I've no other interest in the hotel beyond that.' He stopped again. Lucy's lack of response, or her tight expression, forced him to continue. 'Obviously there's history here, but there's also a lucrative contract that our competitors would have given their right hand to secure, and that's of far more interest to me, I promise.'

He flashed on his smile again, as if his admission might lighten the mood. Lucy didn't smile back. She was in no mood to be charmed now, which Adam clearly recognised. When he continued talking, his comfortable veneer was gone and he stumbled a little.

'Well, like I said, there's history, but it's not a happy one for my family, and it's not one I want to revisit. I can assure you this is a professional project for me, not a personal one. However, if you would prefer RWA to step back because of my personal connections, or for me to step off the project, I can understand it might make things simpler.'

When he stopped speaking this time, he stayed silent and let Lucy weigh up what he'd said. But she was no more comfortable than him, and she didn't have an immediate answer.

RWA had come with glowing testimonials and a track record of gently bringing old buildings back to life. Charlie was close friends with the company's CEO. Unpicking the relationship between the hotel chain and the architects' firm they'd hired, never mind the contract, would be difficult. And telling Charlie there was someone who might cause the chain problems would definitely raise unwelcome red flags, which was the last thing Lucy wanted. Her boss valued her ability to deliver solutions, not problems, and that was praise Lucy liked. She decided, therefore, to play along with Adam's version of events and give herself some breathing space.

'I'm sure that's not necessary. If you don't see your family connections as an issue, then there's no need for me to see them that way either. Why don't we talk about your ideas for the hotel instead, and take it from there?'

The atmosphere immediately lifted. Their ideas and tastes turned out to be aligned, and the rest of their meeting – which focused on how best to return the hotel to a sympathetically modernised version of its glory days – went well. By the end of the morning, they had the outline of a project plan which met Charlie's timescales and budget and, as they both agreed, the foundations for an excellent working partnership.

On paper it couldn't have gone better. Adam certainly went away looking far more relaxed than when he'd arrived. But Lucy's cheerful manner disappeared the moment the front door closed behind him. Because – irrespective of how impressed she was with his vision for the hotel, or what she'd said about his links to it not being an issue – Lucy couldn't get the image of him assessing the foyer out of her head. And she wasn't sure about Adam Wendl, or his intentions towards the Edel, at all.

'Maybe he is completely on the level and he doesn't have any intention of filing a claim. But I'm not comfortable taking his word for that, and I want to know where we stand.'

Lucy had run through her meeting with Adam as succinctly as she could. Not that her brevity made any difference. Herr Heisig – the East German government official who had guided the Compton chain through the Edel's purchase – was barely paying attention. He didn't respond when she stopped talking – he was too busy checking folders off a list and separating the papers scattering his desk into a series of piles. The bonhomie he'd been full of in their previous meetings had vanished. And Lucy wasn't happy about that in the slightest.

'I expected you to be a little more engaged, if I'm honest. You were so helpful when you were pushing the sale through, but apparently now you're too busy to deal with a few questions. It's disappointing.'

Heisig stopped shuffling his papers and sighed. He clearly had no interest in Lucy's levels of disappointment.

'Fräulein Stretton, your company bought a hotel from a collapsing government at a bargain-basement price and your boss was as happy as we were to *push the sale through* as you put it. And yet now you're not comfortable? I fail to see why that's my problem.'

He gestured to his cluttered desk and to the pile of half-packed boxes she hadn't noticed which were stacked on the floor behind him.

'I am busy, yes. I'm leaving. This job won't exist in a couple more months, so I'm jumping ship before it sinks. And I really don't know what you want me to do. The sale is done; we all did very well from it. I suggest you enjoy the win and stop worrying.'

He'd taken a cut from the sale, or a sweetener to speed up its progress. That was obvious and something Lucy had suspected at the time, although she hadn't been party to the final financial arrangements. She also knew that, if she suggested his disinterest was due to the fact he'd taken what amounted to a bribe, he would laugh. Two months navigating the strange waters surrounding reunification and all its current legal black holes had taught her that bribery was a standard business practice in the old East and one its officials were determined to squeeze down to the last available drop. She reined her irritation in and changed tack.

'I suppose that, yes, we did all do well. But I'd still like some reassurance that win wasn't temporary and nothing about the purchase can be rolled back. And also some history on the Rodenberg family, if that's possible, so I've a sense of who I might be up against. If you could help me untangle either of those, I'd be very grateful, and I certainly won't bother you again.'

He sighed a second time, but he got up and went across to a set of filing cabinets at the back of the office, returning with a thin folder stamped *Edel Hotel*. He flicked through it for a moment, then he pushed a sheet of paper towards her, gesturing at it as he spoke.

'As I told your boss when he first approached us – and as it confirms here – private ownership of property wasn't recognised in East Germany, and anything expropriated by the Soviets between 1945 and 1949, which includes the Edel, is now judged as government-owned. Which means we can dispose of it as we choose. Even if a family member came forward and tried to get the hotel back, they couldn't: there's no legal basis for a claim, either for the building itself or for compensation. All this information was included in the sale's paperwork, and Mr Compton was very happy about that too, as far as I recall.'

That was true. Charlie – who liked a good deal and wasn't always forthcoming in his definition of how he defined or pursued that – had been delighted, and seeing the document which proved that the Edel's sale had been done through legitimate channels was reassuring. But Adam's admission that his family's history with the hotel hadn't been a happy one was still niggling, and she couldn't let that go.

'Thank you. I was aware of the legalities, but it's good to be reminded. However, what's concerning me more is that Herr Wendl – who is a direct descendant of the Rodenberg family – has alluded to a problem in the Edel's past which...'

She paused, conscious that bringing up hunches and feelings wasn't exactly a professional approach, even if she frequently relied on hers.

'The truth is I'm concerned that he may have some personal reason for his firm's involvement in the refurbishment which, consciously or not and legally or not, might lead to him causing difficulties for the Compton chain going forward. And I'd like to get ahead of that if I can.'

Herr Heisig glanced at the clock on his office wall. Lucy pretended not to notice.

As the silence stretched, he sat back and gave up. 'You're not an easy one to shake off, are you? Fine. If I make one phone call, will you agree to be satisfied with whatever the outcome of that is? And then will you leave me in peace to get on with the little that's left of my day?'

Lucy nodded. He went out. She picked up the folder to check through it, but there was nothing else inside other than a copy of the contract Charlie had signed and a floor plan of the hotel which she already had. She was considering digging through the filing cabinets when Heisig came back.

'Right, well I don't think you're going to have any problems with the family. According to my source, the story is that the last recorded living owner – Lili Rodenberg, who was the wife of Marius, the heir to the business and in charge up to 1944 – wasn't only a devoted Nazi, she was also a close friend of Hitler and his inner circle. They were frequent guests at your hotel, and she was murdered by the resistance because of those connections.' He kept talking as Lucy gasped. 'There may be some newspaper clippings in the city archive if you want to check, but my contact is very reliable. He was paid to know this stuff before the Wall went down; he probably still is. So, like I said, the family's not likely to be a problem.'

He shook his head as Lucy, who was brimming with questions, tried to interrupt him and ask them.

'Trust me, a past like that isn't one that anybody would want resurfacing. There was no tolerance for Nazis in the East after the end of the war, and I don't imagine that attitude will change, reunification or not.' He nodded to the door which he'd left open behind him. 'I don't think you need to worry about

Wendl. If he has an agenda, I'd guess it's to make sure his family story stays hidden. And – given the bad publicity which could result for the hotel if the truth gets out – you might want to help him with that too.'

Lucy could take no issue with that. She let herself be bundled out of the office and walked back to the hotel with her brain in freefall. *Nazi Hotel Reopens* was hardly the publicity angle she'd been hoping for. She could already hear Charlie roaring. Which meant she needed to speak to Adam Wendl and take control of the Edel's story. Because, whatever agenda Adam might have, she wasn't going to be governed by it, and she wasn't going to leave anything to chance.

'The allegations about Lili Rodenberg are true and – as I'm sure you understand – they're not ones I'd relish becoming more widely known.'

Lucy had suggested a coffee shop on the corner of Friedrichstraβe as the venue for their second meeting: she needed neutral ground. She was also wearing her sternest black trouser suit, the one she wore rather than her usual fitted dress when she needed a protective layer. Whether it was that or the location, the man sitting opposite her and not drinking his coffee was a far less confident version of the Adam she'd met at the Edel. When – without wasting time on pleasantries – she'd asked him if he'd taken on the hotel project because he wanted to hide his grandmother's past, he didn't seem certain how to respond.

'I don't think so, or at least that wasn't my original motivation. When the refurbishment proposal came over my desk, my first thought was, *That's wonderful*. So many of Berlin's beautiful buildings – especially its grand hotels – were lost during the war, we've a duty to the city to reclaim the ones that are left. That's what reunification should be about. But then...' He stared at his cooling cup. 'You have to understand that for most of my life, I didn't know about the Edel, or that my family had ever had any involvement in the kind of world it represented. Luxury hotels like that were completely outside my experience, or at least until I—'

He stopped talking. His face closed. It was obvious there was a story there, and it was equally obvious he had no intention of telling it. Lucy forced herself to swallow her curiosity. Whatever it was, she couldn't let him get distracted and clam up; she needed him to focus on the Edel.

'You said the allegations about Lili were true. What do you actually know about her involvement with the—'

Lucy looked around at the other customers. Nobody was looking her way, but saying the word *Nazis* in a quiet Berlin café felt like it was guaranteed to cause upset. She settled instead for, 'What do you know about her life?'

Adam shrugged. It wasn't a gesture that sat comfortably on him – Lucy guessed he'd been trying for unconcerned; it made him look defensive.

'Very little more than what Heisig told you. Although I do have this, which is proof that what he said is accurate.' He pulled a piece of paper out of his pocket and handed it to her. 'It's a photocopy of an old newspaper article. My mother gave it to me when I first heard about Lili and – because I questioned everything she said – I questioned the story's validity.'

Lucy took it, assuming it was the one from the city archives Heisig had alluded to. The typeface was small, and some of the German phrasing was more archaic than she was used to, but there was no mistaking the woman in the photograph. Lucy had seen the same bright eyes and curved mouth staring out from the wedding picture where she'd first encountered Marius. She said as much to Adam and admitted that it would take her longer to read the whole article than he probably had time to wait. He seemed to have expected that.

'That's fine. Borrow it and read it through later. It's a bit of a rant to be honest, but the name on the byline probably tells you as much as you need to know.'

Lucy hadn't noticed a name beside the article until Adam pointed at the line above the first paragraph. It was hard not to recoil when she recognised it.

'Joseph Goebbels wrote this?'

Adam nodded. He was no longer trying for unconcerned. 'The Reich's Propaganda Minister was apparently a great fan of my grandmother, which isn't the easiest thing to admit. This is essentially a eulogy written by Goebbels, praising her loyalty to the Party to the skies. See what he says about her, here and here.'

Lucy quickly translated the phrases Adam was pointing to. They left no room for doubt.

Lili Rodenberg's loyalty to the Reich knew no bounds.

Her murder is a stain on the city she served.

Our Führer has lost a dear friend, and we will leave no stone unturned in the hunt for her killers.

Adam gave Lucy a moment to absorb those before he continued.

'That this was written is likely why Lili was classified in 1945 as one of the *Belastete*. That was the category the denazification courts assigned to people who'd profited from their Nazi connections. If nothing else, it's proof of how close to Hitler and his acolytes she was.'

He sat back, leaving Lucy staring at a face which no longer seemed quite so beautiful as she'd first thought it. And at an article which also mentioned the Edel by name and painted it in a very uncomfortable light.

'How did she die, do you know?'

Adam sighed. 'It's not clear. Goebbels calls it murder but doesn't give the details, and he blames the resistance but doesn't say who that meant. My mother thinks Lili's body was found on the pavement outside the hotel and that she'd been shot. But her memory wasn't clear – she wasn't there, she couldn't remember who'd told her and she refused to talk about it again, which is understandable. And I've tried, but I've never found any written evidence to confirm what actually happened.'

Lucy couldn't stop herself shuddering. What Adam was describing was a hard fact to square with a photograph of a beautiful young woman. And it wasn't an image she wanted linked to the Edel, in private or in public.

'That's horrible, whoever she was or whatever she did. And it can't be easy for your mother to live with.'

Adam didn't respond to that, so Lucy carried on.

'Do you know what happened to Marius? Was he a friend of Hitler's too? Was he also killed for being one of them?'

Adam shook his head. 'No, I don't think so, although, again, I'm not sure. He was a soldier, and he seems to have disappeared early in 1943, which could suggest he was fighting on the Eastern Front in Russia. He was presumably one of the millions killed there. My mother said...'

His pause was an echo of his earlier *until I...* Lucy expected him to close down again, but he rallied himself instead.

'Well, that's basically all she said. My mother won't talk about her father, or about Lili. I know very little about her life before she had me, and the little I thought I knew turned out to be wrong.'

He bit his lip as Lucy raised her eyebrow – a gesture that made him look suddenly and painfully young.

'I assumed – until she eventually told me otherwise – that the couple who raised her, who I referred to as my grandparents, were her natural mother and father. Obviously they weren't. And as for Lili... What can I say? She was a stain on the family. That's how Nazis were viewed in the DDR, and that's the only way I can describe how my mother felt. Gabi became the most committed citizen in East Germany to compensate for her mother's sins.'

He'd been hesitant while he was talking. He'd been sad. Now he was bitter.

He's carrying hurt, or guilt, or anger inside him. He's carrying a scar that's never healed.

And this was neither the time nor the place to ask him about it, although ignoring his unhappiness went against Lucy's natural instincts. She didn't like seeing him in such obvious discomfort, but delving into his personal issues crossed professional boundaries, which wasn't something she was ever comfortable doing. Adam Wendl's secrets weren't any of her business. The Edel's, however, were.

'You knew about Lili – or about the bones of her past anyway. But you knew nothing about the Edel, or what happened there during the war, until the Wall fell. Have I got that right?'

It was what he'd told her. Lucy was relieved when he nodded. Whatever else was coming, she needed to know that, so far, he'd been telling the truth. Unfortunately knowing his account was true didn't mean it made sense. Lucy didn't like gaps – that was where problems began. But there was no way to explore those without the boundaries between personal and professional shifting. She went as carefully as she could, keeping a wary eye on his reactions.

'I'm sorry if this sounds blunt. I'm only asking because I need to know where the holes are so I can make sure I'm well prepared when it comes to the relaunch. But it does seem odd to me that your mother wouldn't have mentioned the hotel's existence to you earlier.'

She gave him a moment to speak. When he didn't, she pressed on.

'Surely she must have some memories of it? And you said she was a committed citizen of East Germany, so she – and you – must have lived on this side of the Wall. Did you never come close to the Edel? Don't you think it's strange she said nothing?'

She'd crossed the boundaries she'd meant to avoid and she'd misread his silence. His face didn't just close; it snapped shut. *Until I* began chiming through Lucy's head like the peal of a bell, although she couldn't understand what its message was. And then she wished she'd stayed silent when he got to his feet.

'I think I was clear. I didn't know about the Edel until the Wall came down, and I didn't know about Lili until then either. Gabi tells me the little she tells me and resents even doing that. And I don't push her for more. To say we're not close is an understatement.'

He kept saying *Gabi*, not Mother. He'd said earlier that he questioned everything she said. There was a sadness in that. And something too close to home for Lucy to ignore.

'I'm so sorry. It can't be easy to feel separate from your mother. To not be sure that she cares.'

The words were out of her mouth before she realised how personal they were. The lapse in her judgement brought Lucy up with a jolt.

I'm laying my situation over his, and I've no right to do that. I don't know him.

Lucy started to try and backtrack and apologise, but Adam stopped her with a wave and sat back down again as heavily as if she'd winded him. Whether she had any right to speak so honestly to him or not, she'd hit a nerve.

'You don't need to apologise. You threw me – I won't lie; I threw myself with what I told you. But I'm not offended, I promise.' He paused, took a breath, brought himself back under control. 'The issue here isn't about protecting my bruised feelings; it's about protecting the Edel. I don't want my family hurt, and I don't want the hotel's story overshadowed by Lili's when she reopens. I don't imagine you do either. And I don't know how to stop that happening – heading off problematic PR must be far more your area than mine. But maybe we could find out a way together to keep Lili out of the picture? If that would help?'

It would help. Adam understood the likely impact of Lili's *Belastete* legacy on the Edel if it got out far more than Lucy did. But nothing about the problems the Compton chain could now be facing sat well with her. And every instinct told her that, no matter how easy the purchase had been, or how committed she was to the Edel and its relaunch, this wasn't going to be the straightforward project she thought she'd taken on. There were too many secrets jostling around it for that.

CHAPTER 6

NOVEMBER 1938

They're trappings, that's all. They're not permanent. We'll wipe them away when the madness is done.

Lili walked up the Edel's central staircase, nodding to the maids dusting the portrait of Hitler which sat above the balcony and checking that the foyer's swastika banners were hanging straight. Conscious that her thoughts as she wished the Party's symbols gone from the hotel were an echo of her father's advice to 'Be a good German... That's what will count when this nonsense is over.'

Although God knows how he'd define a good German now.

Ten years had passed since Benjamin had died and nothing was over, or looked as if it would ever be. Hitler's hold on power was total, and the rest of the world was apparently as in awe of him as Germany was. The 1936 Berlin Olympics, with their impeccably choreographed displays and the sheer scale of the opening ceremonies, had been hailed across Europe and America as a triumph. Since then it seemed he could do whatever he liked. Nobody had raised a finger to stop Germany's annexation of Austria in 1938. Great Britain and France had turned their heads the other way when Hitler had occupied the

Sudetenland, although the Czechoslovakians who lived there and counted it as their country had begged them for help. Nobody seemed concerned in the slightest that Germany was widening its borders, swallowing its neighbours, hungrier for more land every day. And nobody seemed concerned about what was happening inside the country either.

Germany's Jewish population had been cut adrift, turned into a foreign body, made easy to ignore and to discriminate against. The Nuremberg Race Laws which had horrified Lili in 1935 now ruled every aspect of that community's life. There wasn't a profession or a public school or a public space which would admit Jews. Violence against Jewish businesses had increased. Mobs had roamed Berlin in May and again in June, smashing shop windows along the Kurfürstendamm, daubing antisemitic slogans over the ones they didn't shatter and leaving bleeding bodies in their wake. Nobody had protested, in public, against that either. Or against the Jewish community's increasing isolation, and the indifference to it which had become the country's default. Jewish passports now came stamped with a letter J. Jewish men had to add Israel to their names; Jewish women had to add Sara. Germany's Jews had become both invisible and marked out, and Lili wasn't sure which of those sentences carried the greater threat. The nonsense her father had dismissed and the madness that had led to were a very long way from over.

Lili let herself into the Edel apartment, a place that felt far more like home than the townhouse in Lichterfelde, which had also been handed over to Marius when his father had retired and left the city for a country life outside Hamburg. Gabi was babbling away to her nanny in the sitting room, her three-year-old head buzzing with stories she didn't yet have the words to tell. Lili leaned against the doorframe and let her daughter's music wash over her. She'd come so close to losing her family, to losing everything that kept her alive. That she hadn't was because she had taken her father's, and Marius's, advice. She'd turned Lili Rodenberg into the kind of good German the new Germany prized, and that Germany had kept on rewarding her.

'I don't believe you. I don't believe you would have kept something as important as this a secret. Not from me.'

It was the *not from me* which broke her. Lili had held herself steady all through telling Marius the truth about her past life in Leipzig. But *not from me* suggested that there might have been another way of doing things. That he wouldn't have left her if she'd told him who she was from the start. That he might have tried to defend and protect her, if she'd only given him the chance. She couldn't give him a chance to say any of that now; she didn't think her heart would be able to beat if he did. She had to make him agree to her hastily contrived plan.

'Now you know who I am, and what that means, you have to understand that I can't stay. That you'll be ruined if the truth comes out. So I'll leave. I'll go away from Berlin. You can tell people I'm sick and, after enough time has gone past, you can quietly divorce me. There won't be a scandal that way. Your family, and the Edel, will be safe.'

'Dear God, you've got it all mapped out, haven't you?'

His anger was worse than his initial disbelief. Lili didn't try to correct him; she didn't tell him her plan wasn't something she'd been storing. That it was a new one born of panic, and the last thing she wanted to do. Marius deserved his fury, and she deserved to bear it. Her defence – that fear had made her run from her faith and her people and hide who she was, and that the lie had become too big to see her way round – was a hollow one, but it was true. She wasn't going to insult him by pleading that love had made her blind to consequences, by making excuses that put the blame for her omissions on him. She bit her lip and let Marius continue.

'So this is it, is it? This is how we end? You're going to martyr yourself and break my heart, and I have no say? What about my child, Lili? Are you going to take my baby away from me too?'

The pain etching his face was so pure, Lili couldn't bear to look at it. She had no strategies left to offer him. The baby wasn't a separate being to her yet. It was still part of her body, its breathing and life entwined with hers. She hadn't considered, *What about my child?* Her selfishness had failed him in that too.

Marius shook his head as if he could read her thoughts. 'The baby is part of me. I love it as much as you do. You know that – you've known that since the first moment you told me you were pregnant. If you stopped trying to direct how this goes for a moment, if you stopped pushing me away, you might remember how wonderful that moment felt.'

And then his voice broke. He couldn't speak;, all he could do was shake his head. Suddenly her hands were clasped in his. Suddenly she was inside the warm nest of his arms, unable to tell whose tears were falling the fastest. Deaf to anything beyond his heartfelt, 'We'll find a way through this, Lili – we have to. You're my life, and I'm yours. I can't lose you. I won't.'

And he's never once gone back on that decision or regretted it, or I'd know.

Lili slipped off her shoes. The delight on Gabi's face when her mother tiptoed into the room, appearing to the little girl as if by magic, was a pleasure that would never grow dim.

They hadn't slept that night. They'd tried out every scenario that would keep their family safe. *We could sell up, we could leave, we could go to America.* All of those things were possible. The Rodenbergs were well connected – they had the resources to find sponsors overseas and the money to emigrate.

Nobody would look at quotas and make their passage difficult. That unkindness was reserved for the Jewish families who'd been left with nothing, who were truly desperate to go, an irony that wasn't lost on either of them. At one point somewhere between midnight and dawn, selling up and leaving became the winning plan. It didn't hold in the daylight. When Marius's thoughts turned to the day and what the Edel needed from him, and from that to how much he loved his hotel. He didn't say, *I can't*; he didn't need to. Lili could read him too well.

'We can't live with regrets. However we go forward, we have to be honest about where our hearts lie.'

As soon as Lili said that, neither of them spoke about leaving again. They stayed, and they refused to let that become the impossible choice.

'You hide in plain sight. That's what people do in hotels. Guests become who they choose to be; they pass each other by without noticing. Staff are trained to keep secrets, not to see what shouldn't be seen. Hotels like the Edel – and the families who run them – are judged on our public faces, so we'll make those whatever they need to be, and no one will dare to doubt you or any of us.'

The plan had sounded like madness when Marius first proposed it, but he'd refused to drop the idea. They'd stayed in the suite all morning, combing through Lili's past for stray cousins or friends who could come forward and trip her up, but she couldn't think of anybody. Herr Posner had been an old man in 1929; she doubted he was still alive. And, although neither of them took any pleasure in the thought, it was likely that Leipzig's Jewish community was already scattering. Lili's papers had never been challenged; the story she'd built round herself had always held tight. By mid-afternoon they'd convinced themselves there were enough good strands to hold them, and Marius had been building on that foundation ever since.

He flew the right flags; he hung the right pictures; he rolled out the red carpet for the right men. The Edel became the hotel where the Party threw lavish balls to celebrate the Olympics and the annexation of Austria. Hitler kept his suite on permanent standby. When Göring asked where such a pretty Lili had bloomed, she told him a tale of a young girl from an honest family who had been left alone far too young and brought tears to his eyes. And when Himmler asked when Marius was going to share his flair for logistics and join the SS – where wives were subject to as much scrutiny as their husbands – Marius pleaded the pressure of running Hitler's favourite hotel and no more was said.

'We are happy together. We are safe.'

They told each other that as often as it needed to be told. The first part was certainly true. The second seemed to be holding.

Although that could change in a heartbeat. If I give myself away, or if somebody does appear from the past and recognises me.

She had far more nightmares about that happening than she ever shared with Marius.

'Mama! You is here.'

Lili laughed as Gabi caught sight of her in the doorway and came running. She scooped her daughter up and pressed her face against the child's vanilla-sweet skin. And she pushed away the thought that always came hand-in-hand with, *We are safe,* the one which neither she nor Marius would ever admit.

As long as we don't stray too far outside the world we've built inside here; as long as our secret stays with us.

'Vom Rath is dead and his assassin was Jewish – the streets are about to explode. I've been warned by the Party to keep as many of our guests inside tonight as we can. And they're sending a couple of guards to make sure that none of the trouble spills over our way.'

Lili didn't allow her expression to falter as Marius whispered the news in her ear. She waved at a familiar face checking in. She complimented a passing bellboy on his smart uniform. She didn't need to ask where the warning and the promise of protection had come from, although she wished they weren't so high on the list. The Edel was important to the Party, and the Party looked after its own.

'I'll send a personal note to each room to say that the city is best avoided tonight. You speak to Chef – tell him we'll have a full house for dinner. And I'll arrange extra entertainment and dancing to follow. Nobody will have any interest in going outside.'

Marius kissed her cheek and hurried off to the kitchens. Lili sent a message to her secretary to meet her upstairs.

Everything must look normal, especially when it's anything but.

She repeated the Rodenberg mantra to herself as she crossed the foyer at her usual pace. It kept her face smooth. It didn't stop her feeling sick.

Ernst vom Rath – a German diplomat based at the Reich's embassy in Paris – had been shot two days earlier on November the seventh by Herschel Grynszpan, a young Polish-German Jew. Nobody knew exactly why the attack had happened, and nobody was focused on why, once they heard *Jew*. Hitler had sent his personal physician to Paris. The diplomat's face was all over the newspapers; he'd been turned into a martyr even as he clung on to life. As soon as Lili had heard that vom Rath's assailant was Jewish, she'd known what to expect. And now he was dead.

The streets are about to explode.

It didn't take a genius to work out who was going to pay.

The previous day's papers had been thick with articles stirring up hatred against Germany's Jewish population, and those articles had borne fruit. Shops and synagogues in Hessen and Kassel and Dessau – cities which the papers praised for their long-standing tradition of loyalty to 'old values' – had been looted and destroyed. Now the tension had reached Berlin. Lili had felt it souring the air when she'd taken Gabi to look for conkers in the park earlier that morning. She'd come back so desperate for news, she'd actually wished that this was one of the days she had to play host to Hitler. She was never in the room for long, but she increasingly made good use of those moments.

The men who gathered there were careful how they spoke, and Hitler was the least talkative of all. From what Lili had observed, he preferred to start a conversation and see where it went, rather than taking an overt lead in it. There were certain words, however, that the men favoured, and Lili – although she had no idea what to do with the nuggets she gleaned, and Marius grew nervous when she tried to sew them together – had begun to decipher their meaning. She knew who was meant by *problem*. She was aware that Hitler's key ministers had each been tasked with finding a *solution* to that, and that they were all competing like small boys to come up with the winning idea and secure his favour. She'd heard the words *removal* and *resettlement*. Unfortunately, Hitler was in Munich, so – apart from the courtesy of a phone call from the Reich Chancellery to check its safety – the Edel was as dependent as the rest of the city on rumour and personal contacts.

It was just after ten p.m., as the last dessert was being served and the dancing began, when one of those contacts finally came good and a journalist rang the hotel.

'Goebbels has made a speech calling for retaliatory action across the country. Munich is already burning.'

Lili swore later she heard the first roar and the first cascade of breaking glass in the same moment Marius came to her in the ballroom. Whether that was true or not, from that moment until the skies cleared the next morning and revealed the extent of the destruction, shattering glass and screams were the loudest sounds in her head.

'Tell the band to turn up the volume and not to play any slow tunes, and tell André to open more champagne. I'm going to check on Gabi.'

Lili left Marius to charm the guests and ease their concerns, not that she expected many of the Edel's current clientele to be consumed by those. The world in which synagogues burned and anybody cared was light years away from the world they lived in. And tonight more than any other troubled night, Lili hated that she was supposed to live in that world too. She certainly couldn't sit comfortably in it doing nothing. She went upstairs but – once she saw that both Gabi and her nanny were safely asleep – she didn't stay. She grabbed a coat and slipped out into the streets.

One turn away from the Edel's pretty lights and lively music and into Friedrichstraße and the night's landscape shifted. Lili flattened herself against a wall as the approaching mob drew closer. It was four abreast and deepening. She steeled herself and wriggled forward into a better position. The numbers were increasing every second, the crowd splintering into factions as it grew. Angry voices hurled street names and districts in a rallying cry. Oranienburger Straße, Artillieriestraße, Charlottenburg. Places where there were synagogues, where the city's Jewish population was more heavily concentrated. The faces doing the shouting were shrouded in shadow, but Lili could see the outlines of mallets and clubs. She could smell petrol.

'What in God's name are you doing?'

It was Marius, pulling at her arm, pulling her back.

'The doorman saw you leave and head this way, and he called me. Are you trying to get yourself killed?'

'No, of course I'm not.'

Lili twisted away from him, her whole body wincing as another window shattered in the darkness behind them.

'I had to see for myself what was happening. And I have to help. We have to help.'

Marius's reaction was clear even in the poor light. He was already saying no and shaking his head. Lili ignored him.

'We don't have a choice. This is going to get worse. People are going to be in terrible danger tonight – people like me.'

He gasped with horror as she said what was never meant to be said. He pulled her close again, begging her to be quiet. Lili ignored that too.

'You do understand what's needed, don't you? You've done it before. You made the Edel a safe haven for me; now we can do the same for so many others.' She grabbed his arm and started dragging him towards the corner where the bulk of the mob had assembled. 'Look at the crowd – listen to them. This is much more dangerous than the riots in the summer. They've gathered like lightning on the back of vom Rath's death and Goebbels' speech – the response must have been organised. We can't stop the burning or the looting, I know that, but this is our chance to stop innocent people from being injured or killed. And it won't be hard, not with all our resources. We could send cars to the worst areas; we could go there ourselves and fetch the most threatened ones back.'

She stopped, waiting for Marius to jump onto the same page as her. He didn't. He didn't ask her to be quiet again – the roar was so loud now, it was impossible to pick out individual voices so there was no need. But he didn't listen to her pleas either, and he didn't agree.

'We can't do that, Lili. I wish we could, but it's impossible. We can't do anything to change what's happening. And I'm sorry, I really am, but if we stand up to this mob, if we take a stand against Goebbels and take one Jewish person into the Edel for safekeeping, what do you think will happen then?'

Lili knew, but she didn't care. She'd been waiting for a crowd bent on vengeance to assemble ever since the news of vom Rath's murder was announced. Now that it had, a spark had woken inside her she'd been damping down for too long.

'Don't do this, Marius. Don't let me down, not now. I've said and done nothing for ten years. I've been a coward, living my safe life while so many others have had that right stripped away. It's not enough. I owe my father more than my silence.'

It was said. It was heard. And Marius's face was twisted with misery, but he still shook his head.

'That you feel so guilty breaks my heart; that you think I'm letting you down breaks it too. And I know how brave you are. That you'd risk discovery if it meant we could make the Edel into some kind of sanctuary and save others doesn't surprise me at all.' He suddenly tipped her face up to his, so she was forced to see the fear in his eyes. 'But what about Gabi? Have you really thought about her? She's the child of a forbidden marriage. They could take her away, Lili, don't you realise that? Isn't your silence what she deserves?'

She'd been so caught up, she hadn't been thinking about Gabi at all, and that horrified her. Pain ripped through Lili at the thought of her actions bringing harm to her child. And a sense of helplessness that cut as deep as when she'd watched her father disappear under a flurry of blows.

'But there has to be something we can do. There has to be some way to help.'

She turned back to where the street was steadily filling, the crowd spreading out its hatred like a smothering blanket.

'This thirst for violence won't go away. It will grow bigger. It will do worse.'

The mob was marching, torches lit, voices raised in the songs whose horror had haunted Lili for years.

'I can't stand meekly by as they destroy everything that's decent and good. And I can't put Gabi in danger. So what am I meant to do?'

Now Marius was the one without an answer.

He took her hand. They went back to the hotel, entering it through the service entrance so the SA thugs guarding the front door couldn't ask awkward questions. They went back to the ballroom where Lili did what she was required to do and smiled her brightest smile at all the people who had no interest in what was happening outside their champagne-filled bubble. Who'd swallowed the lies about pure and impure blood so completely, they felt no sense of kinship or obligation to the people whose lives were about to be ruined. Who made Lili sick.

When they eventually returned to their apartment, Marius fell into an exhausted sleep. Lili couldn't settle or find any peace. She abandoned their bed. She stood alone at the window instead, watching the flames bloom across Berlin's dark skies in ragged bursts of crimson and orange, watching the smoke trails spread bruises across the firelight.

Watching the world start to end.

CHAPTER 7

AUGUST 1990

'I know your family history is a difficult subject, but I thought you might like to have these. It seemed a shame to discover them only to file them away again.'

Lucy handed the small album to Adam with more confidence than she felt. She wasn't certain that – just because a photograph was a lifeline for her – the images it contained would speak positively to him. Or help him speak more easily to her. But she did know that the cost of staying cut off from the past was a hard one, and she didn't want that hardship for him.

She watched him open it, hoping that the selections which she'd fretted over were the right ones. The last thing she wanted to do was upset him. The first picture she'd included was a group portrait of Marius as a young boy, in a formal pose with his parents. She'd added the wedding photograph of Marius and Lili after that, and a handful of Christmas and New Year's Eve celebrations which showed the Edel in a happy light. She'd left out a lot of what she'd found. The photo of Marius in his Wehrmacht uniform. One of Hitler and Himmler flanking a beautiful bride in the ballroom which had made her skin crawl.

It was a relief when he thumbed through the pages and didn't immediately hand the little book straight back.

'I've only ever seen the newspaper picture of Lili; this one is a lot less formal. And I've never seen one of my grandfather. I really do look like him, don't I?' He smiled up at Lucy with a warmth she hadn't seen before. 'Thank you. I mean that. You didn't have to go to this much effort, but I appreciate that you did.'

It was a good start, although the pictures didn't appear to be triggering any memories which might help assemble the hazier details of Lili's story. Which meant Adam wasn't the only person who needed to see them. Lucy mentally crossed her fingers in the hope that he'd stay as positive when she mentioned the second part of her plan.

'Will you show them to your mother, do you think?'

She's expected his first reaction to be an instant *no*. She'd expected him to say that his mother wouldn't be interested or that the pictures might be too hard for her to see. Lucy was ready to counter either of those answers, by explaining that Gabi's recollections – of the Edel or her childhood after she presumably left it – could be key to understanding how widely Lili's secret was known, and could flesh out what might be told in the future by others. But she wasn't prepared for Adam's shock at the suggestion, or the guilt she saw flash across his face before he looked down again. And she could only think of one way to explain that.

'She doesn't know you're working on the Edel's refurbishment, does she?'

'No.'

He didn't say anything else; he didn't look up. Lucy ignored the *I'm pushing boundaries again and that didn't exactly go easily last time* which had immediately jumped into her head. A simple *no* wouldn't do. Gabi was the loose thread. The one whose reaction to the hotel's reopening and any revelations that might follow was – for Lucy anyway – a complete unknown. And if there was to be any control over how Lili's past emerged, the last thing Lucy needed was loose threads.

'I hadn't realised that, and I'm sorry if this is too personal a question – I seem to have a habit of asking those with you, and it's not how I normally do my job – but is there a reason why you haven't told her? Are you concerned she might be angry, or upset?'

She paused as Adam shifted in his seat and glanced at his briefcase. He clearly wanted to leave. Lucy put her hand on his arm to stop him, and the surprise of that brought his head back up.

'I appreciate this may be difficult for you, Adam, but I'm not asking out of idle curiosity. I'm trying to get ahead of any problems that could sour the relaunch, and I'm wondering if your mother might know some of those. Or cause some of those.'

Her directness – if not her touch – settled him. His answer did little to settle her.

'I don't know. I really don't. She's my mother, but I barely know her.'

He slipped back into himself as Lucy withdrew her hand and waited, wondering what she had stumbled into. And although what he said next sounded as if he was sharing a part of his past with her, his tone belonged to a man who was pulling his barriers up higher.

'I've lived separately from Gabi for almost half of my life, for all my adult life. And not just separately but completely out of contact. There's a lot of hurt, on both sides. There's a lot still unspoken, and neither of us seem capable of tackling that gulf.'

I didn't know about the Edel until the Wall came down.

There was a great deal that Lucy didn't know about the workings of the Deutsche Demokratische Republik, but she did know that free movement between East and West had ended in 1961 when the Wall went up. She was aware that people had died in the years after that, trying to cross the border and get from one side of Berlin to the other. *Out of contact* was heavy with more questions than she knew how to ask.

I'm out of my depth with him. I can't begin to guess at his story, never mind get to the bottom of Lili's.

That was an odd feeling.

Outside the older and very wealthy circles working for Charlie had brought her into contact with, the men Lucy normally met were – at least on the surface – very like Adam. They were smartly dressed and cosmopolitan, high-achieving and ambitious and – like her too – they held professional jobs at a level slightly above what was expected of people in their early thirties. They were also easy creatures to place. Yes, a few had softened their northern accents when they moved south in the same way she had done, and they also didn't take the London salaries that they were earning and their parents were stunned by for granted. Most, however, had been to the same sorts of schools and the same universities and, if they hadn't, they glossed over that gap as smoothly as Lucy did, and they were old hands at changing the subject. All those factors usually added up to men she could read, men without overly complex layers. Which was why she was rarely tempted to take the relationships she fell into with them very seriously. She was afraid they'd be wary of the too complex layers in her.

But he wouldn't be because he's got his own. And they're not easy to read or place at all.

Lucy didn't know what to do with that thought, or with the confusion on Adam's face as he stared deliberately away from her. He no longer looked uncomfortable; he looked lost.

Maybe this project could be the thing that brings him and Gabi together. Maybe this will be what heals them.

She bit her lip and dropped that idea as quickly as it came. On the rare occasions she'd encountered fractured family relationships before, Lucy's default had been to try and mend them, and the irony of that wasn't lost on her. She also knew better than anyone that wishes stayed as wishes, and Hollywood happy endings were as elusive in the real world as a rainbow's pot of gold. Meddling in Adam's relationship with his mother was no more part of her remit than puzzling at his layers. And no matter how intriguing she was starting to find him, getting personally involved with colleagues was high on Lucy's list of things not to do.

She decided therefore not to respond directly to what he'd said. She gave them both a moment to collect themselves. Then she asked if he would agree to try and arrange a meeting for her with Gabi anyway. She wasn't sure which of them was the most surprised when he nodded.

That couldn't have gone worse if I'd planned it that way.

Lucy rubbed her bare arms and wished she was wearing a jumper. The temperature outside was so warm, her nose was sprinkled with freckles, but the Edel's cellars existed in a damp and frosty climate of their own. Chilly or not, they were still the only place she wanted to be. She needed the soothing rhythm of sorting through boxes and filling in the gaps in the hotel's timeline. She needed to re-establish a sense of control. And she needed to stop picking over the afternoon's frustrations and mistakes, although that was easier said than done.

'She's agreed to meet, but not here at the hotel, or at her flat. She's suggested a café near the Tierpark, which is the East's equivalent of Berlin Zoo and an area she knows. She's rigid, I'm afraid. She has rules.'

Lucy arrived at the rather less than cosy café where Adam and Gabi were waiting, imagining the mother to be an equally

elegant, if more reserved, version of the son. Instead, the real
Gabi was a dowdy and functional-looking woman. Her hair
lacked a style, her face was make-up free; her skirt and blouse
had been chosen with little concern for colour or flair. But what
she lacked in elegance, she made up for in the reserve Lucy had
expected.

Her eyes roamed the café as Lucy introduced herself, as if
she was checking who might be watching or listening. She
didn't shake hands; she barely smiled. And when she started to
speak – cutting across Lucy's explanation of why she'd wanted
them to meet – Lucy finally understood the phrase she'd heard a
number of newscasters use to describe how the reuniting citizens of Berlin regarded each other. *The Wall may have been
dismantled, but it's as solid as ever inside too many heads.*

'I'm not my mother. I've never been her.'

Gabi presented her whole life to Lucy in that opening
sentence and then continued her monologue with an agenda
which made sense of *rigid*. What followed was a description of
a perfectly lived, and perfectly happy, DDR life. Gabi
described her adoptive father's role as a doctor who worked selfless hours and her own career as a teacher helping to mould the
minds of the East's next generation with great pride. She told
Lucy about the teaching medals she'd been awarded in recogni-
tion of her selfless contribution to her country, and about her
and her parents' apartments in the buildings reserved for citizens of honour on Karl-Marx-Allee. She delivered her sermon
in words that were weighty with *duty* and *service* and empty of
Lili and Adam. And then she folded her hands and her lips and
was done.

*That's where I should have left things too and accepted that
there was no common ground between us. And been happy that
I'd got nothing to worry about.*

Lucy carried on unpacking the box on the table in front of
her without registering its contents. Gabi hadn't agreed to meet

to talk about Lili; she'd come to the café to distance herself. To prove that there was nothing between her and her mother beyond a biological tie which brought her no pleasure. It was obvious that, if Lili's story emerged, Gabi would retreat from it in the same way she'd been retreating from its shadows her whole life. She wasn't going to defend her mother. She wasn't going to cause problems. Lucy had understood that at once, but she was curious and irritated by Gabi's blocking of the questions she'd come with, and so set on uncovering the whole story she carried on prodding anyway.

'Don't you remember anything about your real parents? I appreciate this is hard, but I'm trying to make sure we do enough damage limitation to prevent a raft of bad PR when the hotel reopens and there are a lot of gaps in Lili's past which could jeopardise that. Any insight you can offer to fill those in would be a great help in averting future problems.'

She'd forgotten who she was talking to and made a mess of the conversation before it got started. She'd reverted to the kind of business-speak which was better suited to meetings with people desperate to impress Compton Hotels and talked about PR and *damage limitation* to a woman whose values were in direct opposition to such westernised ideas. And she'd said *real* and dismissed the parents Gabi was so evidently proud of as if they were of no consequence. It was little wonder Gabi's stiff veneer finally cracked.

'What do you want from me? Do you want me to tell you that I gave flowers to Hitler with a big smile on my face when I was a little girl? Do you want me to say I saw my mother waltzing with Goebbels? Do you want me to tell you that I loved her, or that I hated her and I wish her name would disappear as completely as she did? Why don't you just tell me which one your precious PR campaign needs?'

That outburst had silenced the café. Realising what she'd

said and done had shocked Gabi to her feet. And her anger at herself had turned her fury on Adam.

'This is your fault. If you'd only been satisfied with the good life you could have had here in the East, we'd all be okay now. But no, you had to follow your own path and destroy everyone else's. Well I won't be party to that kind of disloyalty anymore.'

She'd fled then, leaving Lucy open-mouthed and Adam shaking, and their onlookers buzzing with exactly the kind of gossip Lucy had been desperate to avoid.

And I still didn't have the sense to stop blurring the lines and leave too.

The box was empty now. Lucy began turning over the papers and ledgers it had contained, keeping her movements slow in the hope her heart rate would follow.

'I'm so sorry.'

Adam's voice rang as clearly through her head as if he was sitting beside her. She could almost smell the café's weak coffee.

'She's afraid. Not just of the past, although that's a huge issue, but of the future too. She hates change; she wasn't brought up in a world that embraced it. She doesn't understand why the DDR has fallen, and she doesn't want it to go.' He'd sighed then, as if he was running old arguments through his head. 'She never would accept its worst elements. She'd talk for hours about the good stuff: the full employment and the free healthcare the state provided and how well looked after we all were. But mention the surveillance, or the Stasi secret police, or the people who disappeared into their godforsaken prisons, or worse, and she'd get up and walk away, the way she just did. She'd deny it all. Even though the state abandoned her because I did and reduced her perfect life to ruins.'

Abandoned. A life reduced.

The words and phrases that always strip me bare.

That was where the afternoon had finally collapsed, in a

collision between Adam's failings and hers which had blind-sided her.

Lucy had done well. She hadn't blurted out, *What did you do to break her heart like this?* Or, *Why aren't you more grateful that you have her?* She hadn't said, *Do you know how much I'd give to be sitting in a café anywhere with my child?* She'd held back all the misery that *abandoned* stirred up. And she hadn't run blindly out of the café like Gabi. She'd left abruptly, but she'd left politely. She'd held back the tears at her own mistakes, but now they were here, trickling down her face, splashing onto the cover of a dusty old book which had been buried beneath the ledgers.

I can't keep doing this. I can't keep crying for Emily and doing nothing else. I have to take charge of my life.

She'd thought that before and done nothing. That situation couldn't continue – Lucy understood that; she wanted to change that, but she didn't know what the next steps were, and she wasn't ready to dig for them yet.

I need a distraction. The answers will come if I don't focus on them.

She wiped her face and opened the smaller book's frayed cover. It wasn't another account book, as she'd assumed. At first glance, she thought it was a straightforward diary: the entries were dated and many of them recorded events which had taken place in the hotel. As she read further, however, she realised that what she'd found was far more than a simple social calendar. The dates weren't confined to one year, and a substantial number of the entries – some of which had unfortunately been damaged by dirt and damp over the years – had been written in the form of letters.

My darling Marius... Your devoted Lili

Each letter she could decipher started and ended the same

way. Each entry was in the same handwriting, which clearly belonged to Lili.

Lucy forgot her cold arms; she forgot all about Gabi and Adam. Unsent letters were things she understood.

She began to read through the journal with more care. An hour disappeared, then another. She stopped glancing at her watch. When she finally emerged from its pages, her heart was racing again, and Lili was completely rewritten.

PART TWO

CHAPTER 8

MAY 1940

'Lili?'

She turned at the man's greeting, her polite public smile fixed in place. His next words instantly wiped that away.

'Lili Krauss, is it really you?'

Everything froze with *Krauss*. Berlin became Leipzig, Lili lost her bearings. The man's face was a blank; the busy street was a blur. Her first thought was, *I've been caught*. Her second was to wonder why she'd never planned for such an inevitable thing happening. And her instinct was to run, to put as much space as she could between herself and Marius. To buy him and the Edel time before the storm broke. It was a good instinct, but she couldn't move. Terror had fallen over her like a net and tied up her limbs.

She wanted to challenge the man who was staring at her. She wanted to draw on all her acquired dignity as Marius Rodenberg's wife and dismiss him. She could no more do that than move. For all she knew, he was a catcher, a Jew black-mailed by the Gestapo into catching other Jews. For all she knew, he'd been stalking her for weeks. And if that was the case...

Lili had been right about the hatred which had torn through the city in November 1938, in the co-ordinated attack which was now known as Kristallnacht. It had grown bigger; it had done worse. That night shops and synagogues all over Germany had been reduced to piles of charred bricks and broken glass. In the days that followed, the attacks switched onto the frightened people who'd worked and worshipped in those ruined buildings. Jewish children were finally expelled from all German schools. Jewish businessmen were compelled to hand over what property and money they had left into the hands of *true* German citizens. And then they were ordered to use the funds they no longer had to pay the bill for the Kristallnacht clear-up.

That night had given birth to a new word: *Aryanisation*. The forced transfer of Jewish-owned businesses to non-Jews; the redrawing of Germany's economic landscape and Berlin's streets. It was a word Lili had learned at Hitler's lunches and one that had leaked out into the newspapers who uniformly applauded the policy that went with it. The country became a feeding frenzy as companies like Thyssen and Krupp, who the papers referred to as reputable, raced to gobble up all the stolen Jewish assets they could get their hands on. Lili could hardly bear to walk into the Edel's cocktail lounge for the sound of the bankers and the industrialists crowing. Nobody else turned a hair. Now that Hitler had fooled the French and the British into believing he wasn't a threat and had done what he'd planned all along and taken Germany to war, Aryanisation was being touted as the only safe way forward. The fear that the Jews would use their wealth to sabotage victory in this war in the way the papers insisted they'd sabotaged the last one had become ever more widespread, and acceptable. And not just in Germany.

The Führer's hunger for land had swallowed up Poland and Czechoslovakia. His hatred had swept through the populations of those newly occupied territories as fiercely as Kristallnacht's fires had swept through Berlin. He'd made a speech in parliament predicting that war would bring about the extermination of the entire Jewish race in Europe and brought his clapping audience to their feet. No one thought they could curb his anti-semitism now. No one, as far as Lili could see, wanted to try.

Ghetto. Concentration camp.

She'd grown accustomed to hearing those new words at the lunches too. Hitler was determined to march into the future without any trace of Europe's Jews; there would be no more safe places. And if she had been uncovered, if the Nazis had Marius's wealth in their sights, there'd be no saving any of them.

So I can't let him take the upper hand.

'Why would you call me by that name?'

She waited for the laugh, for the signal to the policeman waiting behind him. Instead, the man froze. He looked round, but – although he was clearly checking the street – he didn't wave or call out.

He's as afraid of being caught as I am.

That realisation unknotted her limbs, but she no longer wanted to run. Catcher or not, there was danger here, and Lili needed to gauge how deep it ran. Now it was her turn to glance around, to look for a place where she could take control of the situation. Luckily there was an old corner bar a couple of minutes' walk away, one of Berlin's dark recesses which refused to move with anyone's times but their own. Nobody from the Rodenbergs' circle would ever frequent it, but Lili hadn't always been a Rodenberg. She nodded towards it; he followed her at a careful distance. Neither of them spoke until they were sat at its gloomiest table, with their backs to the door. Lili was determined to say as little as she could until he'd revealed his hand. She waited for him to start.

'I'm so sorry. I broke every rule greeting you in public like that. It was the surprise of seeing you again after so long – of seeing anybody from the old days in Leipzig.'

Aaron Matzner. His name had come back to Lili the instant she looked properly at him, along with a memory of a gangly, permanently hungry boy stumbling through their Hebrew lessons and irritating the rabbi. Not someone she would ever have expected to see in Berlin.

'Why are you here, Aaron. It is Aaron, isn't it?' She gathered a little more courage as he nodded. He'd been an annoying boy but never a cruel one. 'I thought you'd make your life in Leipzig, not here.'

The pain which flashed over his face told her she had nothing to fear.

'So did I, but there's nothing left of us there. The synagogue has gone – it was burned to the ground in 1938. Anyone from the community with the resources to leave has long gone too. I didn't have the money to get further than here, where I've been for a year now, looking for like-minds and safety in numbers. But none of that's any excuse for behaving like a fool.'

Lili clamped down on her last images of the Leipzig synagogue before they could derail her and kept her focus on Aaron. He gulped down his brandy and poured another generous measure from the bottle he'd brought with him from the bar. His face and body were so thin, Lili wondered if drink was his main source of nourishment.

Aaron saw her staring and shook his head. 'I'm not a drunk, if that's what you're wondering. Despite what I just did, I need to keep my wits sharp. But I still have the hollow legs I had as a boy, and food's not so plentiful now as it was then.'

The well-stocked larders at the Edel popped into Lili's head and she blushed. Rationing had been introduced in August 1939, shortly before the Wehrmacht marched into Poland, but that was a measure designed to conserve not limit resources, and no one classed as a German citizen had gone hungry. The Edel's favoured status meant it hadn't been affected at all. It was a different story, however, for Berlin's Jews. They were only allowed to stop in designated stores, for an hour a day between four and five p.m. when the shelves were severely depleted, and they had to pay higher prices for the privilege.

Maybe he needs help; maybe that's something I could offer.

'How are you surviving? With all the restrictions and the rules, I mean. Do you have work?'

Aaron didn't answer that. He was too busy scanning the diamond clips in her ears and the pearls at her throat.

'Never mind me – you've reinvented yourself, haven't you? You're not Jewish here.' He whistled under his breath. 'No wonder you looked as scared as if I was about to produce a warrant or a gun when I used your old name. Are you in hiding? Are you getting help, or do you need it?'

She'd been expecting his judgement if she revealed herself, but all she could hear was concern. When she quickly ran through who she'd become – because she could sense he was a man who would see straight through lies – his eyes widened.

'So you see, perhaps I could help you. The Edel is wealthy; we've not been affected by rationing. We'd need to be careful, of course, but I could carve out food supplies if you could use them. I'd like to do something. Sometimes the guilt of living so easily when too many of us don't overwhelms me.'

She'd never used *us* before. She'd never had the possibility of an ally, of someone who understood what it was like to live with one eye over your shoulder. She almost cried when he smiled.

'That's very generous, especially given the risks. But what if there was something more you could do?'

'What do you mean?'

Suddenly, having an ally seemed rather less enticing. Lili sat back as she imagined Marius's horror at the way the conversation was going; at the thought she was having this conversation at all. But Aaron had spotted an opportunity, and he wasn't about to give up.

'Worse days are coming. No matter how well you've hidden yourself, you must know that. The race laws and the violence and the seizure of property has isolated us and stripped away the last vestiges of security we were hanging on to. We're the enemy now, as much as the British and the French, maybe more so.' He looked at his drink, but he didn't pick it up. 'Nobody cares what happens to us, Lili. We're already being pushed into specially designated Jewish housing; soon they're going to start rounding us up. Next they'll be putting us into ghettos and those camps they've been building. Hiding us away, making it easier to kill us.'

Lili wrapped her arms round her body as his words sliced through her. The bar was so cut off from the spring sunshine, it might as well have been winter. Her silk dress was too thin. Her blood was ice. His vision of the future was the vision which increasingly lived in her head and haunted her dreams. The one she'd overheard Hitler and his ministers steadily building. She clenched her lips shut as he carried on.

'Some of us are already planning for that future happening. I couldn't get out; I didn't have the money, but I'm surviving, and I can help other people do the same.'

She wanted to say, *Stop, don't tell me.* Instead, she said, 'How?'

'There's a group of us, or more accurately a chain. We find people with the skills to make false papers and map out routes and find food. And we move people to safety, so that at least some of us will still be alive when this finally ends. And to do that we need safe houses.'

'Who's involved? In this chain of yours? Are you in charge of it? And who does the moving? It can't just be you.'

Lili didn't want to know, but she also didn't want him to ask the question she knew was coming.

Aaron shook his head. 'I can't tell you any of that. If you were involved, I wouldn't tell you much either. It's best that nobody knows who's in charge or where they sit in the system. Each link plays its part, but it's an invisible one. And you and the Edel could—'

'Don't Aaron, please. Don't ask what I can't give. I have a daughter to think of.'

Lili hated the disappointment Aaron didn't try to hide. She hated that he said, 'Please.' That he countered her refusal with, 'So do a lot of the people who are going to die.' She hated herself for being so frightened.

'If it was just me, I'd do it. But I can't put her, or my husband, or all the staff who would pay the price if your plans go wrong, at risk. I'm sorry. I really am.'

She got to her feet, unable to look at him.

'Will you at least take this?'

He'd dug a pen from his pocket and a scrap of paper that he scribbled a short message on while she shifted from foot to foot.

'It's an address where – even if I've gone or reinvented myself too – you'll find someone who can bring you on board. When things really collapse. When – as I hope you will – you find the courage to change your mind.'

Lili couldn't see a day like that coming, and she didn't like the implication that she was a coward even if it felt true, but she couldn't refuse the note. She stuffed it into her bag and didn't reply when he asked her not to destroy it. There was so much more she wanted to say. She wanted to explain why she'd hidden herself; she wanted to repeat the offer of food. She needed to ask him not to tell anybody her new name, even though he would likely be insulted if she did. But Aaron had finished with her and turned back to his drink. There was nothing left for Lili to do but leave.

All Lili wanted to do was get home to the Edel, to hug Gabi, to spend the afternoon devising treats for her daughter. To feel safe.

She entered the foyer determined not to notice the swastikas which hung down like curtains. Determined to ignore the uniforms too many of the hotel's clientele now wore. To smile at the house detective who'd been newly assigned to them by the Gestapo – because of the number of American journalists who still visited the Edel, according to the officer who'd taken no notice of Marius's protests that their old detective had done a perfectly good job. To see only the beauty in the building, not what Marius's determination to keep her safe had forced it to become. *If the Edel can adapt, so can I*, was Lili's mantra now.

The Edel, as Marius kept reminding Lili, was used to uniforms and used to war. The hotel had watched hundreds of young officers dance in the ballroom and then march out of the city with their hearts full of victory in 1914. She'd felt their loss four years later, in the empty arms the music couldn't fill; she'd watched their sweethearts grieve. The Edel knew war started with hope and ended with horror, regardless of whether victory was won or lost. She carried her ghosts in her fabric, but she'd survived the first war, and Marius was convinced that she would survive this one too. Lili hoped he was right, but the red flags and the Führer's portrait which dominated the foyer felt like stabs to the Edel's heart and she was worried the scars would run too deep to be mended this time. And today something had stirred the pain up. Half a dozen steps inside the door and she could taste the unease.

'It's Klemens, the pastry chef. He's been arrested. That's not his real name. He's Jewish and someone denounced him. The Gestapo took him away.'

André had lost his usual eloquence. He fell over his words so clumsily, it took Lili a moment to understand what he was saying. She'd noticed him hovering when she came in, but she'd assumed that he'd had another supplier dispute and was waiting for her to resolve it. Now he was sweating and drawing too much attention. She took hold of his elbow and steered him into the corridor beside the lifts.

'Say that again – slowly. Take a breath first.'

He did as she asked. Then he grabbed and wouldn't let go of her hands, which was almost as much of a shock as his news.

'We have to do something, Frau Rodenberg. He's not the only one here at risk. Could you intervene? Could you speak to...'

He ran out of steam; he couldn't say the names.

If we were a safe house, I could have got Klemens away.

Lili shook that thought out of her head. She had no idea if Aaron's scheme even worked, and it was too late to worry at that now.

'Is there anybody else at risk of the same charge, André? Is there anyone else they might come back for?'

He dropped her hands and dropped his eyes. 'Don't ask me that. Isn't it better these days not to know? But do something, please. They'll send him to one of their camps – I know it. Or they'll interrogate him, and he's not strong enough to survive that.'

Invisible links, fragile lives. She could feel their threads stretching through the Edel, threatening to snap.

Lili closed her eyes for a moment. This wasn't Aaron, asking her to help people she didn't know in some future that might not happen. This was a member of the Edel's family, and there were rules about that. She couldn't let fear win again and refuse.

She pulled herself together and found the smile he needed. 'I'll go now. I'll make a good case for him, I promise. But I need you to do something for me.'

André was still shaken, which meant that the rest of the staff would be too, and that could affect the whole Edel. The last thing they needed was a nervous atmosphere that might let this story leak out.

'Would you speak to the staff on my behalf – tell them that everything will be fine? And then will you take Gabi to the kitchens for ice cream? I know Nanny could do it, but she can be very stiff, and nobody will have any fun if she's left in charge.'

Fun wasn't a word many people would apply to André either, but Lili knew he could be trusted to understand the diversion she intended Gabi to be and would let the staff spoil her. The task brought his shoulders back up as she knew it would. Now all she had to do was hold up her own.

SS Headquarters in Prinz-Albrecht-Straße was close by, but Lili called for the Rodenberg's Daimler anyway. It seemed better to arrive in style and remind them of her status. It took her less than five minutes to get there. It took her even less time in Himmler's office to realise what a fool she'd been. The Edel might be Hitler's favourite hotel, but that didn't guarantee her special treatment when the word *Jew* was involved.

'Are you telling me that your hotel detective, the Gestapo officer who made the discovery, is a liar? Or that your head waiter isn't a Jew? Or are you saying that him being a Jew is less important than him being a good worker? I have to confess, Frau Rodenberg, that I'm a little confused as to what you are saying, or doing, here.'

Himmler's patient smile was as false and unpleasant as the overly polite way he'd pointed out what a mistake she'd made in pleading Klemens's case. Neither gave Lili anything to appeal to. She knew she'd lost as his smile spread.

'I do appreciate that this has been a rather nasty experience. It's always a shock when someone we trust turns out to be something else. But your employee is Jewish – that's a fact. He's not entitled to his job and he lied, and that's a crime. And if there is any suggestion that you or your dear husband knew and were protecting him...'

Himmler spread his hands and shrugged and left the threat hanging. Lili stood up. There was nothing she could do to help Klemens, and she needed to leave before she made his situation worse.

'I have wasted your valuable time, Reichsführer. Forgive me. As you say, it's been a shock, and he has always been such a well-thought of employee, so...'

Now it was her turn to let the sentence hang and let Himmler read it how he chose. He got up too and ushered her towards the door with his hand resting far too comfortably at her waist.

'So you let your kind heart overrule your pretty head. Let's say no more about it. I'm sure no one else's loyalty is in doubt; I'm sure the Führer will see things the same way. But it might be best to check your staff a little more carefully in future, my dear.' His smile was bright as he opened the door and horribly at odds with his tone. 'And perhaps it's time to make that loyalty a little more public and for your husband to stop acting as if he's too good to put on a uniform. Even busy hotel owners must make sacrifices during a war.'

Lili managed a nod. She left with her whole body shaking. For the second time in a day, she found herself on a pavement gulping for clean air.

It's always a shock when someone we trust turns out to be something else.

Himmler didn't know her secret; he couldn't. But she'd given him the chance to play games with her and threaten her family, and he'd taken it.

Lili climbed into her waiting car and stared at her hands. They were still trembling, but she wasn't afraid anymore, although she had every reason to be, given the threat that now hung over Marius. Instead, she was furious about that; she was furious about everything. The power these men held and abused was dreadful. Their pursuit of a world filled with hate and based on prejudice and lies was unstoppable.

But it shouldn't be.

Himmler had insulted Marius. He'd made it clear that nobody in the Edel was safe. He'd made her feel powerless. But his arrogance and his dismissal of Klemens – a man Lili had never known to be anything but kind and good, who was as undeserving of the terrible treatment he'd likely now suffer as every other Jew who fell into Party hands – had turned her earlier fear of reprisals into cold fury.

Lili reached into her bag and pulled out Aaron's note. Nothing on the surface had changed. Marius and Gabi still needed her silence and her protection. She had no illusions about what would happen if she revealed herself to the world by making some ill-conceived and foolish protest. But she could no longer live with being powerless. She could no longer pretend that the world outside the Edel couldn't impinge on their lives as long as she kept the world inside it safe.

She picked at the silk lining as the car turned back into Mohrenstraβe and slipped the note down inside the rip she would sew seamlessly back together later. The note was a weapon, a way to say, *This persecution cannot go on.* And she didn't know how, and she didn't know when, but she knew that some day – when the scales tipped beyond the point where saying no was impossible – it was the weapon she would choose.

CHAPTER 9

NOVEMBER 1941

The scales have finally tipped, my love. I can't go on looking the other way.

Lili paused, unsure what to say next. She still wasn't certain how much information she could entrust even to her own private pages. Writing like this was new to her – she'd never kept any kind of a diary before. She'd tried it as a girl because that's what her classmates did, but the discipline of daily entries – which rarely amounted to more than a description of the flowers she'd used to make the day's prettiest bouquet – had bored her, and she'd lost interest in a week. This was different. This book wasn't a record of mundane events; it had become her way of unloading the secrets she couldn't voice, and her way of talking to Marius. It was a place for the outpourings that were meant for her eyes only, and for drafts of the letters she couldn't send, that couldn't be trusted to an army censor. Or to Marius's fears for her. She picked up her pen again and let her heart guide it.

*Oh God, I wish you were here. I need your advice; I need your
arms. I need you.*

If wishes came true, he would never have left.

Himmler had won, or in part anyway. Marius had been
raised with the concept of service baked into his bones and the
Reichsführer-SS's jibe about him being too good for a uniform
had stung. He hadn't waited for another insult. Marius had
taken Himmler's barbed comment as his cue to enrol as an
officer in the Wehrmacht in the summer of 1940, a decision
he'd presented to Lili as being a far more palatable option than
being corralled into the SS. And he'd discovered – to nobody's
surprise except his own – that he was very good at his new role.

He'd come back from the training academy in Munich filled
with new friendships and with a new spring in his step. Lili
applauded that and didn't tell him how much she hated his
uniform. Or that her heart leaped into her mouth every time she
pictured him marching onto a battlefield. Or that his absence
had made her prey to Göring's leering jokes and Goebbels'
attempted caresses in a way they wouldn't have dared try with
him there. She'd thrown Marius a party instead and cried with
relief when his first posting was to France where the fighting
was done. Now she could only hope that the Eastern Front –
where his logistical skills meant that Marius was about to be
deployed – would be as kind to him, even if he hadn't seemed so
sure about that.

Opening a war on a second front had taken everyone by
surprise, including the journalists who sat round the Edel's bar
every night and considered themselves combat experts. Hitler
had presented his about-face decision to turn on his Russian
allies and invade the Soviet Union in June 1941 as an act of
betrayal by them, not by him. He'd given endless speeches
insisting that a second front in the East would be as easily won

as the one he'd already won in the West. That mounting it was the only way to destroy the Russian communists and Jews who'd made a mockery of their earlier pledges of friendship, before they attempted to destroy Germany. He'd made the same declaration at the start of the lunch party he held shortly after ordering the Russian invasion and had waited while Lili and the serving staff clapped. Hitler was obsessed with the victory over the Soviets he was certain was coming. Marius thought the second campaign was a mistake and an over-extension of resources. He'd started worrying about the dangers of a Russian winter while the sun was still high in Berlin's sky.

> *It's rumour; it could be Allied propaganda. But I fear the worst has really come.*

She almost dug the pen through the paper as she recorded that, but at least she now knew what to write.

Lili wrapped her shawl tighter as the frosty air nipped round her shoulders. Her basement office was as cold as the kitchen's fridges compared to the study upstairs in her apartment; her secretary refused to work in it. And that was precisely the point. Cold or not, Lili insisted that she needed to be near the stockrooms when she was placing and checking orders, and she refused to move the ledgers to the suite. The truth was that the basement was the only place where she was never observed, where she could pour her fears out, in Marius's words and her own.

> *I'm keeping a record of what you told me, my love, so that you will see that my change of heart was the right one. You might not have wanted to believe the rumours you told me, but I do. Troops have been issued with orders to kill Jewish civilians – that's what you said, and I know you imagined me with a gun*

in my back when you said it. Thousands of Jewish men and women rounded up in Ukraine, taken to the edges of their villages and shot while the local police played music to drown out the sound of them dying. Special SS squads trained in the techniques of mass murder. You called them stories to stop me from breaking. We both know they are anything but.

It had broken her heart to watch him go back, but Marius couldn't resign or protest, or walk away. That path led to a firing squad. He could do nothing, but doing nothing had become impossible for her.

Hitler had grown so used to her presence at his lunches, he wasn't always as quick as he had been to dismiss her. Lili had learned very quickly that he had little regard for women – he assumed they were simple creatures who knew their place and didn't listen, or understand, when men spoke. She'd taken note of that; she smiled and stayed silent unless she was spoken to. She made sure he never had a reason to question that she was any different from any other good German wife. She took all the extra minutes she could get in the room and listened harder. Which was how she knew there was a new word being bandied around at the lunch parties now. *Clearance.* It was never defined – their coded words rarely were – but Lili hadn't had to puzzle out the meaning of this one. Not since the start of September when the Party had made the task of clearing the Jews out of Germany, and everywhere else in occupied Europe, into such a simple exercise.

Yellow stars. They're everywhere now, and who doesn't find yellow stars pretty?

Gabi scattered them across her pictures, twinkling out of her heavily scribbled black skies. Star-shaped celandines and dahlias went into yellow summer bouquets where they shone like pieces of heaven. Yellow stars were meant to be beautiful; they were meant to be magical. They weren't either of those things now. Now they came as a badge the law decreed had to be worn by every Jewish man, woman and child over the age of six. A sign that singled the wearer out, that said, 'You can see me – I'm here for the taking.'

So you see the stars are filled with poison now, and they're what tipped the scales.

Lili put down her pen and checked her watch. Five minutes to go before another nameless man slipped in through the kitchen door she was about to go and unlock. Before she beckoned him in with a finger on her lips and squirrelled him away into a walk-in cupboard in an unused far corner of the wine cellars that was barely big enough to house a child, never mind an adult. Five minutes to go, and twenty-four hours after that of being the Lili Rodenberg who was always calm and in control no matter how fast her heart was beating, before she sent him on his way again along the chain. Everybody involved in that process as nameless as the cargo she helped to ferry. Nobody knowing about the Edel's new role except her. It was a secret as dangerous as the other one she carried, which was why she needed to record what she'd done for her husband and explain why she'd gone back on her promise.

'Don't do it – I'm begging you. I understand why you might want to, but you don't really know who this Aaron is, and you don't know the other people involved. Anyone could betray you. From that side or from this if the wrong person gets wind of what's happening.'

She'd told Marius about her meeting with Aaron, and what he'd asked of her. And for a moment during the telling, she'd wavered. She'd thought about the Edel's cellars, which were a rabbit warren of nooks and crannies, and believed that the idea of hiding runaways in them was possible. Marius's furious and frightened, 'Don't you dare put us all at risk like that,' had been loud enough to wake up Gabi.

So Lili hadn't done it. Until Marius had left. Until she'd worked out how to manage the risks. Until the yellow stars had blossomed like fungus across Berlin and she'd had to.

She'd dug the note out of her bag and gone to Aaron's address then, wearing a dull hat and a shapeless coat she'd found in lost property. He wasn't there. The man who was had given up expecting her and needed a lot of reassurance she wasn't there as a spy, or as a hopeless want-to-be do-gooder who would buckle and give up the first time the Edel's resources were called on. Lili was never told that the first person who was sent to her wasn't on the run, or that she'd been set and passed a test. She was told not to ask questions, and she didn't. But she would tell Marius the truth when he came home again – she'd promised herself that. There was no point in worrying him with some cryptic message designed to bypass a censor until then.

She glanced at her watch again – it felt as if she'd barely taken her eyes from it – and was relieved that it was finally time to get moving. She put the diary safely away and started to recite her checklist under her breath as she got up, repeating it to herself as she stood by the door. Sometimes the whispered words made what she was doing less threatening and calmed her.

Marius isn't here and doesn't know; he can't come to any harm. Gabi is with her best friend for the night; she can't come to any harm either. No one on the staff knows a thing.

She was careful, she took precautions, she managed the danger. If she was caught, or so she told herself, she was the only one who would take the blame.

I'm helping;, I'm doing good. My father would be proud of me for making this stand.

She'd record that pledge in her diary too. The checklist might waver, but that was the one thought which always worked. Which steadied her hand and her nerve as she drew back the bolt and ushered her next desperate traveller in.

CHAPTER 10

JUNE–JULY 1942

'Is it true that you're there in the room with Hitler and his ministers? That you hear everything they discuss?'

Lili pressed herself closer to the thin wall. *Everything* was an overly hopeful word. The voices were so low today, she could barely catch a clear sentence. This lunch party had been an oddly subdued one from the start. Hitler had barely acknowledged her as she welcomed him into the room; Göring had drained his first drink without thanking her for pouring it; Goebbels hadn't leaned in and whispered his usual off-colour comment.

No, that's wrong. They weren't subdued: they were angry and trying to hide it. The Führer looked as if he was about to explode.

Lili wedged herself in tighter, taking care not to dislodge a dustpan or topple an iron. She didn't waste time wondering what Marius would say if he could see her. She knew all too well how horrified he would be that she'd not only gone back on her promise, she'd done far more in the end than he'd feared. Her only consolation was that he couldn't find out. There was nothing good about his long periods away with the army – the pain of missing him, and worrying over his safety, was a physical ache – but at least his absence from the Edel meant that she didn't need to keep secrets or lie to him.

Aaron's note asking Lili to meet him had arrived three months earlier on a bitterly cold March day when it felt as if the city was never going to shake off its winter chill. The message had been brought to the hotel by a nondescript delivery boy and it had come out of the blue. Lili hadn't seen or heard from Aaron since he'd accosted her in the street in 1940. She'd never known whether he'd reinvented himself and left the city, or if he was still involved with the refugee chain he'd been instrumental in setting up. Not that he'd given her a chance to ask. When she'd arrived at the bar it had taken her three changes of train line to reach, he'd greeted her as if they were partway through a conversation.

'I hear some of it. I'm usually only in the suite with them for a few moments, to greet them and serve the first drink. Once the first course has been served, they help themselves to the rest. And what I pick up is fragmented. They use a lot of words that sound innocent but aren't – *resettlement, clearing, solution,* that kind of thing. But they don't explain them – I've had to guess at the meanings – and I'm never invited to stay. I'm certainly not present when any planning or decision-making goes on.'

Her answer hadn't disappointed Aaron as much as she'd expected it to.

'They talk openly at the hotel then, or not openly exactly, but the way they would in their private offices?' He'd been close to a smile when she nodded. 'That's what I hoped for, Lili; this is what we need. Them with their guard down and a listening ear close by, so we can try to get a step ahead of them. The words you said you'd heard – one of them was definitely *solution?*'

She'd nodded again; his face had tightened and lost even the ghost of a smile.

'That damn word is everywhere. What can it mean except they're properly coming for us? Not with laws and ghettos but with something that's worse, something that we can't yet make sense of.'

His certainty had unnerved her.

'What do you mean, it's everywhere?'

Resettlement had appeared in the papers, but *clearance* hadn't and neither had *solution*. Lili had looked for them, but she didn't have the resources that Aaron did.

'All our networks report hearing *solution* every time SS men get together. But now it's changed. Apparently there was a conference a few months ago, when they stuck *final* in front of it. What else can that mean but death?'

Aaron's words had chilled her then, and they chilled her now, despite the heat in the stuffy storeroom. She'd pushed down the dread which had gripped her in the dark bar as Aaron continued, so that she could carry on functioning as normal when she got back to the hotel. That dread hadn't faded far away, and neither had anything else Aaron had said during their meeting.

'There's a link between all the terms you used. The resettlement part has started, but it's impossible to get a firm idea of how widespread that's going to be, never mind the destinations. Finding out about those is as difficult as finding safe houses. We can't get into the detention centres at Grunewald or Anhalter to see what's actually happening inside them. Nobody who's sent out on the trains comes back or writes letters home. And we don't know where the trains are heading, but we do know that the luggage people are instructed to bring with them is always left behind. That doesn't tell a good story.'

Aaron's eyes had blurred when he'd said that. Lili's eyes had filled too. Everybody in Berlin knew about the resettlement trains, although everybody pretended not to. The Jews didn't appear at the stations those left from by magic – they were openly marched through the streets. The suitcases piled up on the platforms became the property of whoever – rich or poor – got to them first. New tenants moved into suddenly empty houses while their previous owners were being crammed into cattle trucks. And no questions were asked or explanations offered: the city simply adjusted itself to accommodate its new normal.

'It's wrong to call what's happening resettlement. It's removal, which is presumably what they mean by clearance. We're being erased, and the city is papering over the gaps as if we were never here. And I don't believe that the trains are heading for some Jewish paradise in the East, which is what they'd have us swallow, or that anybody who travels on them survives. We need information, Lili. And we need you to get it.'

Aaron's assessment had been frightening, but Lili couldn't find fault with it, and she'd known as soon as he'd said *with their guard down* what he was going to ask her to do. She hadn't said no, the way she once would have. Becoming a link in the refugee network had removed that word from her vocabulary, and Aaron knew it. Stepping over the line into danger the first time had been far harder than moving forward once she was across. But she hadn't known then how to help him.

'I can't stay in the room during the lunch – they wouldn't talk; they'd send me away. I can't listen outside the door – even if that wasn't too thick, there's always a guard posted there. The suite Hitler uses is on the end of the building and doesn't have an adjoining guest room – that's why Goebbels chose it. And the third floor is always kept empty when they come – Goebbels would never admit it openly, but it's obvious that he's paranoid about anyone seeing the Führer behave or sound like an ordinary man rather than the mythical being we're meant to view him as. He's very careful to restrict who gets close.'

'But you'll do it, won't you? You'll find a way?'

Lili hadn't said yes – she couldn't promise him then what

seemed like the impossible. But she hadn't given up considering the idea, and she had found a way. Not immediately. It had taken time to stand in the suite and try and work out if over-hearing what went on in it was practical. It had taken long flights of fantasy into the possibility of hiding listening devices inside the room, but that apparatus only existed in her imagination. It had taken long nights poring over the hotel's floor plans. But once the answer jumped out at her, it had proved to be a remarkably simple – if uncomfortable – one.

The narrow space Lili was shoehorned into was more of a supply cupboard than a storeroom. It had been carved out of the suite with a small partition wall years before when space was at a premium and the wall had then been papered over to look as solid as the rest of the room. It was a perfect listening post, and it was as safe as she could make it. The door was in the service corridor out of sight of the guard. The maids knew better than to clatter around looking for supplies when Hitler was in residence. The partition itself was cardboard thin. When the men in the suite spoke in their normal voices, Lili's perch was almost as well placed to pick up the conversations as if she was sitting in a chair in the corner of the main room. And when – as was happening now – tempers were lost and those voices rose, she had a ringside seat at the fight.

'There's no one with the skills or the fire he had.'

It was Hitler speaking, his voice twisted up in a snarl.

Lili closed her eyes as the anger broke. Two previous listening sessions had taught her to cut out all background noise, including the *What am I doing here?* which inevitably leaped unbidden into her head. She focused on the room on the other side of the wall instead, picturing the seating plan, picking out each individual voice.

'He was my strongest weapon, my hammer against the Jews. I'd wade through blood to avenge him.'

Heydrich. They're talking about Reinhard Heydrich.

Hitler's impassioned declaration was followed by a rumble of assent which spread round the suite like thunder, although Lili doubted any of the ministers present were particularly pleased to be put in their places by *strongest weapon.*

It didn't surprise her that Heydrich was the main topic of conversation, or that his murder was the cause of Hitler's fury. The Reichsprotektor of Bohemia and Moravia was a man whose hatred of Jews and his determination to see them persecuted was so vicious it ran thick as blood through his veins. The assassination attempt against him in Prague in May and his subsequent death from his injuries on the fourth of June was the main topic of conversation across the whole city. Heydrich's funeral had been one of the most elaborate Berlin had ever seen. The coffin had been carried through the streets on a gun carriage to the Invaliden Cemetery, accompanied by muffled drums and watched by a vast silent crowd. Hitler had laid a wreath and given the oratory; he had called Heydrich a man with an iron heart. The whole ceremony had been broadcast live on the radio; the country had been told to mourn him as if they had lost a family member. Wading through blood for revenge was exactly what Aaron had feared would follow.

'There has to be vengeance, of the most brutal kind. His memory must be honoured.'

Lili expected the pause which followed that statement. It was entirely in keeping with Hitler's preferred strategy of stating a wish and waiting for his ministers to find a way to step up and fulfil it. That Himmler, Göring and Goebbels instantly began talking over each other, competing to get their ideas heard like children in an unruly classroom, didn't surprise her either. But the level of their vitriol did. It far surpassed anything she'd overheard before. The civilised masks they wore in front of her were off, and there were no hidden meanings.

'It's easy. Strip out more trains to carry more passengers and increase the deportations.'

That was Göring, his mouth thick with port.

'You keep saying the camps and the machinery arc ready, so prove it. Fill them to capacity and use it.'

That was Goebbels, needling someone. Himmler, Lili presumed – the rivalry between the two of them never took long to surface. She forced herself to focus, not to freeze at *camps* and *machinery*. There would be time to unpick those later. And then Himmler spoke, and there was nothing to unpick.

'They're more than ready. You want proof? Wait till you see the huge increase in efficiency I'm about to deliver. Gas is, after all, a good deal more effective than guns. We'll be able to despatch them in record numbers.'

It was the lack of malice that had Lili biting back a moan. He could have been discussing a new and improved filing system.

Gas.

She could feel a cough rising, her throat closing over; her eyes starting to stream. She told herself to stay calm, that it was only a word, but how could *gas* ever again be only a word? Someone repeated it, someone else added *liquidate* and *final.* The voices melded into one. The words bounced round and round the suite, getting darker and more dangerous. Old ones Lili had heard before; new ones that were terrifying. And all uttered with an unshakeable confidence as each man thrust himself forward to be his leader's new weapon.

Lili had to force herself to listen to it all. Then she had to force herself to leave the stockroom and walk towards the suite, not the bathroom. To be ready and waiting with a cheerful smile and a cheerful goodbye as the puppet master and his entourage swept back out of the hotel. To not lunge for their throats.

. . .

Aaron's messenger boy didn't come, even though Lili – whose nerves had shredded to tissue paper with the waiting – woke up every morning willing him to. And she had no way of getting a message to him without that contact point.

The safe house she'd found her way to in 1940 was no longer in use. Meeting in a pub was discouraged. If she needed to pass information on to Aaron urgently, she added a silk spray of edelweiss to the window box nearest the front door and hoped that the right person noticed it. If a Jewish refugee was going to be sent her way for hiding, she would receive twenty-four hours' notice of a special wine delivery. If that delivery was cancelled, there was never any warning or explanation. Lili waited in place at the garden door and nobody came. She was a tightrope walker with no net, who had to hold her head up or risk falling. She'd learned very quickly that worrying whether a piece of the chain which balanced them all might snap didn't help.

What also didn't help was that there was no instruction book. There was no plan in place if the delivery van made a drop but didn't return the next night for the pick-up. And there was no plan for *Get here now – they're talking about gas, they're talking about machinery, the end isn't coming, it's here,* except a bunch of silk flowers which nobody she needed seemed able to see.

Lili spent the fortnight after her last eavesdropping session moving forward, doing whatever she could to stay busy and stop fretting. Nothing worked. Waiting on Aaron with no idea when she might hear from him was impossible. *Gas is, after all, a good deal more effective than guns* sat like a weight in her stomach, stopping her eating, turning the nights endless. The woman staring back at her from the mirror that morning as she pinned up her hair was too thin; her face was older than thirty-one should look. Lili couldn't live inside that woman any longer. Which was why she decided to abandon Aaron's plan and make one of her own, put on her best hat and her brightest smile, and go out and find him.

Lili came down to the Edel's foyer planning to visit both the bars where they'd met. She was going to find the wine company which was listed on the special delivery notes if that didn't work, because it surely had to exist. And when she finally discovered Aaron's whereabouts and told him what she'd heard, she was going to say: *Send me more travellers; fill the hotel.* She was going to say, *We have to save everyone*, although she hadn't a clue what *everyone* meant. She was determined to keep searching for him until she'd walked every inch of Berlin.

She never made it out of the hotel.

'Lili?'

Another man was calling her name. But this voice was the right one, the only one she wanted to hear use it. She took the staircase's last steps in a leap. She was in his arms before he'd had a chance to put down his bag. Marius. Back at the Edel without warning as if Christmas had come in July. And – when she finally stopped clutching him, stepped back and looked at him – as thin and careworn as she was. The outside world fell away as Lili raised a hand to her husband's hollow cheeks and traced the new lines which were written there. All thoughts of Aaron flew out of her head. Nothing mattered beyond getting Marius upstairs and getting him away from the war.

That proved to be a hard thing to do. Marius moved slowly; his thoughts were scattered. He needed to sit and hold Gabi until his tight arms became a prison and the little girl wriggled away. He needed to eat as if he'd never eaten food. He fell into a sleep that looked so like death, Lili couldn't stay in the room. And, when he woke, he needed to talk without stopping.

'The things we've done, Lili, the things I've seen. We took I don't know how many prisoners after Moscow; from what's been said in the base camps, it could be millions. And I know better than anyone that resources are scarce, but the order was to let them die – by starvation, by exposure, by whatever it took. The brutality keeps ratcheting up. The soldiers are taught to think of Russians in the same way they're taught to think of Jews, as sub-humans, as worthless. It's an open invitation for the worst of them to act like animals. Civilians are being shot, set on fire, slaughtered. I'm starting to hate being German, and God help us if the tide turns.'

He'd gone past tears, although his body was shaking.

'Then stay here. Don't go back. We'll think of a reason. I could go to Himmler, or Hitler if I have to. I'll persuade them you're too sick to return.'

He looked so ill, that excuse sounded possible. Lili was perfectly prepared to try it. But this was Marius, and Marius was duty. She forced herself not to weep when he shook his head.

'I have to go, my love; I don't have a choice. My men are relying on me. We're going to be part of the big push against Stalingrad.'

Lili's heart wanted to stop as he said the name.

It was over a year since Germany had invaded the Soviet Union. The official rhetoric about the invasion since then had been built solely around victory. Hitler's speeches were thick with success, punctuated with the millions of Russians killed or taken prisoner in the battles for Moscow and Leningrad – although this was the first Lili had learned of their treatment – and the thousands of tanks and guns the German forces had seized from the enemy. They were also brimming with the glorious strength of the German soldier, a superman who could march through mud and snow and burning sunshine and remain undaunted and undefeated. Hitler told his audiences a tale of heroes who strode into battle singing songs of the Fatherland, whose loyalty and pure blood made them impervious to death.

Berlin's streets told a different story.

The dead were everywhere there. In the spaces beside the grief-stricken. In the black-bordered envelopes the delivery boys hated handing over and the bereaved families shrank from. In the tears and black dresses the men's widows wore. Those soldiers didn't come home; their bodies were lost on battlefields with names which meant nothing but misery to their mourners. But the wounded found their way back. Berlin was a city of empty sleeves and folded-up trouser legs; of scars which had ripped through and puckered once handsome faces into roughly ploughed fields. It was a city where the young men had been made broken and old.

We're going to be part of the big push against Stalingrad.

Lili's heart wanted to break. It was summer now, but winter would soon be coming. A Russian winter, which meant snow thick enough to swallow a man to his waist and soak through to his bones. Which brought temperatures cold enough to freeze engines, to ice up eyes and mouths and bite away fingers and toes. Marius had been lucky so far, although perhaps not as lucky as Lili had thought until she heard him talking. He hadn't been in the worst fighting at Moscow and Leningrad; his logistical skills had kept him closer to base. But this was different – she knew without him having to say it that *part of* meant he was destined for the front lines. It was hard not to hear a death sentence.

'I won't be able to write to you, my love; you won't be able to write to me. The generals are describing this as the battle to end all battles, as the one which will bring the Soviets to their knees. I don't think it will be as easy as that; I don't think our troops will survive another bad winter. And I don't know when, or if...'

She finally hushed him then. There couldn't be talk of dying; she wouldn't have that spectre in the room. She kissed the forget-me-nots engraved into the gold band of his wedding ring instead and made him do the same with hers.

'These are our blessings, my love. These carry our vows; they join us. We don't need letters to hold us together; we live in each other's hearts.'

She steadied him, as she always steadied him. The love in her eyes and her voice brought him back to her arms and brought him back whole to their bed. And when they'd re-found each other there, and Marius asked her if she'd been in contact with Aaron again, it was that love which kept Lili's lips shut.

She couldn't show him the diary, not yet. She couldn't send him back to war burdened with the risks she was taking. She couldn't tell him about the men who hid in the cellar, or how she hid like a spy in a stockroom. The fear of what might happen to her wouldn't help him keep alive.

So Lili held on to her secrets through the handful of days and nights which were all he'd been given to spend with her. She didn't go hunting for Aaron. She took the edelweiss sprig out of the window box. She surrounded Marius with love and spun the Edel back into what it was meant to be: a place of comfort and calm. She was his Lili while he was with her, and that helped him to walk away when his leave was done. But when he was gone, and after she'd wept herself hollow at his going, Lili wasn't a woman Marius would recognise anymore.

Lili was no stranger to the truth of the war's progress. Like everyone else in Berlin, she listened to the official radio stations in public and the BBC broadcasts from London when she was alone. Soldiers were dying in agony, in their hundreds of thou-sands, and a German victory wasn't any closer to coming, no matter what the rhetoric about battles to end all battles said. The Eastern Front was a nightmare ruled by the weather and Soviet troops who had no interest in surrender. The Allies were starting to push back in the West. The Americans had joined the war. Cologne had been turned into a fireball by British bombers; the centres of Lübeck and Rostock were gone. Three years in and there was no end in sight to the fighting or the suffering.

> *And the men who have charge of that won't stop until they've built their Thousand Year Reich, irrespective of how much blood is sacrificed in the service of their terrifying new world. And they've made us powerless to stand up and stop them.*

Powerless. It was the word that stung hardest every time she wrote it. Except now, perhaps, it had found a new place to sting.

Hitler hadn't only called Heydrich his strongest weapon when the tempers were flying at the lunch party. He'd also called him arrogant and stupid and dim-witted for travelling in an open car without adequate protection. Hitler travelled everywhere in the security of his armoured limousine, including the five minutes it took to get from his office to the Edel. He'd been as angry at Heydrich's lapse in judgement as he had been at the killing. And Lili knew why.

There had been a moment when, despite the barrier of the partition wall, Lili had heard the anger fall away and a sudden rush of vulnerability flood in. When she'd realised that Hitler might be saying *arrogant* and *stupid*, but what he actually meant was: *You were a fool to allow them to kill you; you've raised the possibility that killing us can be done.*

Lili knew that there was a lesson somewhere in that. The challenge lay – as it had with the words she'd collected – in how to decipher and use it.

CHAPTER 11

JANUARY 1943

My darling Marius,

I hope you are warm, my love; I hope you are well. Winter has its teeth into us now. The temperature fell so low last night, there were ice trails thick on the bathroom window this morning, and Gabi is mesmerised by the snow.

Lili put her pen down. She didn't know why she kept doing this, starting her letters with news of home as if they were actually going to reach him. Marius was so far away, the physical distance between them seemed to stretch on forever. There'd been no word from him since the hastily scrawled postcard he'd sent six months earlier, from a Polish border town he wasn't allowed to name. Christmas had passed by with nothing except the dull ache of missing him and Gabi's confused tears. All Lili knew was that he was somewhere deep inside Russia, in the middle of January. So what was she doing writing about winter? Telling him that his daughter had spent the morning pressed against the window laughing at snowflakes, when snow could be as dangerous as bullets to him.

I might not know what to say, but I still need to write.

The urge to be close to him, to unburden herself to the thought of him, remained as strong as ever. She picked up her pen again, searching for a safer topic to start her words flowing. If not the weather, what? The current state of Berlin?

Life here is...

She was defeated before she could find the next word. Maybe *complicated* would do. It was certainly that. Perhaps she could tell him about the way rationing had started to bite. About how the Edel's waiters now wore tiny scissors hung on ribbons round their necks to clip coupons from the diners' ration cards. Or how many of the bottles on the top shelves of the bar were currently filled with coloured water. Or how the chefs squealed in horror if anything labelled *ersatz* appeared in their kitchens as if they'd forgotten where and when they lived, and how reliant they'd become on the game and produce which regularly found its way to the Edel from Göring's huge private hunting estate in the Schorfheide Forest. Except she didn't want to talk about any of that.

Lili also didn't want to discuss Hitler. Or the worsening behaviour of his overfamiliar ministers and the other officers who frequented the hotel. The ones who couldn't keep their hands to themselves and were determined to fill the empty space in her bed. She could hardly tell her husband that there were days when she felt like some modern-day Penelope, warding off unwanted suitors until her Odysseus found his way home. That there were worse ones when she walked round their beloved hotel, smiling at the men who acted as if their presence graced rather than defiled it, and longed to burn the whole building down.

Although I could. I could tell him anything. He's never going to read a single word.

Lili shut that thought down before it took hold. There was a darkness in it she couldn't give in to. One that could conjure up a black-bordered telegram. The journal was important – she couldn't stop writing it now. When Marius came home, after he'd told her about his war, she was going to give the book to him and tell him, *This was mine*. So she had to write, and she had to believe he would come back to her and read it.

Lili rubbed her stiff fingers to get the blood flowing and dug out a pair of fingerless gloves which she'd found among the hotel's gardening supplies. She crossed through what she'd written and started again.

My darling Marius,

It's a year now since I moved the first traveller through the hotel. It's been a strange business. We treat each other like carrier and freight. Few words are exchanged. I know nothing about where they have come from or where they are going. I suspect nobody thinks that far ahead. The other participants in the chain are as equally unknown to me. This is how it must be, for safety's sake, but there's a terrible loneliness to the actual doing. Or there was, until two months ago. Until there was Alice...

'In there.'

The woman flinched for the first time since she'd run through the gardens when Lili opened the cupboard door. It wasn't hard to see why. The tight space had the air of a cell. It was half a dozen paces long and half a dozen paces wide. There was no window. There was no room for a bed. Lili had pushed a chair against the back wall and piled it with blankets. There was a stock of cold food in a box on the floor, a jug of water and a glass, and a covered pail neither woman acknowledged. Those basic items filled it. If any of the people forced to hide inside there carried any more items with them than could be concealed in a hem or a hidden pocket, there wouldn't have been room for those.

'Take this.' Lili handed over a small torch. 'Block the bottom of the door with a blanket before you use it.'

She didn't say, *It's only twenty-four hours – that's not so long*. She'd learned that platitudes never helped.

The woman nodded, went into her hiding place and closed the door. Lili hated to walk away. She hated to leave anyone alone in the cold and the dark. There was nothing else she could do. She went back upstairs as quickly and quietly as she could into the apartment where the width of her double bed felt like a mockery and spent the night curled up in the empty nursery instead.

The planes which had frayed the city's nerves a few hours earlier had passed over without incident. Berlin had breathed out and gone quietly to bed without the fear of bombs falling. But the skies weren't done with them yet. Lili was woken from a dream filled with loss and dead ends by a storm which roared round the building, rattling windows and drowning anyone foolish enough to be outside in a cascade of rain. By dawn, the worst of it was done, but the rinsed-out skies revealed a trail of devastation. Roof tiles and broken branches littered the streets. The staff who managed to struggle in to work reported roads blocked by fallen trees and telegraph poles. The Edel's phone lines were dead.

Lili sent a boy with a message to the friend's house where Gabi was staying to check she was safe. She organised workmen to check the roof and to clear up the rain-sodden garden. She got on with the day as she always got on with the day, but the night was a different matter.

They waited at the back door at the agreed time, and beyond that. Nobody came.

'It's happened before. I can wait it out, if you can.'

The woman who emerged from the cupboard was steely-eyed – Lili had no doubt that she could wait out anything. But she was also shaking with cold and her gloveless fingers were tinged with blue.

'Come upstairs with me, for an hour or two. You can have a bath, eat some warm food. Then, when you're feeling better than you must feel now, I'll bring you back down here a little better equipped.'

Lili made the offer without allowing herself to think it through. The woman stared at her and stepped back. Lili could see the refusal coming, and she didn't want to hear it. She grabbed the too-thin arm and led the way to the service lift so quickly an argument was pointless. Neither woman spoke until they were inside the Rodenbergs' apartment, but Lili's reluctant guest scanned every inch of the corridors they passed through as if she was expecting a trap.

'My daughter is staying with a friend. I always make sure she's out of the building on transfer days. My husband is away. Nobody will come. There's nothing to worry about. You'll be safe.'

Lili bundled her charge into the bathroom, conscious that she was babbling, not wanting to see the luxury she lived in through the eyes of someone reduced to darkness and hunger.

By the time the woman re-emerged, dressed in the far warmer clothes Lili had left out for her and with her skin glowing, she at least looked less haunted.

'Why are you doing this?'

It was a direct question; it deserved a direct answer.

'Because I am also a Jew. Although that's been a closely held secret for almost half my life.'

The woman sank down onto the sofa with a speed that was comical. Then she burst out laughing and lost ten years.

'Well that wasn't an answer I was expecting. No wonder you were so eager to drag me up here and make me more comfortable. Should I presume all this do-gooding is born out of guilt?'

There was an edge to her voice which Lili didn't rise to. The woman, who was staring at her with a mixture of interest and what looked horribly like contempt, had come from goodness knows how many damp cellars into an apartment where there were crystal jars of bath salts in two different colours and a surplus of winter coats. She'd earned whatever digs she wanted to make.

'Yes, it does. From guilt that I've been so well protected while so many aren't. And from hatred of the men who say we are the monsters. And because I can't bear to be made as powerless as this regime is determined to make us.'

The cynical smile softened. 'I'm Alice. I'm supposed to call myself Sara or nothing. But that won't do for tonight.' She looked round the suite and stretched herself out to fit it. 'Tonight I want to be myself again, for a little while anyway. So I'm Alice Herschel, and I'm very pleased to meet...'

'Lili Rodenberg.'

Lili sat down on the opposite chair, filled Alice's cup with hot tea and pushed plates of thickly sliced toasted cheese and apple cake towards her. They could have been friends enjoying each other's company on an unremarkable social engagement, if Alice hadn't fallen on the food like a wolf. Lili sat back and let her eat. She left nothing behind.

'How many others have you moved, before me?'

'Eight.' Lili grimaced. 'It's not enough. And you're the first for a while. I've been trying to tell myself that's because there's a huge network of people ferrying Jewish refugees through the city. I don't really believe that's true.'

The slump in Alice's shoulders told her it wasn't. That the only huge network ferrying people in Germany was the one being used to kill them. The silence stretched; Lili suddenly knew she had to fill it with honesty.

'They come here, you know.'

Alice's head came up at the change in Lili's tone. 'Who?'

'Hitler, Goebbels, Himmler. The whole rotten band. They sit in our most expensive suite and eat lunch, and I serve them drinks. And we all smile at each other as if we're the greatest of friends.'

'You're serious, aren't you?'

Alice's disbelief had given way to something Lili really wanted to be admiration. She nodded.

'Completely. I play the role of the perfect hostess upstairs, knowing I'd disgust them if they knew who I really was. Then I go down to the cellars and help move the people they want to wipe from the face of the earth out of their reach.'

Alice whistled. 'And no one suspects what's going on here?'

Lili shook her head. 'Why would they suspect an establishment as well regarded as the Edel? And why would they suspect me? I'm a woman, and women, in their world, aren't capable of holding a political thought, never mind actively carrying out a deception – you must know that. We're good little girls: we have babies, and we don't meddle in men's work; we do what we're told. They don't have a clue how dangerous we can be.'

Lili had spent so much time quantifying and worrying over the risks, it was the first time she'd articulated – to herself, never mind anyone else – how strong the act of fighting back made her feel. And now she'd started putting that feeling into words, she didn't want to stop.

The two women had moved so far past the rules which were meant to govern their interaction, there was no point in holding the rest back. And the relief of finally telling the truth to someone who was actually present to hear it as opposed to spilling her feelings into unsent letters ran through Lili like balm. She told Alice everything. She described the secret room. She told her the horrors that she'd overhead there and had finally managed to pass on. She wasn't surprised when Alice's response was, 'Is that it? Is that where this ends?' She'd been asking herself the same question for long enough.

'If you mean, could I physically attack Hitler, could I produce a gun and shoot him or set a bomb, I've thought about it. I've imagined it. But it's not possible. I'm not an assassin. I have a child I won't put into that kind of danger. The stakes are too high.'

'The stakes are too high if he lives.'

That could have been a challenge, but Alice's face had closed down on *child*, and her eyelids were drooping.

'I'm sorry. I've been doing all the talking, and I know nothing at all about you.'

Lili had been about to say, 'Tell me your story,' but Alice had slipped sideways on the sofa and into a deep sleep. Lili fetched a blanket and let her be.

Which I shouldn't have done, I know. But the poor thing was exhausted, and November is no time to be sleeping in a cellar. And I almost got her back there without being seen, but...

Lili stopped writing. *But* suggested that what had happened next – being caught in the wine cellar with Alice in the early hours of the next morning – had been a disaster. It hadn't been, although it had come close.

'I'm not here to hurt you. I'm Jewish too.'

Alice had reared up like a lion and grabbed a knife from somewhere inside her coat the second she'd seen the outline of a man in the corner by her hiding place. If André had hesitated even for a second, she would have stabbed him. Instead, her *Dear God, not another one* had allowed them all time to breathe.

That's the story I need to tell you.

Lili picked up her pen again.

'I'm Jewish too'. I was as shocked as Alice when André said that. I'd checked his papers in 1941 when we were finally forced to obey the rules – they were as convincing as mine. And he didn't only sum up the situation in an instant, he took charge.

'The ballroom is crawling with SS men – Brigadeführer von Krailling is holding a bachelor farewell party for one of his men, and they're rowdy enough for a zoo. I was down here looking for one of the more expensive bottles they're demanding. No one will dare to come for you tonight, but I'll get you out of here as soon as I can. I imagine there's a system – Frau Rodenberg can explain that to me tomorrow – and I'll keep you safe until that starts back up. If you'll trust me to.'

Alice did, of course, and he was as good as his word, even though it took two more days to move her on. He won't let me tell him why I've done what I've done. He says there'll be time enough to share secrets after the war and for now all that's needed is to keep faith with each other. I can't tell you how grateful I am for him, Marius, the relief of having...

'Frau Rodenberg, are you down there?'
Lili scrabbled to close and hide the journal as her secretary's voice floated down the stairs.
'I'm coming, I'm coming. Wait for me in the foyer.'
Writing the letter had taken so long, Lili had lost track of

time. She'd missed the lunch service and the kitchen deliveries. That was the kind of absence which made people talk.

But when she appeared in the foyer, nobody was saying anything.

'What is it? What's going on?'

She noted the telegram boy, although she refused to look in his direction. The flimsy piece of paper her secretary was holding out as if Lili might want to take it wasn't edged in black. Nothing bad could possibly be coming. But André's face was so white it looked blue, and one of the receptionists was sobbing.

'I said, *what is it?*'

Her voice was too loud. The words on the telegram were too few. And the only one she could see printed there said, *Missing.*

PART THREE

CHAPTER 12

SEPTEMBER 1990

Finding the journal had thrown Lucy completely off track.

Not only because its contents cast a whole new slant on what they thought they knew about Lili. Or because reading it had produced far more questions than answers. It derailed Lucy because of how deeply personal the entries felt.

> *The bombing raids have intensified; the planes come two or three times a week now. They've already hit the city's outer edges. Everyone is afraid for the children – the Führer wants them evacuated to the country; some of Gabi's friends have already gone. There's rumours he might make it compulsory, and what on earth will I do then? A night or two away from her is bad enough; weeks – or months if the raids get worse – would be impossible, but so is keeping her in harm's way.*
>
> *I'm failing Gabi. The more I pretend my past has nothing to do with me, the worse it gets. How can I teach my daughter to be honest when I stopped being that long ago?*

There were passages of the journal – where Lili feared for

her daughter and felt that she'd failed as a mother – which Lucy could have written herself. Once she realised that, she'd become so obsessed, she couldn't shake off Lili's voice. The more entries she read, the more real this altered Lili became. Lucy began wandering through the Edel's rooms with its previous owner walking beside her, looking over her shoulder, burrowing inside Lucy's head the way she was burrowing inside Lili's. The instinct Lucy had felt the first time she'd walked into the hotel – that the Edel already knew her – grew stronger with every revelation.

It was true that Lili's fears and outpourings weren't always easy to decipher. Even in the pages that hadn't been damaged, her subject matter meandered. She never disclosed why she was moving refugees and exposing herself and her family to unthinkable danger, and a number of the references were so cryptic, it was as if they'd been written with a shield set around them. But it was clear that Lili had loved her daughter deeply. And it was equally obvious that Lili was a woman whose life had been weighed down with even more secrets than the journal had disclosed. Which was where Lucy's problems had begun. It wasn't long before the journal – and her own long-buried emotions which the entries kept forcing her to confront – became a weight on Lucy too.

Lucy had hit a wall and she couldn't admit it – asking for help had never come easily to her. Her normal pattern was to keep on moving, to push forward until she'd put enough space between herself and her demons to pretend she'd outrun them. She couldn't do that anymore – the need to stop was overwhelming. So for the first time since she was seventeen years old and her life had tumbled off track, Lucy not only stood still, she retreated.

She gave her site manager a week's worth of instructions. She cancelled her meetings. She told Adam she was needed in

London and Charlie that she was going to take a rare holiday before the renovation schedule really ramped up. Then she locked the door of the apartment which she'd rented when she first came to the city and did the one thing she'd been avoiding for years. She let the past – with all its difficult memories – come...

'I thought you were better than this. I thought you were too clever to ruin your life, and ours.'

Her father's grim-faced disappointment was as hard to bear as her mother's red eyes.

'I'm pregnant.'

Two words that delivered a bombshell and wrecked a glittering future before it began. And Lucy's protests of, 'I can manage this, I can make it all work,' were a fairy tale no one was prepared to believe in.

The complete shutting down of her dreams had been almost as big a shock as her new body. Even in her darkest moments – when she couldn't keep telling herself that her recurring bouts of sickness were food poisoning and square that with her steady weight gain – Lucy hadn't really believed that the life she could almost grasp was gone. She'd thought there were too many people in her corner for that.

'My condition hasn't impacted on my schoolwork so far; it doesn't need to get in the way.'

That was another myth, and one that snapped her headmistress's lips firmly shut. Lucy's shaky declaration that her plans needn't change carried no more traction than the desperate, 'Other girls must have gone through this and still managed to get to university,' which followed.

Nobody was talking about university anymore, not even for the brightest girl in the year who was guaranteed to get straight As in all her exams. Not once the reason why Lucy was suddenly wearing a lot of baggy jumpers was finally explained. Once she was forced to admit that the baby's father was a summer visitor to the town and wouldn't be riding in to save her with a ring, nobody was talking about her future at all. And those *other girls* who she was so confident she could join? They didn't exist, or they lived in London where the times moved at a more tolerant pace. They certainly didn't live in small northern towns like Morecambe where the moral code still belonged to the 1950s not the 1970s, and a pregnancy at seventeen was a permanent fall from grace.

I'm pregnant.

With those two words, Lucy stopped being her parents' pride and joy, the first person in their solidly working-class family to reach the dizzy heights of further education. She stopped being an almost-adult. She became an embarrassment, a source of shame. She was returned to a childhood where she had no say over her life. She became a problem other people solved.

'There's a home in Preston that will take you.'

That was it. A pronouncement made with no explanation, with no room for discussion. Her father using *home* as if she no longer had one. And a gap in her parents' planning which Lucy never thought to ask him or her mother to fill.

'What happens next? What happens when the baby comes?'

Lucy lay in her blanket nest, her head filled with her lost younger self. That would have been the most obvious question to ask, but she never had.

Because I already knew how they'd answer, and where would that have left me?

She sank back under the covers, her body tensing against a different day. Remembering how the silent drive to Preston – a bigger town where no one would know her – had curled up her insides. Remembering how she'd sat in the back seat of her parents' pine-scented Ford Escort, staring at the backs of their heads, willing one of them to turn round and remember who she was, who she could still be. Trying not to cry as the next set of images flashed up like holiday slides on her father's old projector. Her mother thrusting her suitcase towards her without making eye contact and handing her over to a grave-faced stranger while her father sat pointedly alone in the car. The two of them driving away without looking back, leaving Lucy to navigate a world that, for all the hours she'd spent with her schoolbooks, she didn't have the skills to manage.

Nobody at the home which wasn't a home was deliberately unkind, but nobody was interested in Lucy either. She was simply another in a long line of girls who'd slipped up, or got caught, or who didn't know better than to keep their legs together, depending on which matron was in charge. The bedrooms were clean, the food was boring but plentiful. There were daily lessons which Lucy couldn't engage in. There were cinema nights where everybody laughed too hard at unfunny films. But there weren't any mother and baby classes. There was no attempt to prepare the home's young charges for what was coming.

Because it wasn't coming for us. We were never mothers to them.

That was a hard memory to face. That was the casual cruelty Lucy had never been able to accept. No one – not the nurses, nor her parents, nor the friends who'd fled from her like scalded cats in case her disgrace was catching – had ever thought of her as a mother or called her by that name. Not once in the moments after the baby arrived and Lucy knew that *mother* was who she would be for the rest of her life. Not once in the scant few weeks when her beautiful Emily was allowed to stay with her. Even though Lucy had fed and bathed and done everything for her daughter, and the little girl's head only ever turned at her voice.

Mother wasn't hers because that title was reserved for another woman. The one with the pretty blue coat and the handsome husband; the one who signed the papers which made Emily hers. Who agreed – because the law told her that she had to – that of course the adoption would be an open one, and of course Lucy would always have a place in the child's life.

Who looked hunted when she said it and might as well have disappeared off the face of the earth since.

Lucy lay in the bed she'd spent too much time in, waiting for the self-pity to come. That normally flooded in on a wave with the slightest poke at the past. This time it didn't come at all. Lucy probed at the memories again, digging about in her pain to find the worst parts of it. Her last sight of Emily's tiny face. The newly minted parents, who she had created, walking away with their precious bundle. The bleakness of Emily's empty cradle. Her fury when her parents finally returned to reclaim her and she'd screamed, 'You made me abandon my baby, and I hate you,' at them like a banshee. And the tears that had come after that and wouldn't stop, which had infuriated everybody. Lucy rifled through them all one by one until she'd sucked their marrow out. The self-pity stayed silent. But other words came in their place.

I could have behaved better far sooner than I did. I made a choice, but I could have made that choice earlier and done more. What I'm doing now helps people; it was always worth the risk. Why did it take me so long to understand that?

The sentiments weren't hers; they were Lili's. And they didn't all fit: whatever Lili had chosen to do, Lucy hadn't chosen to give up her baby.

But I didn't fight very hard for her either. I could have behaved differently too. I could have made my life – and hers – turn out far differently if I'd been braver from the start.

That was a shock. That was new. Lucy had been living one version of her life for so long, she'd never considered that there might be another viewpoint. The moment she did, anger at her own blindness propelled her out of the bed.

Lucy scrambled out from under the covers. She turned the shower to hot and scrubbed herself pink. She dressed and reintroduced herself to the outside world and a supermarket. She discovered she was starving and ate almost everything she'd bought. And when she'd done all that, she stopped. She breathed. She allowed herself to think what she'd never let herself think: *What if I'd...* It was very hard to face the way that shifted the spotlight.

Her parents had taken control, that was true, but Lucy had let them. She'd never once said, 'I want to keep the baby,' outside the safety of her own room. She hadn't said, 'Let me try.' She'd been afraid that every back would turn against her and she'd fail, but she'd felt like a failure ever since anyway. And the woman who took Emily was... *not the enemy.*

Another set of memories shifted. Lucy suddenly remembered the gentle hand on her arm, the softly spoken *'I'm sorry'*. The *'We'll take such good care of her for you'* when Lucy signed the papers. What if they'd really meant that? What if they'd been as upset as she was that them leaving the hospital so happily with Emily had turned out to be so final for Lucy?

What's done is done and what's left is a mess, but it doesn't have to stay that way.

Lucy didn't know if the voice in her head was her own or some echo of Lili's. Wherever the words came from, they were a comfort. She opened the journal again.

Lili had fought against her past for years. A lot of the entries were still hard to follow, but the depths of that struggle shone out. Lucy had been fighting her own past for as long, acting as if the narrative she'd been placed inside as a teenager was set in stone. That way of thinking couldn't work anymore; she wouldn't let it. There had to be a better ending.

She got out a pen and a notepad. She began to make notes, flitting between her life and Lili's, trying to make sense of them both. An hour later she had if not a plan, then at least a sense that there was another way forward. And she no longer had one story to rewrite; she had two.

CHAPTER 13

SEPTEMBER 1990

'It starts in 1941 and the last entry was written in April 1944. There's been a fair bit of damage and not every entry is legible – sometimes I could only make out a handful of words – but if you read the whole thing, it's remarkable. And you need to read the whole thing because the woman who wrote it?' Lucy shook her head. 'She's not the Lili we've been presented with.'

Lucy hadn't given Adam any details about the journal when she'd called him and asked him to come and meet her at the hotel, other than that the cellars had thrown up something he had to see. Her caution was partly due to the lesson Charlie had drummed into her about not over-steering first impressions, but it was also more than that. She couldn't yet define exactly who this new Lili was, and she wasn't sure it was her place to do that. Unfortunately, now that he was here, Adam wasn't making it easy for her to find a way in.

What Lucy hadn't yet understood was that Adam – who shared more similarities with his mother than she knew or he would accept – wasn't a man who liked surprises. He'd arrived at the Edel on edge, and he'd said very little when she showed him into the comparative privacy of the ballroom, beyond a question about Lucy's trip to London which momentarily confused her. When she'd produced the journal and explained what it was, he'd withdrawn even more. And although his hand kept hovering close to the table where the now well-thumbed book was waiting, he didn't make a move to open it.

'Then who is she? And why would anyone make up a different version of her?'

Lucy wasn't sure why he sounded so belligerent or what to do about it. She got up and went over to the door which she'd left ajar in case any of the workmen came looking for her. Although the ballroom hadn't yet been invaded by stepladders and power tools, the noise from the restoration work in the foyer was persistent. She closed the door, and gave herself a moment before she turned to try and make sense of why he was acting so defensively. It was only when she returned to the table and noticed his leg was shaking that the pieces fell into place. Adam was nervous. A week ago, Lucy wouldn't have understood his reaction; now, she recognised someone struggling with the challenge of old certainties shifting. Before he could be receptive to anything she was about to say, he needed to relax.

'Here.'

Adam frowned as Lucy produced a bottle of red wine and a pair of glasses from the back of the ballroom's dust-coated bar.

'Don't worry – it's a good one; it hasn't been sat here since the Stasi left. I was saving it until the last bit of repainting was done, but I think we've more need of it now.'

Adam accepted the drink she poured him without argument, took a very large swallow and held out his glass when Lucy offered him a top-up. Once that was done, she sat down again and pushed the journal closer to his side of the table.

'I don't know why anyone would do that, any more than I know who she really was yet. When you've spent time going through this – and you'll need to take time with it – you'll see that trying to put Lili together from what she's written isn't straightforward.' She hesitated, then reached over and opened one of the pages which she'd bookmarked to show him. 'It might be easier if you read this bit first – it will give you a flavour of the rest.'

She sat back and waited while he studied the short extract.

They don't have anything with them and that's hard to see. No clothes beyond what they're wearing and – unless they've sewn them inside their hems or coat linings – not a single personal possession. Everything they were, everyone they loved, it's all nothing now but memories.

Adam didn't immediately look up. Lucy leaned forward and turned to another marked page. 'Have a look at this one too.' She wasn't surprised when he gasped.

I hate them. I hate pouring their drinks and listening to their boasts about the wonderful new world that's coming. What's wonderful about a world that only exists for the pure-blooded? What does that even mean? God, if they only knew what I really thought when they make me stand there and applaud them; if they only knew what I was really doing behind their backs. That would wipe the smiles from their greedy faces.

Adam finished his drink. He poured them both another one before he spoke.

'Is a lot of it written like this? Using *they* and *them* with no clear explanation of who she's referring to?'

Lucy nodded. 'There's some names, and initials, but she frequently writes as if she's worried that the wrong person might read it. There's a pattern to it though, and I think...'

She hesitated. She hadn't intended to be the journal's narrator, and what she was about to say sounded absurd given the story they'd previously been told about Lili.

'Go on.'

Adam had stopped looking at the journal. He was looking at her instead, and so intently that Lucy momentarily lost the thread of what she'd been about to share with him.

'Say whatever it is that you're thinking, Lucy. I know this is my family's history, but you're not overstepping, if that's what's worrying you. And I won't dismiss whatever conclusions you've come to, I promise. I think I may already be there with you.'

That admission made the task easier. And as soon as Lucy started to put her thoughts into words, she knew that they were true.

'I've read the whole thing through loads of times, which doesn't mean that I understand it all, but I have changed my mind about her. I don't believe Lili was a Nazi, or a great friend of Hitler and one of his inner circle – the *they* she keeps saying she hates surely has to be him and the ministers who came to the Edel with him. I think she was hiding behind the pretence of friendship and loyalty, because... Well, I think she might have been moving people – which most likely meant Jews – through the Edel to safety. I think that's what she meant by *them*. Not that I've any clue why she'd do such a dangerous thing.'

Adam did as he'd promised – he didn't dismiss her. He sat back instead, closed his eyes and breathed in what she'd said. Lucy gave him a moment to absorb it, then she turned the journal's pages back to the start.

'This one from 1941 isn't a random first entry. I'm as certain as I can be that this is when whatever she was doing started.' She pointed to the opening entry as Adam roused himself. 'Look what it says. *The scales have finally tipped, my love. I can't go on looking the other way.* She's talking to Marius when she says *my love* – a lot of the entries are in the form of letters to him. And look at the date – November 1941. That's not long after—'

'Jews in Germany were ordered to wear yellow stars, so they

were visible. And presumably, therefore, became easier targets. That's not something you can learn about and forget.'

Adam was firmly with her now. His eyes were alive; his fingers were no longer hovering over the journal – they were flying through it.

'Exactly. She even says further down that the stars were the tipping point – maybe she was scared or unable to help anyone before then, or didn't fully understand the danger to Berlin's Jews. That's never made clear, I'm afraid, and neither is this.'

Lucy gently removed the journal from his grip before he tore the thin leaves, put it back on the table and turned to the final page.

Gabi is safe. Everything is in motion; there's no stopping it now. I can only pray that this isn't goodbye.

Adam ran his fingers over the lines as if he was trying to connect to their author. Lucy remembered doing the same, and she shivered.

'It's dated the tenth of April 1944. If we go with the timescale suggested by Goebbels' piece in the newspaper, that's only a couple of weeks before we think she died. And if you're saying that a lot of this was written for Marius, presumably that's who the goodbye – or the not goodbye – was intended for. As well as for my mother.' He blew out his breath and swallowed hard. *'There's no stopping it now.* She was planning something, wasn't she? Something bigger than moving people, if that is what she was doing up till then.'

Lucy picked up her drink and drained it. 'It looks that way. And if we're right and she died not long after this entry, doesn't that suggest that, whatever the plan was, it went wrong?' Now it was Lucy's turn to sigh. 'Except that none of these scenarios fit with the Lili we've been given and the eulogy that Goebbels wrote for her, and that's where I'm stuck. So I think we need help. I know it's muddled, but your mother really needs to see this. If Gabi reads it, she might draw some comfort from it, and she might remember more about the past and about Lili than she's allowed herself to do since the war.'

Adam had been listening to her so intently, it was a shock when Lucy realised he'd not only stopped paying attention, he'd visibly shut down again at the mention of Gabi. She had a sudden vision of Lili's true story never seeing the light of day – and the courage to find her own better ending vanishing with it – and her voice rose.

'What's wrong? You do see that Gabi has to read it, don't you? Yes this could potentially help limit any damage to the hotel, but it's also far more than that. What's in here is as much your mother's story as Lili's. And I know you said she's rigid and stuck in the past, but doesn't she deserve to know how that story may have changed?'

It was an even bigger shock when Adam's face crumpled.

'Of course she does. But I don't know whether she could bear it, and I don't know how to tell her what you've found. Think about it: what we're saying doesn't only rewrite Lili; it rewrites who Gabi's always been too. Everything Gabi's done in her life was to redress the shame of having a Nazi for a mother. But if that wasn't true, if she'd always known this altered version of Lili and that had made her think or behave differently, then I...'

He stopped. He looked seconds away from falling apart.

Until I had held Lucy back before. *Then I* couldn't. She'd fallen under the Edel's spell; she'd fallen under Lili's. Adam was a part of both of those. And – despite what she'd promised herself about not meddling in fractured families – what else could she do? Adam was a good man, and he was in need of healing. It wasn't in Lucy's nature to gloss over that.

'Then you what, Adam? What do you mean?' She kept her voice soft, hoping a gentle approach might soothe him. 'If your mother had grown up without Lili's shadow hanging over her, if she'd been someone else, how would that have changed things for you?'

His eyes clouded; his teeth sank into his lip. For a moment, Lucy thought he was going to pull back the way he'd pulled back before. It was a relief when he found his voice instead.

'I wouldn't have left her the way that I did. I wouldn't have been so determined to hate everything she stood for, and I wouldn't have ruined her life.'

Whatever locked place Adam had been holding on to had opened. Lucy got up. She moved to the chair beside him. She stopped worrying about boundaries.

It didn't need much to encourage him to talk after that. The directness of her *tell me* had broken through his high walls. And perhaps – from the way he kept staring at it – the hand she lay gently over his was the key.

CHAPTER 14

SEPTEMBER 1990

'Tell me.'

Lucy wasn't the first woman to say that to him, but she was the first woman he hadn't wanted to hide his past from.

Lucy Stretton had got under Adam's skin before he'd known she was there. He wasn't quite sure how she'd done that. Her delight in the Edel was part of it – her joy in watching the hotel's beauty emerge from under its years of neglect, and the way she'd grasped the strength of its bones from the start, had appealed to his architect's heart. She was also clever and had the kind of Pre-Raphaelite curls and pale skin he'd never been able to resist. But more than any of that, she was kind, and her kindness had struck a chord in him which had been lying dormant for too long.

Because her kindness isn't based on the ease of a charmed life. She knows where a lack of it leads.

They might still be in the early stages of getting to know each other, but Adam had a growing sense – particularly after her hasty retreat from the café – that Lucy's past life had perhaps been, in its own way, as complex as his. Despite that, there wasn't a trace of bitterness in her that he could see. Adam had spent years fighting off that corrosive emotion; he'd been the cause of it eating up his own mother. And he didn't want to put Lucy on some pedestal he instinctively knew she would hate, but he was drawn to her warmth, and – in a not unpleasant first for him – he wanted her admiration.

'Tell me.'

Where to start? How could he explain the realities of his upbringing, and the choices that had led him to make, to a woman who'd grown up in a world with no connection to his? He couldn't think of a way to begin, until he glanced down at the journal.

The scales have finally tipped.

Adam knew how that moment felt. He'd never been at risk of the cruel persecution Lili's travellers had faced, and he wouldn't lay claim to it. But he knew what it was like to be lost in a society where he didn't fit. Where the rules and restrictions intended to govern his life had hung on him like chains. He was still struggling for the best way to express that frustration when Lucy laid her hand over his. Her touch had unlocked him.

'I didn't want to be a soldier for their cause, and there was no way forward for me if I refused. That was my tipping point, the moment when I knew the path I'd been put on could only lead down.'

The rest of the story was far easier to shape once he'd admitted that.

"The Party makes decisions on behalf of us all; the DDR is not about individual voices."

Every time his mother uttered those words – and she uttered them constantly – she lowered her voice and bowed her head as if the Party's grandees were listening to check what came next.

Adam had never understood why Gabi would worry about

the wrong people listening to her. It wasn't as if she ever criticised or questioned the Party's directives, or allowed him the freedom to do it. His mother had no more tolerance for individual voices demanding to be heard inside her home as outside it. On the rare occasions when Adam bucked and protested about the stifling limits of his Soviet-shaped school lessons, or the unrelenting dullness of State television, or – in what was apparently the worst crime of all – asked questions about life in the West, Gabi would flinch as if he'd physically attacked her.

'How can you criticise our country when life is so good here? We have homes, and work, and healthcare; we have a purpose; we are protected. How can you find fault with that?'

She'd deliver that opening line, then sit him down and follow it with a speech about absolute faith and absolute trust and the beauty of the socialist system until he was so squashed by her rhetoric, he agreed that the DDR truly was a kind of heaven on earth. After a handful of lectures like those, Adam learned to keep his thoughts about repression and the Stasi and the lack of opportunities beyond a factory floor to himself. Toeing the line – or the appearance of toeing it – at least kept his mother quiet.

He stopped arguing and remade himself into a model citizen, forged in his mother's image. He put on his Free German Youth shirt and marched in their endless parades. He stopped asking for the Levis that his friends – whose parents were less hardline about goods smuggled across from the West – wore and wore the DDR's cardboard-stiff jeans instead. He stopped asking if they could turn the television aerial around and watch Western TV. When Gabi won yet another of the services-to-teaching medals she wore on her lapel like diamonds, he went with her to the award ceremonies where the speeches went on for hours and made his mother sound like a political moderate. By the time he was fifteen, he could parrot all Gabi's lessons and he'd turned himself – on the surface at least – into the son she actually wanted.

All that hard work made his mother as happy as anyone could make her, but it didn't have the same effect on Adam. He was lonely. That loneliness ran as deep through his childhood as his mother's obsessive adherence to her country. There was nowhere he could turn for help or guidance. His one set of grandparents – who were on Gabi's side of the family – were old and as devoted to their socialist ideals as their daughter. His father had died long before Adam had a chance to remember him, and there'd never been another man in Gabi's life – she was too firmly wedded to the Party and its causes for that. As for his relationship with her... Gabi wasn't uninvolved with his progress or deliberately unkind, but she wasn't present, and she wasn't loving. They were far closer to teacher and pupil than mother and son.

Home was a hollow place, and school was no better. The strain of maintaining a public face which was so at odds with his private one kept Adam apart from his peers. The one outlet which comforted him was drawing, and even Gabi had admitted he had talent in that sphere. The slogan-filled posters he drew at school won competitions, but it was the pictures he drew at home and didn't share which were his real joy. Buildings surrounded by greenery and flooded with light and space. Streamlined houses which took their influences from Mies van der Rohe and Corbusier, the Western architects he'd discovered in the banned books which lived under plain covers in his friends' homes. Places to live and breathe in, which were as different from the ugly concrete boxes the DDR specialised in as sunlight from rain. And as he later explained to the friend who changed his life, 'That's where it really started to go wrong, when I forgot where I lived and started having dreams.'

Adam longed to be an architect. He found out the subjects that were required to study the discipline; he was confident with his grades. He tentatively asked his teachers about the possibility of attending architecture school. It didn't seem like an unreasonable request, especially for a student who was a talented artist and had never once stepped out of line. Unfortunately Adam's acting skills may have fooled his mother, but his teachers had been watching him more closely than her. According to them, Adam went through the motions of loyalty, and his sincerity was open to question. Which he'd proved by singling himself out and having his own ideas.

'The needs of the State governs employment opportunities. Good citizens don't choose *careers*; they're thankful for the job that's allocated to them.'

His teachers were robots, churning out factory fodder. It was an insult to them that he wanted more.

'Your good grades are a product of your good education, and what a loyal citizen who works hard should achieve. They don't confer rights.'

Only the best and most loyal students, and only ever two of them in a year group, could expect to continue to university, and suggesting oneself for that privilege was an automatic black mark. Adam was left spinning, trying to find a way through an impenetrable and illogical maze. And then he hit the last hurdle: even if he carried on doing what he'd been doing for years, did it better and jumped through every hoop they asked him to jump through, attending university was impossible without a down payment of three years spent in the military. That was the moment when his mask split.

'I won't do it. I won't wear their uniform; I won't carry a gun. I won't fight the West if that's what they try and force me to do. I won't support a regime that won't support me.'

'Then don't. Get out of here instead.'

Adam had jumped at that unexpected suggestion and knocked over the pail of water he was supposed to be swabbing the floors with. He'd thought he was alone. He'd forgotten that the older boy – Heiko, that was it – was there because he'd also been making a mess of the compulsory pre-military training programme and was on punishment duties in the empty kitchens too. And he hadn't understood, or wanted, Heiko's rather frightening response.

'What are you talking about? Don't you know that even thinking about leaving is a crime?'

His fellow failure hadn't backtracked when Adam trotted out the Party line. He'd glanced at the closed door and pulled a squashed packet of cigarettes out of his pocket.

'And that's another reason to add to the list of what's wrong. Everything that's worth doing is a crime here. So why not do what I plan to do: get out of this dump before it breaks you and go to the West.'

'He made it sound so simple. As if we could just pack a case and be gone. Obviously it wasn't. I thought he was off his head that day, and for quite a while after that.'

Lucy sucked in a breath, and her hand slipped from his. Adam immediately missed the soft feel of her. He picked up the bottle of wine to distract himself and shared the last drops out between their two glasses. Lucy was staring at him as if she'd just completed a challenging puzzle.

'But you did it, didn't you? When you said you didn't know anything about the Edel until the Wall came down, that was because you weren't in the East. You'd escaped.'

She whistled when he nodded.

'I wondered if that's what you'd done; some of the things you said – or didn't say to be more accurate – pointed that way. But I thought it was impossible to get over the Wall. I thought anyone who tried to do that got shot.'

'They did, so we didn't.'

It wasn't meant to sound flippant – Adam had never felt

comfortable discussing what had happened to him even with the very few people who'd had to be told – but Lucy took it that way. Her irritated 'Don't be mysterious' pulled him up.

'I'm sorry. I wasn't trying to be. It's an odd thing to talk about – running away from your country isn't exactly a common rite of passage – and I've largely avoided doing it. Except in the weeks immediately afterwards, when I had to ask for asylum in the West and support and explain myself. And when I came back and had to tell... Well, suffice to say, it's not a time in my life that I dwell on.'

He fell silent for a moment as the insanity of the escape plan and the stupidity – or bravery – of his eighteen-year-old self flooded back. And wondering if Lucy had noticed his hesitation over *had to tell*. When she didn't say anything, he went on.

'But the simple version is that we went underneath. In 1978, a group of us went through a tunnel that ran beneath Bernauerstraβe.'

'No!' Lucy's eyes widened. 'But that's mad. That's the first place I went to when I came to Berlin. The slabs still standing are so high they dwarfed me and the death strip's so wide...' She stopped. Her face paled. 'You could have been caught and killed. Why on earth did you do it?'

The reason was harder to explain than the mechanics. Adam deliberately didn't give himself time to think.

'Because I was desperate – and selfish.'

He'd admitted the first reason before but not the second. That slip hadn't been intended, and he wasn't ready to flesh it out now.

'I suppose the truth is that I couldn't be who I was over here in the East and I thought I was going to drown.'

The compassion which instantly swept over Lucy's face stripped him bare. He was glad that her next question was another, 'How did you do it?' He needed the safety of facts.

'I couldn't have done it on my own, that's the first thing. Until I met Heiko at the training camp, I'd never really thought about leaving, except in a nebulous, *I wish I lived in the West* kind of way. I certainly didn't have a clue how it could be done. But Heiko was further down the decision-making path than me – he'd been in trouble at school and was convinced the Stasi were going to force him to become an informant. His older brother was in the same position.'

Adam paused, as a sudden, *What if I'd never met him? What would my life be?* hit too hard home. He was grateful Lucy waited until the moment passed and didn't immediately jump in with questions.

'Heiko's family had connections in the West and they owned a bakery on the corner of Ruppiner and Bernauerstraße, with a flour cellar which provided a hiding place, for us and the tunnel. And nobody was using tunnels by then, so I guess they thought there'd be a good chance of going undetected. The old ones where the big escapes had happened in the 1960s had been bricked up. The Stasi had made it impossible to get through the sewer and subway systems – there were locked grilles in the sewers and sheets of metal embedded with spikes on the far edges of the train platforms by then.'

He broke off as Lucy shuddered and decided that there were details about the way the DDR had kept its citizens captive she didn't need to know.

'I'm not sure how the tunnel was excavated; I wasn't part of that bit. I think there were some students from the West involved, and the route they chose worked because there was a building site on the western side of the Wall – which is where we came up – which meant that there were places at both ends to hide the soil.' He shook his head as the memories came flooding. 'The tunnel felt endless when we were in it – I do remember that. It must have been about 150 metres long, and I don't know how long it took to dig it out, but the whole escape was nearly two years in the planning. I'd almost given up the idea of it happening when I got the call to go through.'

'What was that like – waiting to go?'

Adam didn't need to think about that, or he thought he didn't. 'It was hellish. I thought I'd lose my mind trying to carry on being a good citizen when I was anything but that in my head. I thought everybody involved would get caught, and that would have meant a very long prison sentence for all of us, and no kind of future at all.'

Lucy nodded at the answer as if she accepted it, but she was also frowning.

She's heard what I didn't say again.

His answer had been too full of himself. He jumped quickly on before she had a chance to ask about the missing piece of the story: how his escape had impacted on Gabi.

'Going through it was pretty terrible too. The first moment of dropping into the opening wasn't so bad – my adrenaline kicked in. But crawling through the mud...' He blinked at a sudden image of walls pressing against him and oozing with a damp that felt centuries old. 'It wasn't completely black; we had torches, but they weren't easy to hold. I was convinced I was going to get stuck or get buried beneath a landslide. And when I got to the middle, under the strip, and I could hear footsteps above me and dogs barking... There were rumours that they'd put listening equipment in the ground when the first tunnels were found; I was certain they could hear me breathing...' He stumbled to a halt and had to regroup. 'We got through, that's the main thing. And that moment when my hands smacked against the wooden ladder on the far side and I knew I was free? That moment will stay with me forever.'

He stopped. He couldn't help hoping that Lucy would be so spellbound by his bravery, she'd forget the things he hadn't said.

She tried. She made the right noises. She acknowledged how brave he'd been; she told him she'd never heard a story like it. But there was no doubt that his use of *selfish* was weighing on her, or that she'd retreated from him a little, and Adam couldn't shake the feeling that she wasn't as impressed with his heroics as she seemed.

'I have to go.'

It was abrupt, but he couldn't think of anything else to do but leave. He could sense an awkward silence coming, one filled with *but what about Gabi* and he wasn't ready for that.

'I'll show this to my mother and ring you once she's read it.'

He didn't let himself dwell on Lucy's puzzled face. He couldn't shake the feeling that he'd slipped in her estimation. And he didn't like that feeling one bit.

CHAPTER 15

OCTOBER 1990

'I'd like to show you something before I take you to my mother's flat, if you don't mind taking a short detour.'

Adam was overly formal as he ushered Lucy into his car, and their conversation stuck to neutral updates about the Edel's renovations while he drove, a topic which was at least safe ground.

There was plenty to discuss about that. The Edel had been swarming with workmen for weeks and had now almost completed its transformation from a shell into a recognisable shape. Under Adam's direction, all the core work – the rewiring and plastering, the upgrades to the ancient windows and heating system – was done. He was now focused on the upgrade to the facade while Lucy was buried in fabric swatches and paint samples, pulling together a colour scheme whose deep emeralds and amethysts both evoked and modernised the lush tones of the hotel's heyday. And when she wasn't conjuring up colours, she was co-ordinating publicity material and tracking down specialist cleaners for the black and white tiles which the workmen had discovered underneath the brown lino, as well as a company who could recreate the teardrop crystal chandelier which had lit up the foyer before the war.

'There's so many decisions to make, my days run past me before I can catch them.'

Her tone as she said that was uncomfortably jolly and tipped them into an awkward silence that sat between them like a third passenger.

Is this how it's going to be now? Conversations about work and that's it?

It had certainly been the pattern in the fortnight since Lucy had shown Adam the journal. Other than him acknowledging that he'd given that to Gabi, they hadn't once strayed beyond budgets and building decisions.

He thinks I'm judging him, but I'm not.

That wasn't strictly true, but Lucy had no idea how to say, *I'm only judging you a little bit,* so it seemed safer to say nothing at all. Which meant they were both stuck.

Lucy glanced across at him. Adam was concentrating on the traffic, but he must have been aware she was watching him. He started to discuss the Edel again, saying something about sourcing new internal doors from an architectural salvage depot his company had a deal with. He quickly ground to a halt when Lucy didn't respond. His body was as far away from hers as it was possible to be inside the narrow confines of a Porsche 911. When she glanced at his hands, it seemed impossible that she'd held them.

Selfish.

That was the word hanging over the journey. That was the word which had tarnished their last meeting – for Adam as much as her, or so Lucy assumed given how quickly he'd left.

Because of the silence it left around Gabi.

Lucy had been stunned by the story of Adam's escape. She'd heard the desperation that had spurred it, and the bravery. But he'd said *selfish*, and she'd heard that too, and –

although she didn't want to cast shadows over what he'd been forced to do – the more digging she'd done into the realities of life in the DDR, the more apt *selfish* felt.

Lucy's workmen were a taciturn bunch. They'd shrugged and tried to avoid the question when Lucy had asked what the consequences had been for families whose members broke the rules and went West. The response she eventually elicited was a stark one.

'It was tough for anyone left in that position. The authorities couldn't punish the people who escaped, but they had to punish someone to prove they were in charge, so they went after the ones who stayed.'

When Lucy asked what *punish* meant, the men threw a handful of hints around that they wouldn't explain and quickly changed the subject. *Resettlement. Surveillance. Marked out as failed citizens.* Whatever those threats had meant in reality for Gabi, Lucy was certain the life Adam had dumped her in hadn't mirrored the success he'd gone on to find.

And he didn't acknowledge that. He spoke about his decision to leave as if he was the only person affected by it.

She didn't want to judge him for that – she'd never lived in an oppressive society; it wasn't her place to judge anyone who'd been faced with the kind of restrictions Adam had described. It was still hard not to wonder.

'We're here.'

Adam had stopped the car while Lucy was still trying to fit all the sides of him together. She followed him out of the Porsche, paying very little attention to where they had parked, needing to clear the air and unsure how to do it.

'This is Karl-Marx-Allee. This is where my grandparents, and my parents, lived and where I was brought up.'

The street's name caught her attention. Gabi had spoken with such pride about her flat there, it had stuck in Lucy's memory. She stared around, her jaw dropping, trying to marry the word *street* with the reality of where she was standing. Karl-Marx-Allee was a grand sweeping boulevard with a stretch of immaculately mown grass separating its two sides. White art-deco-style buildings rose in tiers above her, their fronts decorated with thin pillars and delicate carvings, decorative gold-tipped tiles and floating balconies. Lucy could see a pair of green-topped towers flanking the far end which wouldn't have looked out of place on a palace.

'Wow.' She turned this way and that, wishing she'd brought a camera. 'Wow, this is incredible, unreal. What a place to grow up – it's no wonder you became an architect if you were surrounded by this every day.'

Adam frowned as if he'd never considered the idea before. 'Maybe. I think I see its beauty now better than I did then. When I was a child, it was just somewhere else to get indoctrinated.' He stopped as his cheeks coloured. 'God, I really do sound like a privileged brat. That wasn't my intention, I promise. And I know I didn't mention Gabi when I told you about my escape and I should have done. I suppose you think *selfish* was the right word.'

'Not really. Well maybe a bit. But I don't think you're selfish now. And I can't begin to imagine how difficult it was...'

Lucy tailed off as Adam shook his head.

'I honestly wouldn't blame you if you think I acted badly. I did, and I need to face up to that. Which is why I wanted you to see this, not because I lived here, but because Gabi did.' He gestured to the buildings as the sunlight flashed across the top row of tiles and turned their golden edges into little fires. 'This was a magical place for her, not only because of how lovely it is but for what it represented. "Exemplary buildings for exemplary workers", that was the saying when these were built. It was an honour to be allocated a flat here – she wasn't exaggerating about that. And I took this beauty away from her. I ran away, and she lost her home and her status. One action led directly to the other. I might not have considered that then, but it's all I think about now.'

He looked so drawn, Lucy was suddenly sorry she'd judged him at all. She scrabbled around for something that might offer him a way out. 'Which is horrible, and I suppose what I'd guessed. But you couldn't have known, could you, what would happen after you went?'

His smile was too sad to be called that. 'Don't be kind, Lucy, not about this. I don't deserve it, and I haven't earned it. Not yet. It's true I didn't know the exact details of how much her life had changed until I came back almost ten years later, but that's no excuse. I wasn't blind to how things were done here – the DDR's faults and its crackdowns were why I couldn't stay. And I was hardly the first to go or cause problems for those left behind.'

He paused for a moment, staring around at the buildings as if he was listening to them. 'The DDR was a dictatorship – it had to control its citizens to survive. Nobody was safe, no matter how grand an apartment they lived in. There was always a story about someone who'd fled West and how their family had paid the price for that. Jobs lost, homes taken, people relocated to some unknown place – disappearing for want of a better word – and then rumours spreading that the parents who'd failed to keep their children loyal and in line were criminals too.' He cleared his throat and took a breath. 'I knew all along what could happen to her – let's not pretend that I didn't. So selfish is what fits.'

Adam fell silent; he disappeared inside himself. His honesty was so raw, Lucy wasn't immediately sure what to say, although she was certain that the last thing he needed to hear was platitudes. She gazed around her, trying to imagine what it must have been like to live in such a beautiful place. Karl-Marx-Allee – unlike every other major street she'd walked down in Berlin – was a haven of quiet and calm. No one was bustling along the carefully swept pavements. There was no music blaring from an open window or a shop doorway or a car.

The street has slipped out of time, and so have we.

Adam had peeled off another layer; he'd trusted her with himself. Lucy was suddenly conscious, in a way she'd never been conscious before, that she'd been given a moment in which she was the one in charge of the way the next steps would play out. She could focus on choices he'd made long ago which cast him in a less flattering light and keep him at arm's length. Or she could listen while he acknowledged his mistakes, acknowledge her own and make a deeper connection with a man who was far more than his flaws.

I like him. I want to keep on liking him. He's worth that effort.

That realisation made what came next the simplest thing. As she'd done when the journal had unlocked a hidden part of him and Adam had needed a prompt to move on, Lucy reached out and took hold of his hand.

'But you went to the West anyway. And when you first told me about that, and left out any mention of your mother's feelings and future, then yes, it's fair to say I wasn't sure that sat well on you. But that was only part of the picture, and I've made wrong choices that I don't think make me a bad person. I certainly don't think that about you.'

She felt him physically come back to her. And she saw his pain rush in.

'Ten years ago my only focus was myself. My relationship with Gabi was broken, and I used that as a catch-all. I told myself she wouldn't care if I left. I told myself that her record here was so exemplary, she'd be fine when I was gone. It was cruel and heartless. I let myself believe lies because it suited me to believe them.'

The man was judging the boy, and he was judging him too harshly.

'Don't.'

He blinked and looked away. She bit down on the urge to spill her own mistakes, because it wasn't the time, and contented herself with a 'What happens now? What do you want to do next?' which could have applied as much to her as it did to him.

His head came back up; his grip on her tightened. 'Everything I can to repair the damage.'

She had to force herself not to add, *Me too.*

Marzahn, where Gabi now lived – according to the little Adam seemed to know about it – had been built to solve the problem of East Berlin's chronic housing shortage with homes that offered a far better standard of living. Whatever the planners had intended, it was an isolated place and a long way from anyone's notion of a workers' paradise.

'It's not what I expected. I thought it would be more along the lines of that village-style suburb we just drove through – not as old-fashioned maybe, but softer and with more green spaces. I didn't realise that it would be so...'

Adam stopped. They both knew that the word he was looking for was *bleak.*

The estate was on the eastern fringes of the city, little more than a twenty-minute drive from Karl-Marx-Allee but a complete world away. Lucy stared out of the car window at the sea of giant grey-and-mustard-coloured concrete blocks which appeared to stretch out for miles. There were wide roads linking the towering complexes; she could see a sign for shops and a playground and a patch of grass here and there. The area wasn't run-down or desolate, but it wasn't welcoming either. Despite the paths and the walkways, there wasn't a soul around, and there was a brutality to the buildings' sharp edges and sheer scale which made Lucy feel unpleasantly vulnerable.

'You've never been here before?'

Adam shook his head. 'Gabi's never wanted me to; she's always been cagey about it. It was a surprise she suggested coming here today. And I think I've been kidding myself, imagining that Marzahn would be some pretty garden enclave. I could have found a photograph of it easily enough if I'd tried – I'm an architect after all. I didn't. That should tell you a lot.'

He paused, his hands twisting. 'Nothing's been easy about this, although that's not any fault of hers. When I first came back, before I knew she'd moved, I went to the old flat, but nobody knew her there. And when I did track down a colleague from her teaching days...' He slipped into a memory it took him a moment to pull out of. 'Well anyway, she certainly wasn't pleased to see me. "Your mother was a marked woman from the moment you fled." That was her opening volley, and I'll never forget it. She did at least give me Gabi's phone number in the end, although that took some persuading, and she threw "I hope the West was worth it" after me as a parting shot. I deserved that, but her contempt for what I did made it impossible to ask questions.'

Lucy gazed up at the soaring tower blocks, hoping that Gabi's flat was at least close to ground level. The woman she'd met had been loyal to her country whatever it did, but she'd also been proud. Being removed from Karl-Marx-Allee to Marzahn – where everything and surely everyone was faceless – must have been a hard and humbling blow. When she glanced back at Adam, his strained face told her he was thinking the same thing.

I don't know enough about where their relationship stands to manage the conversation about Lili that's coming.

Lucy was about to sit down with a woman who'd had her life rewritten too many times. She had no idea if the journal had upset Gabi, or made her angry, or made her want to run from or re-examine her past. She couldn't walk into that – or watch

Adam walk into that – without knowing exactly how their initial reunion had gone. She turned round and slipped her hand inside his again. The gesture was becoming a shorthand for asking difficult questions.

'You've mentioned your return to the East a couple of times, but we've never discussed the details. Obviously I've a sense of how things stand between you and Gabi now, but there's a lot of gaps and – if we're about to go in there and really pull the past apart – it would help to have some of those filled in. So I'm sorry if this is too blunt, but what was it really like when you finally saw each other again?'

Adam took so long to answer her, Lucy wasn't sure if he needed re-prompting. When he did eventually find his voice, it wasn't a steady one.

'It was almost impossible, if I'm honest. We met in that awful café near the Tierpark. We didn't know whether or how to touch each other, so we didn't try. Every conversation we attempted collapsed under the weight of my guilt and her sense of betrayal. And when she told me that she wasn't a teacher anymore, that they'd made her clean classrooms instead after I left...' He broke off, his eyes blurred. 'I should have apologised there and then, but I got in my own way. Even after everything that had happened to her, she didn't want reunification, she didn't want her world to change, and that made me crazy. And she refused to talk about how her life had been. She trotted out some ridiculous line about the State having to preserve itself and make an example of the people who failed it, like she was glad to be a martyr. I think she only told me about the Edel in the end to stop me asking anything more personal about her. It took another meeting – which I pushed for and I'm not entirely sure she wanted – before she told me the truth, as she knew it then anyway, about Lili.'

He stopped again. His face was drained; he clearly needed a moment to gather himself, but Lucy couldn't stay quiet.

'When you saw her, after all those years, did you feel...'

It was too hard to ask: she'd seen the two of them together; she already knew the answer. Lucy cut the question off, scared she might turn the truth into a bad omen and hating how irrational that thought made her.

Adam answered her anyway. 'Did I feel like her son? That's what you were going to ask, wasn't it? No, I didn't. And she didn't feel like my mother. And – although we've gone through the motions of meeting up since – that stalemate doesn't appear to be changing.'

Lucy couldn't look at him. 'Would you like it to?' was the obvious response, but that was unsayable. She didn't want to know a man who could answer *no, I don't* to that question. She didn't want to add to his hurt if *yes* was what he craved but finding a connection was proving impossible. But Adam was a step ahead of her.

'It will change though; it has to. I want my mother to find happiness. I hope that Lili's journal can help her to do that. And – as old as I am – I want a mother. Which means I'm going to have to be the son she deserves, and I'm going to keep trying to be him until she believes that I mean it.'

There was still uncertainty in Adam's voice, but there was also a long-buried love for his mother which desperately needed to find a safe place to settle. Lucy followed him out of the car, hoping with every fibre of her body that Gabi would be able to see it.

Gabi's flat was decorated in the same sour-cream-and-brown palette which had swallowed the Edel. The woman who greeted them was stiff and formal. The front room they were ushered into was small but immaculate. Its furnishings – a built-in wooden unit housing a television and a radio, a rather rigid sofa upholstered in dark green and a too low Formica-topped coffee table – reminded Lucy of the terraced house she'd grown up in. Except that there was no comfort or sense of home here. There were no personal touches.

'I was only allowed to bring what I could carry.'

Gabi had noted Adam's frown at the same time Lucy did. He was staring round the room, presumably searching for familiar items, and she immediately did what she'd done in the Tierpark café. She presented the unhappiness which had coloured her life in one impossible-to-argue-with sentence. Her son's face instantly closed down.

How do they paralyse each other so quickly?

Lucy didn't have time to worry at that – somebody had to rescue the situation. And skirting around the issues didn't feel like the right way to do it.

'It was good of you to invite us here, Frau Wendl. I've seen Karl-Marx-Allee now; I understand how hard this move must have been for you. We both do.'

Gabi – who was clearly unused to anyone speaking so plainly about her changed circumstances – glared at Lucy as if she would happily throw her back out of the flat.

Lucy didn't give her the chance to shut her down too. She carried on talking.

'And maybe it's not my place to say it, but it strikes me that you've been dealt more than one unfair hand in your life. Which is why I felt it was so important for you to read Lili's journal for yourself. Not only because of the way it rewrites her, but because it's obvious from what she wrote in it that you were very deeply loved.'

There was a moment of complete stillness as three people held their breath. Then Gabi's face crumpled. She slid into a chair as if her body had no substance to it. When Adam rushed to her side, she didn't melt into him, but she didn't push his steadying arm away either.

'She wasn't a Nazi, Mum. She wasn't the Hitler-lover she was made out to be. How incredible is that?'

It was *Mum* that made Gabi jump and find her bones again. She twisted round and stared at Adam as if he was the enemy, not her son. She didn't recoil from him, but the impulse was visibly there. And she didn't spare him her fury.

'*Incredible?* Well that's one word for it. And now what? Am I meant to be grateful that I was *deeply loved*? Am I meant to be happy that my mother was the victim of lies? Or that she was in fact the good person I remember when it's too damn late to do anything with it?'

Her pain was so vivid, Adam froze, but *I remember* gave Lucy an opening. She moved to the sofa on the other side of Gabi's chair. The woman's hands were shaking; her skin had receded to parchment – even from a distance her taut body felt cold.

'She's in shock. Go and make some tea, Adam, and bring her a glass of water as well.'

Adam uncoiled and jumped up. Lucy kept a careful watch on Gabi, unnerved by her ragged breathing. She didn't say anything – she didn't want to lead another conversation without Adam there to hear where it went. Fortunately, when he came back from the kitchen carrying a tray loaded with glasses and cups and a packet of biscuits which Lucy hoped were high in sugar, he was far more in control of himself. Between the two of them, they managed to get Gabi to eat and to drink until her skin finally pinked up again. Lucy was bursting with questions, but she glanced over at Adam and waited for his nod before she started to speak.

'You've lost so much, and I'm very sorry for that. But you said, *I remember*, Frau Wendl, as if your memories of your mother were happy ones. Is that true?'

Gabi raised her head and – for the briefest moment – the years fell away and a far younger woman emerged.

'Yes, it is, or the early ones anyway. That's what's so hard. I loved her very much, and the things that were said about her – that terrible newspaper article – never made sense to me. My mother didn't have a cruel bone in her body, so how could she have been a close friend of Hitler?' Her voice caught on the name, but she pulled herself together before either Lucy or Adam could intervene. 'She was a ray of light – that's how I remember her; she was beautiful and warm. And so loving. No matter how busy the hotel was, even after my father went away to fight and she must have been working all the hours in the day, she made time for me, for the two of us. She was popular with everyone, with the guests and the staff – she could even make André, who was the head wine waiter, laugh, and he was a great one for standing on ceremony. But then she...'

Gabi's face rearranged itself back into its old set lips and stiff lines, and her body followed.

'Then she what, Frau Wendl? Please tell us. Maybe the truth isn't as bad as you think.'

It was a brave try, but Gabi shook Lucy's words off like cold water.

'How can it be not as bad? My mother abandoned me – that's the truth. I didn't want to leave her, and I told her that in no uncertain terms, but she still sent me away. I was nine years old, and she packed me off to live with a family I didn't know, in Potsdam where I'd never been. And she never came back like she promised she would, even though I waited for her every day, until I was told not to bother because she was dead. Why would she treat me like that? Was I really so bad? All these years, and I've never known what I did wrong.'

And there it was, the despair Gabi had lived with for almost fifty years. *I've never known what I did wrong.* Her voice had stripped back to a child's as the words poured out, laying open a wound which ran far deeper than the other crimes which had been laid at Lili's door. Lucy began instantly scrabbling for some words of comfort which wouldn't diminish Gabi's pain, but Adam got there first.

'You can't keep torturing yourself like this. You didn't do anything wrong. The real story is all there in the journal. Think about what she said in her last entry: "Gabi is safe... I can only pray that this isn't goodbye." We think Lili was planning something, Mum, and whatever it was clearly went very badly wrong. She sent you away to stop you getting caught up in the danger she was in, I'm certain of it. But she was also desperately hoping to see you – and your father – again.'

This time Gabi didn't flinch at *Mum*; she seemed to latch on to it. She sat forward, gazing at Adam with more gentleness and hope in her face than she'd shown since he and Lucy arrived. That change in her pushed a new confidence through him.

'The journal must have been so hard for you to read. And maybe it was easier for me and Lucy to pick out some of the nuances in it, because we're not as close to what happened as you are. Does that sound fair?'

Gabi nodded. 'There were parts I skipped through, that I couldn't square with my memories. And I wanted to believe she loved me, like she said. But I suppose I wasn't sure, after everything I'd been told to believe about her, how much of what was in there I could trust.'

'I think you can trust Lili. I think what's in the journal is her real voice.'

Adam's expression was so loving as he spoke, Lucy found herself blinking as hard as Gabi.

'But can you help me understand something, Mum? The family she sent you to – was that the Stiefels? The couple I thought were my real grandparents?'

Lucy could see Adam's brain ticking as Gabi said yes.

'You said that you didn't know them before you went to

Potsdam, so I'm guessing they weren't regulars at the hotel? Or part of your parents' close circle?'

Gabi thought for a moment, and then she shook her head. 'No, they weren't; they couldn't have been. When my mother told me I had to go and stay with them, I think she said that they were old friends of my father's, but I've no memory of meeting them before I was sent to their house. She couldn't really explain why I had to go, and I didn't want to – I really fought her, although I can't remember why.'

She stopped for a moment, searching her memory, but nothing seemed to resurface. 'I don't know, maybe it was some sixth sense. She said she was busy; I do remember that because she was never too busy for me. She said I'd have a better time, which I refused to believe. As to why she chose the Stiefels?' Gabi shrugged. 'That wasn't clear either. Maybe it was because I had no grandparents I could go to. My mother didn't have any family still alive, and the Rodenbergs had been killed in the Hamburg bombing.'

Gabi paused, her face softening again as a memory flooded back. 'She did say she trusted the Stiefels to look after me while she couldn't because they were kind, and that was what counted in the end more than whether I knew them or not. I do remember that. Oh...' She sat back suddenly as if the past had come at her too quickly. 'And that was when she gave me her wedding ring. I remember that now too.'

'She did what? What wedding ring? The one that you're wearing now?'

Gabi stared down at the plain gold band she still wore on her ring finger as Adam frowned. 'No, this is the one your father gave me. You've never seen Lili's; I've never worn it. That one is engraved with forget-me-nots and it has the date of their wedding and their initials engraved inside. I loved it as a child; the flowers were so pretty, but she'd never let me try it on, even though I begged her to. I used to see her kissing it sometimes after my father went to war.' Gabi suddenly looked up, her face creased in confusion. 'She was always so certain he'd come back, she refused to accept he was dead, even after the telegram came to say he was missing. So why would she give me a ring that meant so much to her, that she said was her link to him?'

'It was an act of love.' Lucy couldn't stop herself breaking in. 'I think she sent you somewhere nobody would think to look for you, except for your father if he managed to make it home. And she sent you with a ring that carried their love in it. She must have known she was in danger and her main thought was to protect you, and to save him from losing you in whatever chaos came next.'

The room shifted to make room for this new Lili whose heart kept getting bigger. And for a man who may or may not have come back to Germany but had lost his entire family if he did.

Gabi leaned back against the armchair's straight back and briefly closed her eyes. Her skin had turned to milk again, and there was a blue tinge around her lips which sent Adam running for more water. But when she drank that and rallied, she smiled at Lucy for the first time.

'That sounds like the kind of thing my mother would do. Thank you – that helps. And she did make a good choice. The Stiefels were kind, and they treated me as if I was their own child. But they were also fiercely loyal to the new DDR, which meant putting as much distance as possible between me and what was being said about Lili and changing my name to theirs.' She took another gulp of water. 'I can't condemn them for that. Being associated with a known Nazi wasn't just a taint in those days; it could have meant a prison sentence or a gulag. If they hadn't protected me so well, my life would have been ruined. But the fear of her set me on a path I couldn't get off.'

Gabi turned suddenly to face Adam. The sorrow engraved on her face as she gazed at her son made Adam gasp and Lucy look away. It was as fresh as if she was still caught inside those haunted days.

'I thought I had to be more than loyal to escape my mother's legacy. I thought I had to belong to the Party, body and soul. Even when I knew you were struggling to find a place for yourself, that your dreams couldn't fit with what your life was going to be, I couldn't bend, I couldn't help you. It was more important to me to be a good citizen than to be a good mother. I didn't see the damage that belief caused until long after you left. I'm still not sure I see it all now. And I'm more sorry than I can say about that.'

Lili disappeared. Lucy faded into the background. There was no one in the room except Gabi and Adam. Lucy got up and slipped away while they were edging around the words they needed to reframe each other. It was too personal a moment for witnesses.

She went downstairs and waited by the Porsche, watching clouds swirl around rooftops that were too high to see, wondering exactly how lonely Gabi's life had been and hoping this was the day that loneliness changed.

When Adam finally came down to join her, he looked exhausted, but there was a new lightness in his body. He didn't say anything until they were both out of the wind and inside the car's warmth.

'That completely threw me. I didn't expect her to say sorry first; I don't think I expected her to apologise at all. And she listened to mine with more openness than I've ever found in her before.'

He rubbed his eyes as Lucy asked how Gabi was now.

'She's better, I think, although I'm worried she's not well, not that she would let me ask any questions about that. She's agreed to come to the Edel, and she's even talking about trying to find her father, which may be wishful thinking, but I said we'd do what we can to help. There's a lot to work out still – not just about Lili but about our relationship – and a lot that needs mending, but I think that we'll get there, with time.'

Lucy didn't ask him where *there* was. She wasn't certain either he or Gabi knew the answer yet. It was enough for now that the stalemate was broken, and that the will to break it had come from both sides. And none of it was Lucy's story, but the hope it carried ran like quicksilver through her.

'Thank you.'

Adam's sudden switch from worrying about Gabi to focusing on her took Lucy by surprise.

'I mean it. I would never have got this far without you. You've a way of cutting to the point which makes even the hardest task seem possible.'

The warmth in his face wrapped round her like a blanket.

'I didn't overstep then? I've been told that I have a habit of charging in.'

He smiled for the first time since they'd arrived at Marzahn. 'How could you overstep when everything you do comes from kindness? Isn't that what Lili said was all that counts in the end? It's certainly all that counts with me.'

He won't judge me; he's been through too much himself to do that. He'll help me move forward too.

It was time to meet his honesty with hers. Lucy put her hand on the steering wheel as Adam reached for the ignition.

'Wait a minute. Don't drive off, not yet. There's something I want to tell you.

CHAPTER 16

DECEMBER 1990

The Edel was blooming, and so was its newly forming family.

There's something I want to tell you.

It had taken over an hour to lay her past bare, and clouds had cloaked the towers before she was done, but her leap of faith worked. Adam hadn't judged her; he'd helped her open up. Lucy told him about Emily, and the shock of losing her so quickly, which was what she'd planned to do. But she also told him what she'd never revealed to anybody else. That she'd lost her baby twice...

'The adoption was an open one, although that term is misleading, as the openness was only ever intended to be on one side. What it meant in reality was that I was allowed to have what's called indirect contact. I couldn't initiate anything, but Emily's new parents agreed to send a photo of her to me once a year and a progress report. And to tell her that she was adopted when they thought she was old enough to understand, so she can get in touch with me herself when she's eighteen, if that's what she chooses to do.'

She wasn't surprised when Adam frowned at her explanation. Everything she'd told him so far had been full of Emily's absence.

'That can't be easy, to always be so reliant on what they decide to do. But at least you know how Emily is getting on, even if you can't see her yet. That must be some comfort, isn't it?'

'It would be, if that's how things happened. But there's no contact any—'

Lucy stopped herself. This was the point where her attempts to talk about Emily – something which she rarely did – normally ended. With a *there's no contact anymore* she'd never let any previous relationship move past. Except the truth wasn't so clear-cut.

So tell him that. Don't make excuses, for yourself or anybody else. Simply tell him what happened. If he's going to think badly of you, it's best to know now.

Telling him everything was what she wanted to do, but she had no clue where to start. Until Adam took a page out of her book and reached for her hand.

'Whatever it is, you can say it, Lucy. You've heard some raw stuff about me, and no one's run yet.'

Now she was the one feeling unlocked.

'I never heard from them at all. But that wasn't their fault.'

Once that much was said, the next step seemed a little easier.

'I didn't live at home again after Emily was born. I couldn't beyond a couple of weeks – we'd all disappointed each other too much. I'd had a part-time job at the Midland Hotel in More-cambe for a while, so after I left school – because I couldn't go back there either – that became full-time and they let me live in.'

She smiled as a vision of the white hotel glowing against its seaside backdrop popped into her head. 'The Midland was where I met Charlie Compton. He was considering buying the place – it's the most beautiful art deco building and, like the Edel, it was famous up to the 1930s, but then it fell on hard times. Charlie decided not to go forward with the purchase in the end – the restoration was too much, and he wasn't a fan of the town – but he offered me a job with his company as a junior manager, and I took it.'

She hadn't just taken it; she'd leaped at the chance. Two years learning her craft at the Midland had – as Charlie put it – run the hotel trade through her blood. Lucy had swapped Morecambe for London without a second thought, and nobody had tried to dissuade her.

'Where I went wrong was that I didn't change my details with the adoption agency – my parents told me hotel addresses didn't sound stable and it was important for me to sound responsible. It was simpler not to argue, so we agreed that the annual letters about Emily would continue to be sent to their home, and then they'd send them on to me. Except they never did.'

'What? But that's terrible. Surely they had a legal obligation to do that?'

Lucy shrugged. 'They had a moral one maybe, but they never signed anything. And I did ask if anything had arrived, but when I did... The truth is that my parents lied to me. The letters did come, for a few years anyway, until my lack of response must have made the exercise feel pointless. But they told me Emily's parents had never written. That they'd broken the contract, and that the agency was trying to remedy the situation but there was very little they could actually do. And I know I should have fought harder and asked more questions, but...'

Lucy stopped again, trying to find some pity for a young girl who'd been out of her depth, who couldn't live with the hope of a letter and then the crushing disappointment which always followed when nothing came.

She couldn't find a drop.

'I gave up instead. I never stopped missing my daughter – or loving her. I've worn the one photograph I have of her tissue thin. But I accepted what I was told, I poured myself into my job and my new life, and I did nothing about my baby.'

Adam's hand stayed in hers. The softness in his voice made her eyes fill.

'Oh, Lucy, please don't. You're being far too hard on yourself. You were so young – you had no real power; of course you believed what you were told. Only a very hard heart could blame you for that. But what about now? Whatever your parents were trying to do – which was surely some misguided attempt to protect you – they must feel awful about it, or they wouldn't have told you the truth. Can't they speak to the agency and set the wheels rolling again?'

'That's the thing though – they didn't tell me; they didn't get a chance.'

Lucy stumbled. She never let herself think about the end of her parents' story; she'd never tried to explain it. But Adam was holding her hand, and if she couldn't tell him now, she never would.

'Our relationship was non-existent – we barely had any contact beyond stilted phone calls once I joined the Compton chain, and I always made up reasons not to go home. And then they were killed. In a car crash in 1985 – their car skidded on a patch of black ice and went down an embankment.' She shook her head as Adam tried to interrupt: if she stopped again, she'd never get to the end. 'That's when I found the photos and the letters they'd hidden from me, when I cleared out the house. I tell myself they'd kept them because they were going to change their minds one day, but I've no proof of that.'

'Oh, Lucy, you poor thing. What a dreadful mess.'

Now it was her turn to say, 'Don't.'

She couldn't bear his sympathy, not yet. There would be a

time when she would be able to share the spiral of loss those days had turned into, but it wasn't now.

'I did contact the agency myself after that happened, but it seemed everyone had given up on me. Emily's parents had moved, new staff had taken over my file and were too over-worked to prioritise it, and nobody seemed to be able – or willing – to find out their new address, although it had to be on record somewhere. And yes, I should have made demands and made a fuss, but I was numb. I gave up again. That seems to be my default.'

'It's not. It doesn't have to be. Look what you've done for my family.'

Suddenly he was pulling her into an embrace that felt like coming home.

'Whatever you want to do – whether that means finding Emily again now, or deciding that you'll wait until she comes looking for you – I'm here to support you. If you want me to.'

She did want him to. There was something about having Adam in her corner which, as he'd said to her not so long before, made the hardest task seem possible. He'd certainly been in her corner at Marzahn, and since then...

He's lodged himself in my heart, and I think I've lodged myself in his.

Lucy looked up as the Edel's newly re-stained and polished doors opened, and Adam led Gabi in from the snow. This was her third visit to the hotel since October, but her first steps inside were still reluctant ones. It was as if she needed to breathe the Edel's air for a few moments each time she came in before she could properly place herself there.

She's getting frailer.

Adam's hunch had been right: Gabi wasn't well. When he'd finally persuaded her to let him go with her to the doctor's appointment that she'd tried to hide from him, it was also clear that she'd known she was sick for a while. It was heart disease. The doctor wouldn't give a prognosis because Gabi wouldn't let him. But he'd told Adam in an aside on the way out that he should cherish the months that they had, and it didn't need a specialist to see that Gabi was fading.

'We have to try and track down the names from the journal, as well as any leads that might still exist for Marius, and we have to move quickly. I need her to see I'm doing everything I can.'

Adam had arrived at the Edel from the doctor's office, white-faced and shaken but determined to move heaven and earth for his mother, which fixed him even more firmly into Lucy's heart. She'd come up with a plan to place adverts in newspapers in key German cities – and in hotel publications at home and abroad in order to widen the search for Marius – that same day. But – although it was a relief to be doing something – neither of them had felt particularly hopeful about the plan's success, particularly when it came to Marius, who had been missing for so long he was surely dead. They had avenues to explore from the journal which sounded positive: Marius, André, Alice and someone who was only known as FK. Unfortunately, as soon as they factored in all the years that had passed, plus the limited information Lili had left them and the vanishing act that was Marius, those avenues felt closer to dead ends.

What would I do without André? He's become my right hand.

Talking to Alice Herschel might have been wrong, but thank God for her. If things were different, I could have been her. She's the only one, except Marius, who knows the truth, who can understand why I'm doing this. I know I should be sorry for confiding in her, but I'm not.

Both André and Alice were mentioned more than once in the entries dating from the end of 1942. Some of those pages were so badly marked by mould, especially a longer letter written to Marius, that the details were smudged and lost. But it was clear that both relationships had been important to Lili, and that she'd spent time with Alice in a way she hadn't done with the other travellers who'd passed through the Edel. Lucy wanted her to be the key to the puzzle, but André was only a vague memory for Gabi, and neither Alice Herschel nor FK meant anything at all.

'André was in charge of the wine cellars. He was kind to me, and my mother must have trusted him because it was André who drove me to Potsdam. But I don't know why he and not the chauffeur did that, or whether they were friends. And as for the others? I've never heard of them, I'm sorry. They must have been more of my mother's many secrets.'

Gabi wanted more from the journal than it would give her, and she'd grown frustrated with its gaps. When Lucy suggested to Gabi that Alice or FK might have been one of the refugees Lili had helped – and that they'd grown close because of that connection – the idea had deeply upset her.

'You keep talking about her smuggling people through the hotel as if it was a good thing, but I can't see it the same way you do. If Lili had stuck to what she was meant to be doing – running the Edel, being a mother to me – all our lives would have turned out differently. How am I meant to forgive her for that?'

There wasn't an answer which would fix Gabi's pain and confusion, or the anger with herself which always followed her anger at Lili.

'I'm selfish and I'm sorry and I don't mean what I said. I'm proud of her if that's what she did, of course I am. But it's all such a horrible mess.'

Adam and Lucy couldn't mend that feeling either. They'd

both realised, on her hesitant first visit, that Gabi would need time to find a sense of peace and accommodation with Lili, and with the Edel. Except that time was something she didn't have an indefinite amount of. In the end, they decided to focus only on her happier memories when she visited the hotel, and to pore through the diary by themselves.

Alice and André were at the top of the search list. FK was too slippery to attach a strong hook to. Lili had used *she* to describe her, so that at least identified the mysterious contact as a woman. Beyond that, they had nothing, and the entries about her were some of the most oblique Lili had written.

The contact I was told to expect finally turned up today, but she – which was a surprise in itself – wasn't what I imagined. I don't understand how FK fits in or what she wants from me. And why does it matter to her how close I am to the inner circle when she's even better connected than I am?

So now I know. Now my involvement makes sense, but surely what they want is impossible? Even if it could be managed, are they right, would nobody really suspect me?

We want the same end, but we're not fighting the same war. FK cares no more about the Jews than the rest of them. She feels no sense of responsibility for their fate, and neither does her husband. What if I do what they want and nothing changes?

That was all there was to go on, a series of entries which were filled with confusion, but FK still felt more present in Lili's life at its most dangerous point and more tangible than Marius did. Lucy had done some digging into the timeline around him and everything pointed – as Adam had suggested – to his being lost at Stalingrad. The notice that Marius was missing had arrived in January 1943, only weeks after that battle and, according to an entry from the previous July, Marius had definitely been sent to the Eastern Front.

I can't name the place where he's going – it's too awful. I can't think about him trapped there in the winter when everyone's so afraid of defeat.

That entry had been smeared, as if Lili had cried as she wrote it. Lucy could easily imagine that was true. The battle for Stalingrad had been a ferocious thing. Even with the cushion of almost fifty years and the dryness of a textbook account, Lucy's stomach had tightened when she read about the disaster. The German 6th Army encircled in the snow. Attempts at an airlift of supplies defeated when freezing rain coated the cargo planes with ice. Soldiers half-starved and half-frozen and under constant bombardment. Hundreds of thousands killed or captured and marched deep into Russia and even more atrocious conditions. Stalingrad was a monument to inhumanity.

But some of the men survived and nobody knew that for the longest time. Prisoners were still coming home years after Lili died and the war ended, years after everyone had given them up for dead.

That was the one ray of hope in Marius's unfinished life and the news Lucy was planning to greet Gabi with.

She smiled as Adam led his mother over to the new armchairs Lucy had piled with cushions and the table ready-laden with hot tea and Gabi's beloved *Bienenstich* – a custard-filled, honey-glazed cake which Lucy had also grown rather fond of. She put the letter she'd been writing to Emily's parents – in the hope the agency would send it on when they finally replied to her – into her handbag as Gabi settled herself. She would share that with Adam later. What mattered more now was showing Gabi the adverts she'd drawn up to help find the missing pieces of the Rodenberg story.

> *Berlin's Edel Hotel is reopening and we're trying to track down her stories to celebrate at the reopening. If you knew the hotel in the 1930s and 1940s and the names André or Alice Herschel or the initials FK mean anything to you, please get in touch.*
>
> *The relatives of Marius Rodenberg, whose family owned Berlin's prestigious Edel Hotel, are trying to trace anyone who had contact with him after January 1943. If you have any information about him, please get in touch.*

So much felt as if it was coming together. Charlie had agreed to pull the Edel's opening forward so that Gabi could take centre stage at it. Gabi and Adam were still finding their way back to each other, but there was a bond forming between mother and son which had softened them both. Lucy had made renewed contact with the adoption agency, and she wasn't going to be thwarted again by their lack of response.

The Edel's new family was blooming, but it wasn't steady yet, and it wasn't complete. Lucy watched as Adam and Gabi read through the adverts she'd written. She noted how naturally Gabi reached for Adam's hand when the mention of Marius brought her father too vividly back. She didn't say what they were all thinking: that they could send out a hundred messages and nothing might come. Lucy knew all too well how deeply silence could hurt.

But we're trying, and we'll keep trying. And if there's any trace of her left out there, we'll find her. We'll bring the real Lili home.

PART FOUR

CHAPTER 17

JANUARY 1943

They'd been battling two enemies for more weeks than Marius could remember. The Soviet Army which was unstoppable. And the weather, which was worse.

Nothing Marius had learned about war at the training academy in Munich, or in the subdued cities of occupied France, or from Goebbels' tub-thumping speeches was true. War wasn't glorious. It wasn't won because one side had heroes and the other had cowards. The truth was that no side had more right to victory than the other. No man had more right to live than the man he was trying to kill. War was pain and fear and dying men screaming for their mothers. It was the stink of blood and the screech of shells. It was filthy foxholes and relentless rain, thick sucking mud and blizzards which swallowed up the sky and the ground and reduced the world to a scream.

'I envy you, Marius, I really do. You're going to look the enemy directly in the face and destroy him. What an honour that will be.'

Goebbels – whose twisted leg meant that his envy would never be tested on a battlefield – had been grandstanding for Hitler when he'd said that to Marius. Sucking up to the Führer and staring at Lili as if he was readying himself to swoop the second Marius marched off to the East. Marius had wanted to kill Goebbels that day. The thought of leaving Lili alone with the vultures like him who he knew flocked around her when he was at war – who would have her deported without a second thought if they knew the truth about their beautiful hostess – had terrified him more than the prospect of fighting. Her promises to be careful and to stay safe had done little to quell that fear. But at least he no longer wasted time imagining taking a dagger or a pistol to Goebbels. The act of killing no longer needed a name or a face in its sights. Killing was now simply what Marius did, with no purpose except to stop it happening to him.

'It's not so bad here. The people haven't turned on us yet, and at least there's plenty of wide open spaces so we can see the Russki troops coming.'

Marius couldn't remember which of the men he'd led into the nightmare had said that as they climbed off the troop train. Whoever he was, he was presumably dead by now, his body lost to one of the ravines which scarred the landscape and was all anyone could claim for a grave. Marius's unit had been deci-mated and re-formed so many times, he also no longer knew who he was meant to be commanding, although men swarmed to him in some misguided belief that his continuing to live wasn't some random act of fate and might bring the same luck to them. Marius took no notice of that, but the dead man had been right: Russia in October hadn't looked like the worst place to be.

The farmhouses they'd encountered as they moved through the countryside were few and far between, and no German would have chosen to live inside their dilapidated walls. The steppes they crossed were scrubby and brown and endless. But the sun had shone on their arrival, and there'd been thick straw under the groundsheets at the rest stops and meat that hadn't come from a can. Even their first glimpse of Stalingrad hadn't been as fearful as the rumours had said it would be.

The battle to take control of what was left of the city had been raging since the end of the summer. According to the reports Marius had been instructed to read to his men, the place had been largely destroyed by the Luftwaffe, and its broken citizens were on the verge of surrender. There was no immediate sign of the destruction which had led to that point, or not from where they were standing. The sky hung bright with stars, and the distant buildings glowed with the same rich red Marius remembered from paintings of Moscow. He'd stood with his men on a ridge on the night before they entered the fighting, wrapped in the warmth of a quiet evening, seeing beauty where they'd imagined a beast.

It was an illusion, of course. A trick of the senses they'd longed to believe in. The German army was ferocious, but so were the Soviets, and they were fighting back on every street corner, refusing to let a single building fall into enemy hands. The lights Marius and his men had smiled at weren't stars but tracer fire. The red glow was a city in flames, its centre reduced to a furnace. And the quiet which had greeted them was no more real than the light show they'd smiled at. It was – as they soon came to realise – no more than a momentary pause while the *Stalinorgel* reloaded. An intake of breath before the massive rocket launcher released its barrage of weapons and saturated the air with its howl.

Hell was unleashed over them before morning. The roar came, the rockets came and then the weather followed. A fine drizzle for a day or two and then heavier downpours which pounded through the men's clothing and left a dampness which never quite dried, which could too easily freeze as the night temperatures started to plummet. The ground turned to treacle, boots sank and became sponges, exhausted legs struggled to move on. The rain was never-ending; the wind grew teeth.

Sleep was impossible beyond a snatched hour or two. But that was nothing compared to what followed.

The frost arrived in filigree sheets which coated the living and the dead in its lace. Then the cold gathered itself up into a storm and snowflakes with a weight that was closer to iron than feathers started falling. The steppe turned white; the fighting was silenced. Everything slowed as the air and the ground thickened. The horizon disappeared first. Then the straggling rows of men which stood for a front line vanished, and finally the soldier who was only an arm's length away disappeared into the swirl. The snow fell and chaos reigned.

The world lost its limits; the land lost its structure. Armies slid past each other a hair's breadth away, unheard and unseen. A mound of white became a hill or a tank and then shifted again and may as well have been an army of ghosts. A man glimpsed in an instant could be an ally or death.

Marius turned into a purely physical being, his movements blind and reactive. He stumbled, losing his footing and losing his bearings. He waved his gun but had no idea in which direction to point it. He couldn't tell if he'd been fighting for hours or days. He couldn't tell if he was moving forwards or backwards or in circles. He couldn't get a fix on anything, until an explosion which he felt in every cell of his body blew the white veil away. Marius threw himself face first into the snow, burying himself deep into it as a tank roared past him in its dying throes. Black smoke oozed from its body. Ammunition exploded, bursting out of its gun turret in a fanfare. Screams flew from inside its shell whose agonies had lost all connection with any sounds a human should make.

Marius didn't stop to discover whose flag the broken tank wore. If they were his comrades, they were long past his help; if they were the enemy, then retribution was coming. He rolled away from the fire and the noise instead, pushing himself through the snow towards the outline of a building which the explosion's accompanying flash of light had revealed. Ice turned to stone as he flung himself inside. His clothes were sodden; his ears were ringing. His gloves had been ripped off as he scrambled towards safety. But his wedding ring was still there on his finger, and Marius's breath came choking back at the sight.

I'm alive.

The realisation ran through his body like a drug. His hands were numb, but his wedding ring – his lifeline to Lili – was where it should be, and there was a warmth in that beyond price.

I'm alive and I'm coming home to you when this madness is over. Nothing's going to stop me from that.

Marius closed his eyes tight and conjured up Lili until she was as solid as the hut's walls.

She was there with him, in the blue silk dress which turned her skin to porcelain, when the Russian soldiers began shouting outside. She was wrapped inside his embrace, her body moulded to his, when they crashed into the hut and began yelling. And her arms were around him like a barrier when the soldiers dragged Marius to his feet but didn't shoot.

Lili loved him; Lili was there. That knowledge was all Marius needed.

When they dragged him away from the stone floor and threw him into another ruin full of prisoners who were equally as dazed as he was, Marius kept breathing. All through the march deeper into the nightmare that followed, Marius kept breathing and he kept himself alive. Because his Lili was with him, holding his hand through every step.

CHAPTER 18

JULY–SEPTEMBER 1943

Missing is not final. Missing is simply not here, not yet found. It's not a permanent state.

The early morning sun inched its way through the curtains, waking Lili from another restless sleep. She turned to Marius's side of the bed, her eyes still bleary, her arms ready to hold him, only to surface clutching at empty air.

Oh God, when will this stop?

Too many days started the same way. A moment of waking, a moment of forgetting. Then a chasm which opened beneath her the instant reality crashed in. Marius was missing somewhere deep inside Russia, too far away for her empty arms to reach.

The words she'd taught herself to say when that blackness blew in were all that stopped her from falling. *Missing* had become the stumbling block in her life. The charm or the mantra or the prayer which took away its power were all she had to fight back with. *It's not a permanent state.* She repeated them every time the space in the bed or the longing for news of him threatened to overwhelm her. She wore them like armour. When Hitler had expressed his concern for her well-being a few weeks after the message about Marius arrived, she'd offered them to him – only because the more widely she said them, the truer they would be – and had managed a smile when he'd called her the perfect wife for showing such patience. Nobody could have believed in her charm's power to keep Marius safe more than Lili did, but the waiting was still a terrible struggle.

But what if I stop reaching for him? Isn't that worse? Won't that mean I've given him up for dead?

It would be more logical to do that than keep hoping. Hundreds of thousands of German soldiers had been sent to fight at Stalingrad in the winter of 1942, but now it was summer 1943 and only a trickle had so far come back. News of what had happened to the rest was as patchy and hidden as the reasons for Germany's disastrous defeat. Months had passed since that disaster, but nobody knew for certain how many of the 6th Army were dead and how many had been taken prisoner. And nobody dared to discuss those numbers in public or to speculate on the survivors' fate.

The soldiers are taught to think of Russians as sub-humans, as worthless. God help us if the tide turns.

Lili got out of bed and tried to calm herself with the rituals of getting ready for the day, but it was hard to push Marius's fears for what might be facing his men out of her head. The horrors he'd shared with her before he left for Stalingrad came back to her as frequently as her private prayer.

She'd heard Marius's voice in her head whispering, *He's lying*, on a freezing February day when she'd newly lost him but still had to sit ramrod straight in the vast auditorium at the Sportpalast, listening to Goebbels trying to spin disaster into the certainty of future victories. The impact had hit her like a punch, but she hadn't allowed herself as much as a gasp. She'd carried on smiling and clapping and cheering with the rest of the faithful. She'd had no choice. With Marius gone, Lili was the face of the Edel and that demanded even more of a public show from her than it had when she was a new bride.

That show was why she forced herself to get out of bed every morning. It was why she put on the body-skimming silk dresses Marius loved and let her maid style her hair into soft waves, even though all she wanted to do was hide from the world with Gabi. That was an indulgence she couldn't afford, although their brief morning and afternoon hours together remained sacrosanct.

Lili had to be visible. She had to keep smiling whether her heart was in pieces or not. She had to applaud Goebbels' nonsensical speeches demanding huge sacrifices from the German people as if they weren't already making them. She had to agree that happier days would soon be coming when the war was won. She had to do that for her own standing, and for Marius. *If the Edel falls, then he falls too,* was another mantra she held tight to, to fuel her through the days.

Lili let her maid fiddle with one last diamond hair clip and then she went to her study, to check the reservations book and the restaurant's supply needs before Gabi woke up and bounced in. Many of Berlin's smaller hotels had given up the struggle to feed their dwindling customers with their dwindling supplies and had closed up their doors, but not the Edel. She was still standing at the head of the pack, but she was no longer the place – or the sanctuary for Lili – she'd once been.

Her older, gentler guests had retired to their country estates and an illusion of safety as the war's hardships worsened. The Edel was an officers' paradise now and a watering hole for the rich businessmen who'd fattened their wealth on other people's misery. Worse than that, the old codes of civility which had always operated within the hotel's walls were breaking down. Lili had started to avoid the impromptu parties which increasingly packed out the ballroom. That ran on into the early morning and grew louder and darker as the hours progressed.

The gathering two nights ago had led to a fight and a girl screaming in terror. Lili had ordered the hotel's handyman to put a new lock on her suite.

She ran her finger down the list of bookings for that evening, hoping for a quieter night, but so many of the same names cropped up as they had on that awful evening, it was doubtful any peace would arrive.

Which would be manageable if the Edel was still of some use beyond providing a place for brutes to get drunk in.

The sense of hopelessness which pushed in with that thought was almost as dark a shadow across her days as not knowing what had happened to Marius. Lili's public face was as perfect as ever, but nothing behind the facade was holding firm.

Hitler was no longer the regular guest at the Edel he had been a year ago, which meant that his ministers largely stayed away too. Although the hotel was still his preferred port of call in Berlin, the Führer came to the city less and less, apparently preferring the seclusion of his private retreat at Berchtesgaden in Bavaria. He was rarely seen in public outside Goebbels' carefully staged set pieces. Lili had heard the rumours circulating through the kitchens that Hitler was suffering from depression and some kind of palsy and was too shaken by Germany's collapse in Russia to face his own people. Goebbels clamped down ruthlessly on anyone overheard repeating those stories, and Lili didn't mourn the man's absence on a personal level – the freedom from having to shake his hand was a blessing. But it also meant that she had less access to his private conversations and was no longer a conduit for information. Whole weeks had gone by without any chance to go eavesdropping.

Whole weeks had gone by, too, without anybody seeking shelter in the Edel's cellars. Not because the need for a place of safety had disappeared, but because the Nazis had cracked down so ruthlessly on the last remnants of Berlin's Jewish population, their actions had outmanoeuvred the chain. The losses at

Stalingrad had needed a scapegoat and – once Hitler had brooded long enough on those to retaliate – a target hadn't been hard to find. Blame had landed on blameless shoulders once again.

'If the Jewish conspiracy succeeds, Europe will be lost forever.'

'The fight will only end with the extermination of the Jew.'

His hatred thickened with every speech he gave. And that hatred needed feeding.

> *They're planning to purge the factories, on a scale like we've never seen. There are thousands of lives at stake, both the workers and their families who'll be swept up too. Be ready for whatever instructions follow this, and be ready to act quickly.*

That had been the second message to arrive in February which had almost made Lili's heart stop. Because of its wording, and because the way it came to her broke every rule.

The note had arrived as the breakfast service was about to start and the hotel was bustling with staff and guests. The envelope was addressed to Lili, but it wasn't sealed, and it was delivered by a boy who ran into the hotel at full pelt and was cuffed by the doorman for his trouble. If Lili hadn't already been in the foyer, tending to the new flower arrangements and waiting to greet a pair of regular visitors, the doorman might have read it. The thought of what could have happened next, especially if he'd handed the note straight to the hotel's detective, still made Lili's blood run cold.

The message hadn't been disguised as an invoice, and it hadn't been couched in the usual bland vocabulary of *new package* and *upcoming delivery dates*. It had so clearly been written in a panic, it might as well have been stamped with a label marked, *Traitor!* Lili had sprung into action anyway. There were thousands of Jewish workers still employed in

Berlin's armament factories; not offering help to them was unthinkable. She had immediately despatched Gabi to her grandparents in Hamburg for a week, She and André had hauled water and food down to the wine cellar. She'd stopped caring about being caught. She was ready, but they were too late. The clearances had already started by the time the warning was sounded, and the round-up was ruthless.

Lili closed her eyes as the memory of what had happened flooded back, and how powerless she – and every other invisible link in Aaron's hidden community – had been.

The Jewish workers had been snatched in an expertly organised operation which struck every factory in Berlin at the same time. Then – according to Aaron, because Lili had broken the rules too and gone in search of him – they'd been marched to six different holding centres across the city where the security was watertight. The packed trains steamed out of Anhalter and Grunewald stations for a week after that. Nobody could get close. Nobody could help. Nobody made it to the Edel. And nobody in the city seemed to care. Lili had brought Gabi home because she needed somebody to hold on to. She'd arranged a dance to celebrate the start of spring because that was what she was expected to do. And she'd cried as she'd ordered pink and yellow streamers to be hung around the hotel when the days deserved only black ones.

The cellars had been empty since then.

Lili had managed one more clandestine meeting with Aaron, who had become even more elusive since the attacks against the factories in February. She'd offered whatever help she could give, but he'd had no suggestions to offer her. There were rumours that some Jewish workers had manged to escape the round-up, but they were hiding too deep for even his connections to find. His defeated, 'All we can do is wait and hope we'll be needed again,' hadn't comforted either of them.

But it can't keep crippling me either.

Lili pulled herself together and forced herself to focus on the tasks in front of her as her secretary appeared, clutching the inevitable stack of papers which seemed to grow bigger every day.

She might be worn thin but – whatever her views about its current clientele – the Edel was thriving, and it needed her attention. She glanced at the invoices on the top of the pile first. Most of those were marked *paid* for the sake of keeping the ledgers straight, although no money ever changed hands. The regime had continued to protect the hotel's supplies so that everything would be in order if Hitler did decide to visit. The Edel's wine cellars were full. There were still chocolate and sugar-laden desserts to be had and unlimited French champagne. There was bacon and butter from occupied Denmark, salmon and caviar from Norway, and an unlimited supply of looted Polish honey to coat the breakfast pastries. Nobody ate badly at the Edel, except Lili, who could barely eat at all.

'There's this note too, Madam. I was asked to give it to you personally by a very charming young lady who met me on my way in. She said she was from a new wine supplier who has apparently been recommended by Reichsführer Himmler himself, and that this was his letter of introduction.'

Lili took the envelope and retreated into her bedroom. Using a girl to deliver it was clever, and using Himmler's name – and a seal which was grand enough to be convincing if no one looked closely – guaranteed that it would be put straight into her hands. It was a relief that Aaron – because it had to be him who'd sent it – was acting with caution again.

The message was short and to the point, and as cryptically worded as she'd hoped it would be. Lili read it through once before she took the note and the envelope into the bathroom and burned them to ashes over the sink.

There's a new task for you. Trust the contact who comes.

She glanced into the mirror as the water rinsed the evidence away and wasn't surprised to see a new light flare in her eyes. The note promised her a role again; it promised her purpose. It was the first time since Marius had gone missing that she finally felt alive.

Nothing happened quickly this time; it was September before the contact arrived. And, when she did, she blindsided Lili.

'I am Freya von Krailling. It's such a delight to finally meet you. My husband adores your darling hotel – he says you throw the best parties, which is why I'm here.'

Lili had the full complement of the Edel's beauticians and hairdressers at her beck and call; she had an open invitation to Berlin's best dressmakers. Lili knew herself to be an attractive woman who knew how to present herself well, but Freya von Krailling set the bar high. She was glossy – Lili couldn't think of a better word to describe her – every inch of her shone. Her chestnut waves gleamed. Her red patent shoes had never encountered anything as vulgar as a pavement. And her skin – which was perfectly made-up to look completely natural – was luminous. She was also in total command of the palm court tea room by the time Lili arrived there, to the point where Lili considered reminding the spellbound waiters that there were other customers present. The woman was sparkling and revelling in the attention flooding her way. And she was also totally impossible.

'It's his birthday in two weeks and I want to throw him a very special *do*.'

Freya extracted a cigarette from a leather-and-gold case and carried on talking while the waiters flocked to light it. Her behaviour was so deliberately theatrical, Lili had half a mind to ask where the cameras were hiding. Instead, she opened her engagement book and fixed on a smile as Freya's requests grew increasingly preposterous.

'I want a sit-down dinner for fifty, and then a dance after that with an additional one hundred guests. Only champagne to be served, obviously, and every course must be French. I know that's frowned on nowadays, but who on earth wants to eat cabbage and dumplings? Only roses in the flower arrangements and they must all be yellow – my darling Flori does love yellow. In fact, if the serving staff could be wearing that colour too, that would be perfect. And there must be a yellow-iced cake, of course, with five tiers. I assume you'll have our monogram embroidered on the table linen, and...'

On and on she went. Demanding items Lili would have struggled to source in two weeks even without a war, and changes to the decor she would have been reluctant to provide if Goebbels himself had requested them. She carried on smiling and making notes anyway, hoping that – once Frau von Krailling ran out of steam – they might be able to start a more sensible conversation.

'You're very good, aren't you? Aaron said you were, but you've surprised me. Does anything disturb that calm mask?'

Lili stopped writing, her pen blotting an unfinished sentence. She couldn't think where she was. She didn't know whether to respond first to *Aaron* or *mask* – she couldn't work out which was the most dangerous.

'I don't know what—'

Freya's sudden burst of laughter and her 'Aren't you delightful' stopped Lili's barely thought-out response and turned smiling heads. She kept the rest of what she said to a whisper.

'I must have been driving you crazy with all this spoiled nonsense about a yellow-themed party, but you didn't flicker once. I doubt anyone can read your thoughts at all. It's no wonder you're such a good people-smuggler.'

Smuggler was the worst word of all. Lili's instinct was to jump up and leave, to grab Gabi and run before the Gestapo burst into the tea room. Freya shook her head before Lili could move and laid her hand over Lili's as if they were sharing a confidence.

'Don't do anything foolish. This has to look like nothing more than two rich society women taking tea and planning a party. I'm on your side, Lili; I'm the contact Aaron said was coming. But our arrangement only works if nobody looks past our pretty faces.'

She waved at one of the hovering waiters and ordered two glasses of champagne, 'to celebrate the start of a charming new friendship'. Lili had smiled and clinked glasses, but she didn't appreciate how Freya had toyed with her, and she wasn't about to drink up and roll over.

'You could have told me who you were from the start. Now that you have, I'd prefer it if you'd stop dropping hints and tell me what exactly you know.'

Freya's smile remained bright for the benefit of the room, but she kept her voice low as she answered. 'That you've been an invaluable link in moving a number of people out of the city. That you've been moving information too. That you're inventive – and brave.'

Lili waited, but nothing else came.

She doesn't know I'm Jewish. Aaron must have held that bit back.

Lili sensed a warning in that omission, a hint to carry on keeping that part of herself hidden no matter what the task turned out to be. And even if that wasn't what he'd intended, Lili planned to keep her secret close anyway. There were more ears listening than hers nowadays; denunciations had become the city's lifeblood. Even the closest friend could be turned into an enemy, no matter how loyal they'd promised to be. And Freya was a completely unknown quantity.

'We'll all win if this plan works, Lili.'

Freya must have noticed her hesitation; she'd switched gears to a more confiding tone.

'You must have your reasons for doing what you've done with the refugees, but they don't interest me. All I'm concerned with is how close you are to the inner circle. And how much closer in you can get.'

Lili kept up her mantras about Marius to give herself strength, but – beyond crossing her fingers and trusting to luck when bombs threatened, or when she'd been afraid that the next escapee through the door could be the one who got them all caught – she wasn't generally a woman prone to fits of super-stition. She'd learned to rely on her wits rather than bad feelings and ill omens. But the slight pause Freya had left before *And how much closer in you can get* had raised prickles round her neck. *Task* suddenly felt like far too small a word for whatever this woman had brought with her.

'What is it you want, Frau von Krailling? Why has Aaron sent you to me? And what did you mean by *this plan?*'

But Freya shook her head. She gathered up her things and despatched a waiter for her car.

'Not today. There are steps to this. We have to be seen enjoying each other's company; we have to be talked about – because we will be talked about – as good friends, as socialites with our heads full of dresses and fun. As women above suspi-cion. And there are other people you need to meet, who will want to test out your resolve for themselves. There'll be plenty of time after that to tell you the rest.'

She stood up and leaned over to kiss Lili's cheek, pressing her lipsticked mouth close to Lili's ear as she said a more public goodbye.

'What you need to do in the meantime is to keep smiling, and to keep listening at whatever doors and walls that you can. And encourage your special guest to come back.'

CHAPTER 19

JANUARY 1944

If they turn around and arrest me, they know and it's over. If they don't, we'll survive.

Lili stood in the Edel's doorway, taking a moment to prepare herself before anyone noticed she was there.

'You need to come back to the hotel at once, Madam. The Gestapo are here, and they're making arrests.'

Lili had slipped away from the Edel to the flower market for some much-needed quiet. She had moved on from there to the Spittelmarkt shop she still owned but no longer visited often enough and was making bouquets with her manageress – enjoying the peaceful absorption that task demanded – when her secretary's panicked phone call burst through the work-room. She didn't waste time asking questions. A police raid and arrests was a too-familiar scenario.

The scene playing out in front of her was, however, a very different one from the day when Klemens had been taken and Lili's attempt to cajole Himmler had rebounded so badly on Marius. The foyer had been crowded with shocked staff members then, and there had been a sense that something could be done to right what was so clearly a wrong. André hadn't been alone in believing that, with Lili's help, justice would prevail. Four years on and the shock was still there, but few people believed in the certainty of justice anymore or stood around watching when the Gestapo appeared unless they'd been ordered to. It was too easy to get unwittingly sucked in. And unlike the first time, the mood today wasn't only shocked and fearful; it was ugly.

Three dark-coated Gestapo officers were barking at the staff members lined up in front of them, while half a dozen soldiers fanned out across the foyer with their guns at the ready. One wrong move and a bloodbath could follow. Whatever was coming for her, Lili would not allow that. She steadied her shoulders and stepped forward, nodding to the doorman to announce her as soon as there was a suitable pause. Praying that the secret which sat like a fire in her stomach hadn't spilled out and burned them.

'A bomb? You want to use the Edel to plant a *bomb*?'

Lili stared around the satin- and velvet-swathed room, wondering if one of the equally elegant men and women gathered in it had slipped a narcotic into her drink. Or whether she had been invited to the von Kraillings' sprawling country estate in Spreewald as some kind of loyalty test and Himmler was waiting behind the curtains to pounce on her answer.

Nothing in the two very public lunches she'd sat through at the Edel with Freya, or at the far too long and over-elaborate dinner she'd attended at the von Kraillings' Berlin home had pointed to a bomb plot as the crux of Aaron's plan. If it even was Aaron's plan, which Lili was beginning to doubt. Jumping from moving people to organising a murder – as she'd once explained to Alice – was a very big leap. And why had there been no hint of the scale of what was intended before? Lili had sat through a number of social engagements with Freya, but she'd refused to discuss anything of meaning at them at all. And now Lili was supposed to believe that the von Kraillings had cultivated her company because they wanted her to help with a plot to assassinate the Führer? She put her drink down, partly in case the champagne really was the source of the problem and partly because her hand wouldn't stop shaking.

'That's exactly what we want. We need to get rid of Hitler and his henchmen. We need your help or, to be more precise, we need your hotel to do it in.'

Florian Graf von Krailling had been an exemplary host all through lunch. Until the final course – a honey-soaked *Bienenstich* which Lili had always found too sweet for her taste but was Gabi's absolute favourite – had been cleared away and the servants dismissed and he'd finally unveiled the task Aaron had hinted at in his note.

Lili had been speechless at first, not least because Florian was hardly her first choice for the leader of a coup. He was a Brigadeführer in the SS; the von Kraillings were one of Germany's oldest and most respectable families. The circles he and Freya moved in were drawn entirely from the same stock. The men easing their waistcoat buttons were the wealthy sons of Prussian nobility and high-ranking officers in the army and the Luftwaffe; the wives who'd barely eaten a bite were the daughters of bankers and government ministers and ruled Berlin society. They were the Nazi Party's noble elite and they wanted to murder Hitler? It made no sense, and Lili said so.

'But why would you think that, Frau Rodenberg? Because we've sworn oaths of allegiance to him?'

Lili tried to say, 'Yes, I thought that might be a brake on you.' Florian barely stopped to listen.

'An oath has no value if it's been made to a man without honour. Hitler is Germany's biggest enemy – surely you can see that? He's a far bigger threat to our future than the Soviets or the Allies. He's the one, after all, who's sending our men to fight in a war that's already lost. He's the one whose brutality has brought shame down on German heads all across the civilised world. Do you honestly expect men like us – whose families have always stood for duty to country before anything else – to be loyal to a man like him?'

She couldn't argue with von Krailling's logic; she wouldn't weep for a second if his assassination plan worked. But the place he had chosen to carry it out in? Lili shook her head.

'But why would you choose to mount an attack like this at the Edel? I understand why you want rid of him, and I've no argument with that if you think you can succeed, but why do it in a busy hotel where innocent people could get hurt too? Why not attack him in the open, like the partisans did with Heydrich, and minimise the risk?'

As soon as she said it, Hitler's fury at his deputy's stupidity in Prague came rushing back, and Lili answered the question herself. 'Because you can't. Because he's far too well shielded. And the Edel is where he lets his guard down.'

She didn't have time to add, *Or it is if he comes.* Freya jumped in first.

'Precisely. That's why the Edel was in our sights in the first place. Imagine our delight when we discovered that you, not just your hotel, could be a very good match for our little group. No one goes unwatched, Lili, no matter how careful they think they're being. My maid saw you meeting with Aaron in a pub she frequents but was a very odd place for Lili Rodenberg to be visiting. And she told me she saw you there because that's what I pay her to do.' Freya tapped a cigarette out of her case and waited for her husband to light it. 'Dear Aaron was pretty resistant at first to telling Flori anything, but he wanted to keep his little rescue operation running – and he wanted to stay out of a camp – so he gave you up and did what we asked of him in the end.'

Freya's sneer at *rescue operation* told Lili instantly why

Aaron had made himself hold back at least some information about her life. She was still trying to switch her understanding of Freya's relationship with him from ally to blackmailer when Florian picked up the thread.

'I hope you're not going to play the shocked innocent. You've been moving Jewish escapees; you've been listening in on private conversations and passing on what you heard. By any benchmark that makes you a traitor. What difference will another step further over the line make?'

She couldn't let that stand as permission. Not with Gabi's safety at stake. But when she said as much, Florian dismissed her protests once again.

'You're not the only one with children, my dear. I have two sons, heirs to a quite considerable fortune and a very important name. Do you think I'd put their lives at risk? Do you think anybody else at this table wants to see their family line end?' He gave her a moment to study the stern faces staring at her, and then adopted a more conciliatory smile. 'But we'll keep your daughter as safe as we'll keep you – don't worry about that. There'll be passports ready for you both, and a route out of the country, if that's what's required. But it won't be, I promise you. We're going to succeed. Once that first blow's been struck, the army will follow us. Our new regime will be in place before the literal dust settles.'

He leaned forward and dropped his voice. There was just enough menace in it to stop Lili offering any more arguments.

'The plans are made – every detail of what comes after their deaths is in play. But the Edel is essential to our success – you do see that, don't you? The Edel is where he brings the rest of them – Göring, Himmler and Goebbels. There's no point in doing this if we don't clear out all the poison. We have to bring them all down at once, root and branch. And, with your help, that's exactly what we're going to do.'

· · ·

Nobody asked if I'd do it. They simply assumed that I would. Or they didn't care if I objected.

Lili waited for the Gestapo officers to finish frightening her duty manager and acknowledge that she was there. Two weeks had gone by since her introduction to the conspiracy – there was no other way Lili could frame her invitation to the Krailling estate. No timescales had been set; no plans had been made. Or none that they'd shared yet with Lili.

'It needs to happen soon. And now that you know...'

That had been Florian's parting shot. Lili had no doubt that he would force her to give them access to the Edel if he had to. A man who could contemplate murder would have no problem with blackmail – he'd already proved that with Aaron – and he had no shortage of information he could use to destroy her. And if she tried to save herself and Gabi and counter an officer of Florian's impeccable standing with talk of a bomb plot? There was nothing at the end of that road but a prison cell.

She looked around the foyer. There were scuff marks on the tiles. Two ceramic vases had been knocked over and smashed. Her duty manager was shaking. This wasn't a police visit; it was an invasion.

'Could somebody please tell me exactly what is going on?'

Lili was tired of waiting to be spoken to. She was sick of the cruelty and the inhumanity which had taken hold of her country and of deferring to men who thought they were gods. She had no idea which of her staff members had been taken, but she was as certain that they were innocent as she was that the Edel would outlast them all.

I'll be careful, I promise. I won't do anything to put myself in harm's way.

Lili had lied to Marius because she loved him. She had sent him to war knowing nothing about the smuggling or the spying activities she was involved in so that he would focus on his own safety, not hers. But what had he said to her when he'd told her how brutally his men had been ordered to treat the Russians? *I'm starting to hate being German.* Wasn't that how von Krailling and his fellow officers felt? Weren't the families whose members had come together in the privacy of the Spreewald estate, with their devotion to duty and honour, drawn from the same pool as the Rodenbergs?

So wouldn't Marius be part of this plot too, if he could be? If he was the one still in charge here?

The Gestapo officers finally turned as she spoke. Lili put on her public face and insisted on shaking their hands until their manner towards her at least touched on respectful. She didn't remind them that the hotel was one of Hitler's favourites and how furious he would be that its reputation was threatened. This wasn't the time to start flexing – or risking – her status. Instead, she listened while they ran through a list of charges against her hotel manager and head waiter which she knew didn't carry an ounce of truth. She listened while they told her that the investigations could run wider, that everyone in the hotel could come under suspicion and the hotel detective smiled at their threats. Lili carried on nodding and looking concerned until they left. But there was only one thing in her head while she held on to her mask: *I'm starting to hate being German too.*

'I demand to see Brigadeführer Graf von Krailling immediately. My hotel has been thoroughly insulted, and I simply won't stand for it.'

If there was one thing Lili had learned from Freya, it was that if she wanted the world to dance to her tune, she had to act as if she owned it. She'd never seen a secretary move as fast.

'This comes under the Security Minister's jurisdiction, not the army's. You should have gone to Himmler with it, not me. Which everyone who heard you shouting the odds out

there knows. Why are you drawing attention to our relationship?'

Lili took no notice of Florian's terse greeting. She was
exactly where she intended to be, whatever the lines of
command dictated otherwise. But she lowered her voice once
the door was closed.

'Precisely because of it. Presumably everyone out there
knows we are friends – that is what you've been spending weeks
proving to the world after all – and what do friends do except
help each other out in a crisis? Besides, the last time I went to
the Reichsführer with a problem like this, he took my husband
away. He has a vindictive streak and a nasty habit of treating
people like puppets who only exist for his entertainment. But
you know that, don't you? I assume you've studied all their
habits very carefully.'

Florian's office in the palatial Bendlerblock, which served as
the headquarters for both the army and the navy, was light and
airy and panelled from floor to ceiling with the same gold-tinged
wood as his desk. He looked perfectly at home in it. Lili could
easily imagine him presiding over a cabinet meeting and issuing
proclamations on behalf of a new German state. He was still,
however, a long way from securing that position, and the pitfalls
ahead were deep. Which was why Lili was in his office trying to
pretend she was in control of the situation and not terrified.

'Who else am I supposed to bring this to if not you? Two of
my staff members have been arrested on charges of smuggling
Jewish refugees through the hotel after the February factory
clearances. That's not true, but it's awfully close to home. That
smuggling's even been mentioned could suggest somebody
other than your wife has had eyes on me. And if the Gestapo
believe – or choose to believe – that's what's been going on, or if
someone has genuinely tipped them off, then what else do they
know?' She drew a deep breath, but it didn't stop her pulse from
ricocheting. 'I don't want to end up dangling from a rope, and I

don't think you do either. So you need to stop worrying about whose jurisdiction this comes under and behave like the friend you've been pretending to be. You need to find out how serious the charges are, for all our sakes.'

Florian's switch from irritation to problem-solving was so quick, Lili began to understand why he was the one co-ordinating the plot. He sent her to the seating area in the furthest corner of his office and went immediately to work. It took well over an hour of phone calls, which Florian turned his back to make so that his voice was muffled. Lili listened hard, but she couldn't make out the names of his contacts or the details of whatever favours he was calling in. Her lips were bitten raw by the time he turned round again.

'The charges don't hold up. Both men have watertight alibis for the dates the Gestapo were given for the alleged smuggling operation, and no amount of beatings will change that.'

He shrugged at Lili's 'Why were they arrested at all?'

'A false denunciation by the look of things, made by a disgruntled porter who was sacked a few months ago. Berlin is swimming in this kind of malice. God help him when he's brought in, which he will be – they've no patience at Prinz-Albrecht-Straβe with time-wasters, and I doubt there'll be much left of him when they're done. But your employees are safe, if a little bruised. And, more importantly, there's no further investigation coming.'

He nodded at Lili's heartfelt 'Thank God.'

'Obviously we need to stay on our toes, but I don't think we should over worry. It's not uncommon apparently for hotels to be targeted like this – as you know better than anyone, they're ideally placed to hide people, so malicious gossip often sticks. But it would help me going forward to know if there's anyone on the staff you've been working with. Who could be a weak link or an asset.'

He sighed when Lili stayed silent.

'Just give me the name – it'll save us both time. I'll make it my business to find out who it is if you don't.'

The man was ruthless – Lili was under no illusions about that. She was grateful in many ways that he was – turning the bomb plot from a plan into reality and keeping them all alive would require nerves of steel.

'André, the head wine waiter, has been helping me move refugees for the last year. Nobody else is involved. And he wouldn't betray me; he's loyal to the bone.'

She could feel Florian's question waiting.

'He'll help with this, if I ask him to, although I'd rather he wasn't involved. And you'd have to guarantee his safety the same as mine if things go wrong.'

If things go wrong sounded even more damning when she said it out loud than it had done swirling round in her head. There would be no safety for any of them if the plot failed. All it took was for one of the conspirators to panic and backtrack or one of the targets to survive and she and the others would be running for their lives. She didn't share that concern with Florian. She doubted he'd be interested; she was certain he wouldn't reconsider.

'You're going to do it then? You're going to give us the Edel?'

He was watching her carefully, as if he was looking for cracks. He shrugged again when Lili asked him if she had any real choice. It was the curtness of that dismissal which finally made up her mind.

'Yes. But I'll do it on my timeline. I'll get my daughter clear first. I'll find a date when I can invite Hitler to the Edel without looking pushy or raising suspicions. I know the anniversaries that matter to him and how he likes to celebrate them better than you. And I'll be the one who places the device in the suite.'

Lili wasn't surprised when Florian's jaw dropped and he immediately said no, not that she cared. It wasn't a negotiation. The Edel was hers. What happened inside the hotel's walls, what affected the family who kept the hotel running, was Lili's responsibility. Florian wouldn't understand that; she wasn't going to make him try. He also wouldn't understand – because he didn't and couldn't know what lay at the heart of her – that Lili had lived with hatred for so long, the risks she faced kept shrinking. And that she wanted an end to the horror story Hitler had plunged her people into even more than Florian wanted to create another new Germany.

I'll tell him who I really am when the time is right. When he owes me a debt. When I can do some good and make sure that, whatever this Germany he's going to build turns out to be, there'll be a place in it for its Jews.

Lili sat without speaking as Florian continued to pour scorn on her decision. She let him bluster and, when he finally stopped, she repeated her terms. And then she pointed out what surely should have been blindingly obvious to such a clever man: that she was the only one of them who would be able to enter the room without either Hitler or his entourage wondering why. For all his planning and plotting, Florian had no answer for that.

CHAPTER 20

JANUARY 1944

I've survived this before; I can survive it again.

It was a challenge to believe that as the world outside the hut blurred to white and the snow thickened on the windowsills and every step that was coming would take him further from home, but Marius was no stranger now to hard challenges.

'Pack up your things. We're moving out.'

Pack up had been a nonsense. Nobody had *things*. Neither he nor his fellow prisoners had much left to their names beyond a bowl and a spoon and the motley collection of rags and looted clothing they wrapped themselves in. The only difference between this march and the first one was that at least this time he understood the instructions. A year ago, the orders delivered in a guttural Russian had meant nothing to Marius, except the possibility that his ignorance of the language could very easily lead to his death.

The march out of Stalingrad after he'd been captured in January 1943 had seemed endless then. He'd been herded out of the ruins where he was found and thrown into the midst of a straggling column of prisoners who barely registered his presence or changed step. Marius had copied the rest. Moving without speaking, keeping his eyes fixed to his feet, trying not to draw the attention of the Russian soldiers who marched on each side of them and used their sub-machine guns to prod any man foolish enough to break ranks and stumble. The silence was new; it was a relief. The ground had stopped dancing beneath him that day the way it had done when the tanks came thundering. He was no longer expected to run, to zigzag his way through a hail of bullets. All he had to do was walk, and that felt like a blessing, even though the earth was frozen solid and sent ice in numbing waves up his legs.

Marius hadn't known where he was going that day, and he hadn't cared. He'd been oddly euphoric simply to have survived the battle. He'd marched in a haze, imagining himself set on a road that would eventually end with Lili.

Who wouldn't know me now. Who would surely pass me by in the street.

Marius hadn't seen his reflection in over a year, but he could feel the ridges in his face where hunger had stripped the smoothness away. He could feel the tangles which matted his hair and his beard.

She might not know the look of me, but please God the heart she loved is still intact.

That hadn't always been a certainty: Marius had doubted for a long time whether his lost heart or his soul would come back. The march out of Stalingrad had stripped more than his flesh away; his state of euphoria hadn't made it until sundown. The first shot which felled a struggling prisoner had come as a shock. The noise had cracked through the snow-silenced air and snapped even the weakest heads up. By the time the fifth man fell with a bullet in his neck, Marius no longer flinched. Moving forward without breaking step and without lagging behind became his one driving force. Until hunger arrived, and then the only thing driving him on was the pain twisting his howling stomach.

The Russians didn't starve their prisoners, or at least not deliberately. They were given bread, but it was frozen solid and – without any means to cut it because none of them had been allowed knives – the lumps took hours to thaw before they disintegrated. They were given salted herring, but the salt burned the men's lips and their throats. Sometimes – at the rest stops which were no more than holes dug out of the snow – they were given hot food. Meat and potatoes cooked into a stew. Marius's stomach had turned somersaults the first time he smelled that; his mouth had flooded. But the potatoes were black and the meat was a shred, and the disappointment only made the cravings harder.

The Russians had treated them like animals, which was degrading and frightening, but – given how the Germans had treated the Russian prisoners they took and the villages they occupied – Marius had expected far worse. The men were confined to pens ringed with barbed wire when the march halted for a few hours at night; they were thrown slops which he fought for as hard as the rest. At some point, on some day and at some time which he no longer recognised, Marius had felt his hold on what it was to be human slipping away. He didn't have the reserves of energy or thought to mourn over the loss.

Days whirled past him. He had no way of keeping track of them and no interest in trying. He ate what he could grab. He snatched sleep for the few hours that the cold would let him and tried not to imagine sleep sliding into death. He moved when the barked orders clearly meant move. The march became his whole world; he stopped expecting an end point.

The only thing that keeps me living is you.

Marius touched his wedding ring to his lips before it disappeared back under the gloves which he'd snatched from a dead man and never let out of his sight.

'Watches. Rings. Hand them over.'

Marius hadn't needed that order translating: the soldiers had grabbed fingers and wrists to make its meaning clear. But – unlike the constant shout to *move* – it wasn't an order he was prepared to obey. He'd stepped outside his hunger and his exhaustion as the soldiers began separating the prisoners from their belongings. When the Russians reached him, Marius had refused to remove his ring. His *nyet* – the one word he'd learned because it was the answer to every request – had made the soldiers laugh. Then he'd rolled his hands into fists and the laughter had stopped.

Nyet.

He'd kept saying it, even after he lost the first tooth. The ring was Lili; without Lili he was lost. It was a very simple equation. Marius would have taken the bullet he was threatened with before that happened. It was lucky for him that his captors – or the one in charge, whose mournful eyes grew darker with each sip of vodka – possessed a romantic soul.

'Hey, lover boy, get moving. You don't want to miss all the fun.'

That was his nickname now. *Lover boy*. The man who would rather die than surrender his wedding ring and had somehow become a hero from Tolstoy. The Russian officer's amusement had kept Marius alive long enough to reach a camp where there were huts with walls that were made from wood not from ice and floors made from concrete not snow. Where the food was still terrible and never enough, but it wasn't frozen and it appeared three times a day.

Heads came up when that reality set in. Names were exchanged; conversations became less transactional. One morning the snow stopped falling and the sun shone through the dirty windows. White vanished, and blue and green and pink returned to the world. *One day the war will end and we will go home to our loved ones* took root and spread.

And now the camp which had housed them for months was

emptying out into hastily assembled columns and they were marching again. Back into the nothingness of a Russian winter. Off to another work placement or so Marius assumed and, please God again, to the warmer confines of a factory and not the wood cutting which had been this camp's reason for existence and had sapped the prisoners' precious strength.

But not into the unknown. Not into the abyss I walked too closely beside a year ago.

Marius was alive, after endless months as a prisoner whose deprivations had broken and killed more men than he could count. He was alive and, despite the odds stacked against him, he was still wearing his wedding ring.

That wasn't a guarantee his luck would hold, but that didn't matter to Marius: he'd given up on guarantees a long time ago. It was a flicker of hope, and a flicker was all that he needed. Marius picked up his bundle and marched.

'I don't want to go away without you! I don't want to go to Potsdam; I don't even know where that is. Why can't I stay here with you?'

Lili opened the French doors and stepped out onto the balcony, shivering as the evening breeze plucked at her thin dress. The changeable spring temperatures had plummeted again, and the air carried a chill that was unseasonably frosty.

Where are you, my love? Why won't you come home to me?

She stared out over a city whose streets had darkened quicker than the sky as people fastened their blackout curtains in place and turned down their lamps. As hard as she tried, she couldn't sense Marius; she barely knew which way to turn to call him back to her. He was a long way from her reach. And so now was Gabi.

Lili held on to the balustrade and closed her eyes as the tears and tantrums which had turned Gabi's departure into a battlefield threatened to buckle her.

Gabi's fury – and her very out-of-character fear – at the prospect of being separated from her mother had shaken them both with its intensity. Gabi had always been an easy-going, happy-natured child, with a sense of adventure which had made sleepovers with her friends and trips to her grandparents in Hamburg a treat. Not this morning. This morning Gabi had clung to Lili and cried as if she could sense that this parting carried too much weight with it.

Lili had tried to reason with her. Mindful of the terrible disaster which had overtaken Marius's parents in Hamburg's firestorms the previous summer, she'd asked if Gabi was afraid that there might be bombing raids over the city which would put Lili in danger while she was gone. Gabi had dismissed that with a curt, 'You said our shelter was the best in Berlin, so why would I be worried?' and carried on sobbing. Her fear was nameless but real; her tears were inconsolable. She had worn the two of them out.

Which was my fault. I should have told her about the trip sooner. I should have given her more time to get used to the idea.

The wind began throwing needles of rain at her. Berlin's switch from busy city to the black carpet spread out below her grew increasingly unsettling.

Lili abandoned the balcony and retreated into the guest suite, although she felt no more comfortable in there. It was too late now to worry about what she should have done. It was too late to second-guess any of the decisions which had led to this point. Lili hadn't told Gabi sooner because she'd been hoping against hope that she wouldn't have to send her daughter away. She'd been waiting for the note which said, *The plan is abandoned*. She'd been waiting for that note for weeks. Instead, a bunch of white roses had arrived for her two days earlier with a message hidden inside the stems that she'd immediately burned.

A small thank-you gift to celebrate the twentieth.

It was the signal to proceed Lili had known was coming, not the exit she'd wasted weeks wishing for. And it had barely left her any time to tell Gabi that she was going away, never mind explain who she was being sent to.

'The Stiefels are kind people. You'll like them a lot.'

How many times had Lili repeated that line this morning? How many shrill *But who are they?* and *Why haven't you ever mentioned them before?* questions had she had to fudge her way through? Her answering, 'They're old friends of your father's and they miss him and want to get to know you,' had cut no ice with Gabi.

Lili went across to the sideboard which was set ready for the following day's lunch party with the drinks Hitler would avoid and Göring would head for. She poured herself a measure of brandy that was probably too big and sat down on the edge of a chair. For all the false excitement she'd offered to Gabi, she hardly knew the Stiefels at all. It was Marius who had told her they were kind. They were his godparents and the closest thing he'd had to an extended family growing up.

'We've lost touch since the war began, but – if you're ever in real need of something that my parents aren't well enough to provide you with – go to them first. They'll help you without question.'

Marius had given her the Stiefels' address and watched her lock it away in her jewellery box before he left for the East. She'd kept it then to humour him, never thinking she would use it. But she was certainly in real need now. And the Stiefels weren't in Berlin, and they weren't in her circle, which almost counted more than kind.

It will be very hard to trace Gabi back to them if this fails and I'm taken.

Lili got up again, unable to settle. She hated that she'd had to make plans for failure, but refusing to accept that failure might happen put Gabi at too much risk. And she'd cried when the Stiefels' first response to her out-of-the-blue call – which was filled more with gaps than explanations – was a simple and immediate, 'Whatever you need, we're here.' She'd known from that moment Gabi couldn't be in safer hands. Unfortunately, she hadn't been able to construct a story about the Stiefels which would satisfy her angry daughter, because she couldn't tell her even a shred of the truth. Her 'Mummy has a very busy week and won't have a moment for you' had sounded as hollow to her as it had to her child.

Lili sipped her drink and began another inventory of the room in an attempt to distract herself from Gabi's distress, although it wasn't needed: she and André had been over every inch of the preparations countless times and everything was perfect. The table was set with the Führer's monogrammed linen and the embossed silver cutlery which was the exact weight he liked. Each place setting had a silk sprig of edelweiss tucked into the napkin ring, a special touch which always made him smile. There was even a small birthday gift wrapped in gold tissue paper waiting by his plate. Everything was in place except for the guests. And the centrepiece, which was a task for tomorrow. There was nothing else to do until then. Lili could retire to her private rooms. Or, better still, she could go down to the public rooms and be visible.

The most important thing in the run-up is to act normally. Don't break your patterns. Don't alter how you dress or behave. Treat the twentieth, and the days leading up to it, like any other day.

That was easy advice for Florian to hand out. Once he'd co-ordinated tomorrow's delivery, his role in the Edel's side of the operation would be done. He wouldn't be at the hotel. He wouldn't be required to smooth out staff problems on the day, or to smile at champagne-fuelled guests tonight while his heart raced and his mind couldn't get past the death-knell of *tomorrow*... He didn't have to be on show.

Lili shook herself before she spiralled, and swallowed the rest of her drink in one gulp. This backwards and forwards and grinding over details wouldn't do. This was no time to lose her nerve. She was the owner of the Edel. She couldn't hide away, whatever was coming tomorrow. She gritted her teeth and put the dirty glass into the dumb waiter ready to despatch it down to the kitchens so the room would stay perfect. She would go downstairs and do her job – that would at least fill up the hours. Then she caught sight of her hand in the serving hatch's light and she froze.

Don't alter how you dress.

It was no wonder she couldn't sense Marius: her wedding ring was gone. She'd given it to Gabi when she was trying to calm the child down. Lili – in a fit of inspiration which now felt badly timed – had slipped it off her finger and onto a chain, dropped that round Gabi's neck and told her to take good care of it and bring it safely home. When she'd called it 'Mummy's magic charm', Gabi had finally stopped crying. She'd consented to go to the car where André was waiting to drive her to Potsdam. Lili had been so relieved in that moment, she hadn't considered how empty she would feel without the ring which tied her to Marius. Or how naked her finger would look. One of the predatory men who constantly flocked around her would surely notice its absence. And misread that as the invitation they all angled for.

I can't go down there. I can't risk that kind of attention, not tonight.

But there was a silver wedding party in the palm court, and a birthday dinner in the dining room, both of which involved very demanding guests. And Chef would need coaxing to replace the too fussy dessert he'd been planning to serve with the chocolate cake the birthday girl actually wanted.

The curtains rustled as Lili stood in the centre of the room paralysed by indecision. The breeze blew a chill over her neck and her arms.

Gloves.

Her whirling brain snapped itself together again. A different, longer dress – something more elaborate than her afternoon gown, the one with the silver embroidery on the skirt to honour the happy couple – and a pair of elbow-length gloves and her problem was solved. No hiding. No suspicions raised. Business as usual. Lili Rodenberg in command of her hotel, wearing her most glamourous outfit in spite of the war and celebrating with her guests. What could be more normal than that?

Afterwards.

Lili had been holding tight to that word since she'd woken not long after dawn. Every danger the day brought with it had to be balanced against the freedoms that would come afterwards. If she could manage that, she would survive it. And Florian was wrong: there were some patterns that had to be broken.

She turned to Marius's pillow and refused to let her heart sink. Instead of weeping over an empty space, she conjured up his face, turning to meet hers and smiling. Older and wearier perhaps, bearing the marks of the imprisonment she'd convinced herself he was confined to. But alive. Well. Hers.

With the day's opening moments rewritten, she got out of bed and drew the curtains onto a chiffon-blue morning. She would do exactly the same thing tomorrow, but everything else would be changed. Tomorrow she would open the curtains onto a world where Hitler and his acolytes were dead. Where his party was broken and there was a new sense of hope.

A world where afterwards will be real.

Now the plan's completion had finally come, she was determined to strip away its black edges. Lili had spent weeks stuck on *What if it fails?* Now that there was no turning back, she clung to a different thought – *What if it succeeds?* That outcome was surely as likely.

Lili moved round the room slowly, taking her time to select the perfect outfit and jewellery to wear at the lunch. A simple straight-skirted dress in loden green, a colour that nodded to both the Führer's beloved Bavaria and his Austrian birthplace. An enamelled edelweiss brooch, the flower set with pearls and amber. No other adornment except plain gold studs in her ears. Nothing that demanded attention, nothing ornate. Her hair in a neat bun at the nape of her neck.

A picture-perfect German wife.

Lili secured a fine net over her coiled hair with a pin and squeezed a tiny drop of mascara onto a lash brush. She normally checked her appearance with her eagle-eyed maid rather than in the mirror, but she'd given Josi the day off. She'd given as many of the Edel's staff the day off as she possibly could and told the ones still on duty that the third floor – which would be empty of guests by mid-morning check-out – was out of bounds until the evening. No one had raised an eyebrow at that. Closing the third floor to anybody but essential staff had been common practice when Hitler came regularly for lunch. His presence in the hotel had rarely been announced or confirmed then, unless he chose to make it into a public appearance. It wouldn't be announced today.

'I understand that he's terribly busy and the burdens of war must be taking a toll. But he will be in Berlin for his birthday on the twentieth, won't he? It's so rare he has time to visit the city nowadays; we would love to celebrate his special day too.'

Lili hadn't worn a plain dress in March when she'd called on Goebbels in his sumptuous office in the Ordenspalais. She'd wrapped herself in velvet and furs then and hung diamond drops from her ears. She'd applied the deep-red lipstick all his actress favourites wore and outlined her eyes with dark kohl.

Lili knew the Propaganda Minister's tastes, and she knew how to pander to them. Which was why Goebbels had been her first choice for securing the Führer.

'And forgive me if you hear anything in this other than the compliment that's intended, but your preparations for the day are so marvellous, and so thorough, I did wonder if he might value an hour or two of quiet to better appreciate them.'

Goebbels' preparations for Hitler's fifty-fifth birthday celebrations had certainly been something to marvel at, but not in a way that was likely to endear him to Berlin's ordinary citizens. His plans were overdone and too busy and out of step with a population exhausted by the war's increasingly frightening direction. Florian had slipped her an outline of the day's events when she'd first mentioned the idea of April the twentieth as a target date for the bomb. Lili had read them feeling like she was holding the last piece of the puzzle.

Goebbels had decided to use the Führer's birthday as a way to boost Hitler's sagging image as a 'gift' to the German people. There were troops to inspect and a parade planned on the Unter den Linden which Hitler would lead from his car. Goebbels had arranged for banners bearing the slogan *Our walls broke but our hearts didn't* to be displayed across all the bombed buildings in the city. Lili couldn't decide if that was a master stroke or madness, but she'd praised it to his face anyway. And she'd praised the speech he was going to give at the State Opera House before his beloved leader was treated to a two-hour performance of Beethoven. For a man who was supposedly in poor health and no longer comfortable in close contact with his people, it was going to be a very long day, which suited Lili's if not the Führer's needs perfectly. Their frantic scope had offered her a way in, and *an hour or two of quiet* had been enough to sow the seed of doubt in Goebbels that drove him into her hands.

'Given that, I wondered if a small lunch gathering might be

acceptable? The four of you perhaps? He always seemed to enjoy those so much, which was no doubt due to how carefully you guarded the time he spent with us.'

Lili had smiled her prettiest smile when she said that, before she tipped Goebbels' easily flattered ego over the edge.

'He always ushered you into the room first – do you remember? That must have felt very special.'

She'd had him as neatly as a butterfly on a pin. He'd said yes to her suggestion straight away, then wrapped her triumph up in a ribbon.

'Very well, but it will need to be a completely private visit. Unannounced. As few staff present as possible. There's some truth to the rumours about his ill-health and – although his mind is as brilliant as ever – the illnesses that plague him have created a frail appearance which does his image no favours. It's my privilege to preserve that image for the world, and nothing must shatter it. Can I rely on your discretion with that too, my dear Lili? Can I count on your protection?'

Protection.

She'd wanted to laugh at that, but she'd let Goebbels kiss her hand while she said, 'Always,' instead. Protection, however, was foremost in her mind. It was the other way they would all get to *afterwards*.

She'd followed Goebbels' instructions to the letter, but with the safety of her charges in mind, not his. She'd instructed the doorman to clear the foyer when André asked him to. She would serve the opening drinks with André's help, and she'd arranged a meal that they could help themselves to. Nobody else would attend the room. And once the guests were settled, she and André would politely withdraw, giving her the few seconds she needed to—

The telephone rang, jumping Lili out of running through the sequence in her head for the tenth time in the last hour.

'It's arrived. I'll take it directly to the suite.'

André put the phone down without waiting for a reply, as they'd arranged. Time was of the essence now.

Lili glanced at her watch. An hour and a half to go and finally there was a timetable to follow. First, she had to meet André and check the floral centrepiece's position and contents. Once that was done, and the suite door was locked, she would go to the kitchens and check through the menus as a courtesy to Chef. And once those tasks were complete, she would return to her rooms and wait, which was the hardest part. For the first car to arrive. For André's call. For the final act to play out.

I'm not an assassin.

She'd said that with such certainty to Alice what felt like years ago, but apparently it was no longer true.

Lili walked down the stairs to the third floor, the plan now a series of steps to be ticked off. She checked the flowers; the flowers were perfect. A low silver bowl filled with a dome created from pink peonies and cream roses. Nothing too high, nothing so heavily scented it would distract from the food and need moving. She checked the mechanism nestled under the dome's canopy, being very careful not to touch its components. She went to the kitchen and checked the menu, which was as perfect as the flowers. Spring vegetable and cheese tart; apple and carrot salad; mustard seed potatoes; rhubarb compote. Nothing too heavy, nothing too grand; perfectly suited to Hitler's increasingly austere tastes. Everything ready to be slotted into the dumb waiter and laid out on the side tables.

With half an hour left, Lili returned to her sitting room, sat in her favourite chair beside the window overlooking the garden and closed her eyes. All the pieces were in play, including the bomb. It was an unremarkable-looking thing given the expectations it carried. A lump of plastic explosive; an acid detonator inside a time pencil. All Lili had to do before she left the room was fluff up the flowers and touch the pen to the plastic. Then...

She wasn't entirely sure what came then.

Florian had talked her through the bomb's construction and the detonation process, but not the devastation it would cause. He'd estimated twenty to thirty minutes from touch to explosion, so not long to wait at least. After that...

Lili tried to imagine the suite with its eggshell-blue walls and gold moulding reduced to splinters and carnage. The bomb was centrally placed, in the middle of a table laden with glasses and china and close to a window whose wide panes ran directly behind Hitler's chair. She assumed that there would be flying shards and flames. That the injuries inflicted at such close quarters would be severe. She would have to go in and see those for herself – Florian had been very definite about that. There was to be no room for doubt or for cover-ups. He'd told her to take a pistol in with her in case any of them had survived. André had volunteered to do that in her place. Both of them hoped it wouldn't be needed.

Although I'll do it, if I have to. If it's what's required to keep everyone safe.

The telephone rang three times and then stopped. That was André's signal. Lili got up slowly; smoothed her hair and her dress. She stopped thinking. She arrived at the third floor with her keys in her hand and her smile in place in case Goebbels came fussing. She allowed herself one brief pause, one *please let this work*, and then she reached for the door.

It was unlocked. When she touched the doorknob, she realised too late that it was also ajar. It swung open the moment her fingers connected.

Later, when she had more time than she wanted to think, Lili knew that was the moment when she should have run. It didn't matter where to. She should have doubled back and hurled herself down the service corridor and out through the Edel's back door. She should have flagged down a car, bought herself a few minutes. It might have been enough.

Instead, she told herself that an unlocked door was nothing

to worry about. That it would be André, who also had keys to the suite, waiting on the other side in case anything had required a final check. Instead of running away, she walked in. But it wasn't André who was waiting for her by the empty table. And the centrepiece was no longer a perfect pink-and-white dome.

It was a pile of shredded petals on the floor.

PART FIVE

CHAPTER 22

FEBRUARY 1991

Lucy had given very little thought to how she would spend Christmas – she rarely did. And if she'd been asked what was top of her list, she wouldn't have said going tree shopping with Adam. So when he'd asked her to meet him outside the KaDeWe department store on a snowy December afternoon, Lucy assumed he wanted to discuss lighting designs or something else Edel-related. Instead, he'd launched straight into a plea for her help.

'I don't have a Christmas tree or a single decoration, which is probably a standard male line, but it's true. Could you help me up my game?'

He'd laughed at Lucy's confused, 'What?' as if he'd been expecting it. 'It's for Gabi. We've not had much practice at Christmas, at least not at a decent one. When I was a kid, she seemed to be on a permanent mission to turn it into the plainest day of the year, as if she was single-handedly battling the forces of capitalism. It was miserable. I'd like to change the script this year and make it special for her, and you're the one with the decorator's eye.' He nodded at the store's bauble-packed window. 'Will you help me navigate my way through this?'

It was a lovely idea, and a kind gesture towards Gabi, but Lucy's first reaction was still to look for an excuse not to do it.

Her memories of Christmas were as complicated as Adam's. The holidays she'd loved as a child had soured in the bleak ones which followed Emily's birth. And – once the split with her parents had widened beyond repair – Lucy had refused their and any other invitations and thrown herself into work instead, taking on the shifts everybody else was desperate to avoid. The anonymity of a hotel dining room saturated in tinsel and manu-factured bonhomie had always seemed preferable to the empti-ness of anything personal. But saying no to Adam had proved to be rather more difficult than resisting her parents.

The shadow of Gabi's illness, and the prospect that this could be her last Christmas, was there in his eyes. And although Adam hadn't said, 'And it would be twice as special if you were with us,' the hope of that was there too.

Which was where, as always, he had me.

Those eyes, plus Adam's determination to make better memories with his mother, would have been difficult enough on their own to ignore. But there was also Berlin, and Lucy was as powerless to resist Berlin's pull at Christmas as she had been when she'd first arrived in the city, almost a year ago.

The city had approached December as if it was auditioning for a movie. The grey skies had turned white at the start of the month and – instead of the snow dissolving into the grey mush she was used to – it had settled thickly enough to turn even the drabbest street from tired to enchanting. The Tiergarten had transformed into a parade of silver-wrapped Christmas trees and, inspired by its favourite park becoming a winter wonder-land, Berlin jumped head first into the holidays. The shops had turned into grottoes packed with giant nutcrackers and outsized baubles. Christmas markets popped up all over the city. The air round the most popular one at the Kaiser Wilhelm Memorial Church was so heady with *Glühwein* and chestnuts, the scent had turned Lucy giddy. In the end, she hadn't been able to resist the charms of a bauble-decked Berlin, and she certainly hadn't been able to resist Adam.

Not that I really wanted to.

Lucy had an hour in hand before she was needed to oversee the fitting of the new curtains in the Edel's bedrooms and the installation of the stair carpet. She made herself a cup of orange-and-cinnamon tea from the supplies in Adam's now considerably better-stocked kitchen and curled up on the sofa. That was a comfy nook she'd grown very fond of, even if the latest batch of replies to their newspaper search looked somewhat less inviting.

Adam's home on Rüdesheimer Straße – where Lucy increasingly spent more nights than she did at her own apartment – was the perfect setting for an architect. The street, which bordered the western boroughs of Wilmersdorf and Charlottenburg, was very different in style from Karl-Marx-Allee, but it was equally as lovely. The turn-of-the-century houses which lined it were four and five storeys high, painted in shades of ochre and cream, and finished with red-tiled roofs and wrought-iron balconies. Adam's top-floor flat had high ceilings and polished parquet floors and an original set of arched windows running the length of the living room. It was beautifully proportioned and elegantly finished.

'But I bet you think it's a bit too austere?'

Adam had asked her that with a nervous smile as he opened the door and they'd lugged in a tree which had seemed too big when they'd bought it from the street vendor and now seemed too small. Lucy hadn't argued with him. The place was far more functional than homely, although the Christmas tree had softened the room's contours on Lucy's first visit. Since then – with a little gentle encouragement – Adam had transformed the apartment with the candles and cushions and lamps Lucy had tactfully picked out for him.

And we've transformed ourselves along with it.

She began opening the envelopes, distracting herself from the disappointing smallness of the pile with memories of the night they'd decorated the tree together and their relationship had shifted gear. Distracting herself with thoughts of Adam had increasingly become one of Lucy's favourite hobbies.

'The DDR used to tie itself in knots trying to avoid the word Christmas – the holiday was officially known as a "festival of peace". All my friends' families ignored that but, of course, Gabi was determined to follow the guidelines on how to celebrate in a suitably loyal manner to the letter. Even my Advent calendar was decorated with pictures of Young Pioneers.'

He'd told Lucy that anecdote as he was hanging a particularly lurid glitter-coated sugar plum fairy onto an already thickly laden branch, but instead of gritting his teeth at his mother's rigid codes of behaviour, he'd laughed at how peculiar his childhood sounded. That was Lucy's main memory of the hours they'd spent completely over-decorating the apartment – how much they'd laughed together while they did it. The time Adam had spent with Gabi had softened the way he felt about her. He'd begun to try and reframe his past – starting with the Christmases he'd spent with his mother – so that he highlighted the moments of kindness she'd shown him, rather than shaping all his memories from criticism. The anecdotes he'd shared that night were proof that his relationship with Gabi had deepened. They had the same effect on Lucy's growing feelings for him.

'Stollen was my absolute favourite Christmas food – it still is – but getting all the dried fruit needed to make it wasn't an easy job in the East. My mother would start the search in September, and I'd start hunting for all the goodies she'd been able to buy the minute I spied her trying to squirrel in the first bag. Her hiding places got more inventive every year; they had to – the best one was on a shelf behind all her political books. She knew I'd never go near those.

'We didn't have Father Christmas to bring us gifts; we had Father Frost instead. She used to leave little bits of silver foil on the stairs and insist they were his footprints.'

Adam had been generous with his childhood that night. Lucy had picked up on his cue and responded with happier stories of her own. She'd made him laugh as she described the presents her parents had saved for months to spoil her with, and her equally as determined attempts to search through the house and uncover them. And the joy of a day without rules: Christmas cake for breakfast; Christmas dinner in her pyjamas; being allowed to eat all the pink-wrapped fudge pieces out of the festive tin of Quality Street without sharing.

An unspoken agreement fell into place between them which meant neither mentioned the more difficult years until Christmas was over and Gabi – to her delight – had been thoroughly spoiled. Adam had waited until the quiet days which meandered up to New Year before he described his first, unnerving, Christmas in the West. He'd spent that in the Marienfelde Detention Centre, caught in a half-life between prisoner and asylum seeker. Sleeping on a metal bunk bed; sharing a kitchen and a bathroom with an ever changing cast of equally displaced men and women. Queuing for food rations and donated clothes and pinning all his hopes on a permit to stay which wasn't guaranteed. Dreading a rejection and a return to the East and a prison cell.

Lucy had waited until he'd shared the loneliness and confusion of that experience before she'd let him into the holidays when she'd tried – and failed – not to think about Emily. The ones she'd spent crossing the street to avoid toy shops and theatres showing pantomimes and anywhere likely to be filled with small children. And sobbing over adverts for dolls' houses and teddy bears. It was Adam's 'Those Christmases with her are coming – I know it' which had finally sent her properly into his arms. And given her the last push she needed to stop writing letters to the agency which were too easily ignored and pick up the telephone instead.

'I am very sorry, Miss Stretton. It seems your file slipped between case workers and new administrative systems and slipped out of review. That's not good enough, but you've reached my desk now and you won't disappear again – you have my word on that.'

The woman who responded to Lucy's phone message was brisk and efficient and – although she was cautious and wouldn't promise the moon – she was able to reassure Lucy that there was indeed an updated address for Emily's parents on file, and that she would follow up on it personally.

'Emily is eleven now. She may have been told about you, or she may not, but she's of an age where these conversations – in my experience – often start. I'll come back to you in a month with a progress report, and let's all keep our fingers crossed shall we for the right outcome.'

That conversation had taken place a week ago. Lucy was doing her best to hold on to the reality of *a month*, but it was hard not to run into the hall every time her letterbox clattered. It was hard not to do that in both of the flats she commuted between. They'd given Adam's address as the point of contact for the newspaper adverts, which had first appeared in the week before Christmas. As hard as it was to remember the feeling now, waiting for the responses to those had been as exciting then as waiting for news of Emily.

Neither of them had been particularly concerned at first when nothing came. Mail was a haphazard affair over the holidays and – once Lucy had found her way to Adam's bed and agreed to stay there – they had no interest in a quick return to the world. They'd managed to shut that out so completely, New Year's Eve passed them by. They re-emerged bleary-eyed in the first days of January as if from an illness, so caught up in their newly blossoming relationship they felt limbless if the other was away for too long.

The first advert came and went. When the second appeared in the press, their hopes rose again. They manufactured excuses to hang around the flat and laughed at each other for doing it. Now it was two months into an increasingly frustrating search and it was rare for either of them to waste time at Adam's flat waiting for the mail.

Lucy smoothed the latest crop of letters out anyway, hoping she'd find a better outcome in this batch than they'd found in the others but not counting on it. The response to the pleas for help which they'd placed, and kept placing, had never turned into the flood of responses they'd all been hoping for. The letters which did come arrived in a trickle. None of them had so far shed any light on Marius. None of them had really shed any light on the search for Lili's contacts at all.

Most of the replies to the adverts were from people with fond memories of staying at the Edel which they wanted to share, but they contained no helpful information about its owners or other visitors. One or two of the respondents claimed that they knew André or Alice, but they'd wanted money in exchange for the details and they'd wanted that up front, so those letters had gone – reluctantly at first and then less so as their numbers increased – straight into the bin. And now, despite she and Adam and Gabi constantly reassuring each other that it was still early days and the hunt wasn't over, even the trickle had started to dry up. Lucy would have pulled out her tongue rather than admit it, but she was secretly starting to believe that André and Alice and the mysterious FK were all dead, along with everybody who'd known them.

My name is Alice Herschel and I met Lili Rodenberg in November 1942 at the Edel Hotel.

She was halfway down the page – skimming not reading it – before Lucy properly absorbed what the letter said. She had to close her eyes and steady her nerves before she went back to the beginning. The date when the women appeared to have met hadn't been quoted in the advert, which made it more likely that this Alice was real. The first line was the gold they'd been waiting for. But it was the second which sent her running for the telephone, and then out of the door to pull Adam out of the meeting his secretary refused to disturb.

And whatever lies you've heard about her, I don't believe they're true – Lili is the reason I'm still alive. Lili Rodenberg saved my life.

CHAPTER 23

MARCH 1991

I settled in Hannover in 1945 with a group of other Jewish survivors from the Bergen-Belsen concentration camp. None of us had families left by then, but we have a thriving community here now, centred round a synagogue we founded ourselves in the early 1960s, to replace the one the Nazis destroyed in 1938. I have lived a good life, or I've tried to, but not perhaps when it comes to Lili. Hers is a story whose wrongs still haunt me. I should have told it before.

Lucy folded Alice's second letter into her bag as the train pulled into Hannover's central station. In the two weeks it had taken to arrange a visit to Alice's home, she and Adam had spent hours speculating about the woman they were about to meet. They'd also invested a lot of hope into *I should have told it before,* even though that statement was very open-ended. Lucy couldn't shake off the feeling that this could as easily add more questions to Lili's story as tie it up. Adam was equally insistent that Alice's input would solve it. The journey from Berlin had turned into a tense one.

'We're a bit early. We could walk to her house if you want – it's not that far. We could take a detour through the old town on the way.'

Lucy looked back at the station as Adam studied a street map and tried to find his bearings. The three huge arched windows which dominated the station's facade glittered in the sunlight. The lower but equally elegant wings which flanked the building's centre were beautifully proportioned. The station was an impressive piece of architecture, but it left Lucy cold.

'Does the whole city look like this?' She waved at the busy concourse behind her as Adam frowned. 'This is all very grand, but I thought Hannover was bombed to bits in the war and so would look very modern. The station could have been transported here from the nineteenth century, but the plaque over there says it's a reconstruction and dates from the 1960s. If that's what they've done everywhere else, how *old* is the old town actually going to be?'

Adam glanced at the notes printed down the side of the map.

'That's a good question. Not as old as you'd think or as it presumably looks. You're right about the bombing – it says here that Hannover was a major manufacturing centre in the 1940s, and the factories and the rest of the city were targeted dozens of times by the Allies. Over ninety per cent of the centre was destroyed, but a lot of that was rebuilt in the early sixties, like the station.'

He glanced up at the building, taking in the features Lucy had now decided she actively disliked and slipping into professional mode.

'It's a difficult one. There doesn't appear to have been any consistency across the country in how the war's destruction was managed. Some places decided to reinvent themselves; some places preferred to reinvent the comfort of the past. It looks like

Hannover chose the latter and decided to restore as many of the historical buildings back to their original state as they could. So it's fair to say that Hannover is modern, but not in the way you perhaps expected.'

Lucy stared across the bustling square, with its ubiquitous statue of a man on a horse, over to the raft of gothic-style spires she could just make out in the distance.

'I don't want to see it, and I'm sorry if that's disappointing. I know you're probably interested in seeing how the renovations were done, but it all feels very fake to me. I don't want to go hunting for the truth about Lili in some Disneyfied version of history – that just sounds like another cover-up. And I appreciate I'm being illogical, but will you let me have it anyway?'

For a moment, Lucy thought Adam was going to argue or slide into another of his lectures on architectural principals. Her heart – which was already his – swelled when he nodded and flagged down a taxi instead.

Alice Herschel was seventy-nine years old and complained of 'unreliable knees' which looked perfectly healthy as she bustled around fetching coffee and a large platter of pastries. She was formidable – her 'Let's not waste time on unnecessary chatter about how everyone's doing; let's get down to the matter in hand' bore testimony to that. But she was also warm and quick-witted, and she'd lived a fascinating, if heartbreaking, life.

'I grew up in Berlin, in a pretty house on the edge of the Tiergarten, which was as idyllic as it sounds. My family were wealthy and well thought of – or at least they were until Hitler decided we weren't to be thought of at all. My father was a professor of physics at the Humboldt. My mother's parents owned a string of art galleries, and she was a highly respected artist in her own right. She ran literary salons that – in her words – collided deliciously with my father's too stuffy scientific ones.'

Alice described her parents so vividly, Lucy could picture them laughing and sparring and engaged in the matchmaking which she said was her mother's favourite pursuit and drove her father to distraction. She described them with a warmth which lifted the couple out of the numbers on a too long list of the dead and back into living, breathing people.

'They were also very progressive, which meant that I was allowed to choose my husband for myself and was also allowed to study for a profession, both of which were quite scandalous for girls in those days, especially as I was their only child. I took full advantage of their good nature, of course. Much to my poor mother's horror, I became a physicist like my father and – to her delight – I married a musician. A man with the voice of an angel and the looks to match. Who I adored and was adored by in return.'

Neither Lucy nor Adam needed to ask what had happened to Alice's laughing, vibrant family. She carried their loss on her face. And the past for her was still all too present.

'The war put an end to my scientific ambitions and, after I was released from Belsen, I was ill for a very long time. When I finally recovered, I wanted a quieter life, and I retrained as an archivist – I suppose I wanted to catalogue the past, to make sure nothing gets forgotten. And I gave lectures too, sometimes, about the camps and the regime that built them.'

She paused for a moment and glanced round at the crowded bookshelves which cluttered the room. 'All these words, but I wonder if anybody learns anything. And when I try to explain what it was really like...' She shrugged. 'It's hard to recreate the past for those who didn't live through it. People do their best, but it's difficult in a world where television shows pictures of conflicts thousands of miles away the instant that they happen to understand how different it was in the war. The German media was completely under Goebbels' control, and so much was hidden.'

She gestured to the bookcase nearest her. 'Look at all those books with *Holocaust* in the title. We didn't know that word then; we didn't know what was waiting for us. We could see the small acts, of course – the restrictions on our freedoms and our jobs – but the bigger picture? We weren't prepared; we hadn't a clue. And even when some of us did start to piece the clues together, it was still impossible to accept that a genocide was coming. Who thinks in such terms without hindsight? It's one thing for a historian to trace a line from one law and one restriction to the next and plot a course that says, *This outcome was inevitable.* I can do that myself easily enough now the evidence is there. But then?'

Alice's sigh seemed to come from her soul. 'We had such full lives; we were such good Germans. We'd no idea how fast that could change. That we could be reduced to nothing. That we could be cut so completely out of society, we became invisible. And so demonised, our removal became an acceptable, desirable thing. Who could?'

Nobody speaks up, nobody's ever dared, and that silence has created a terrible power.

Lucy flinched as a line from Lili's journal jumped into her head. Alice noticed and nodded as if she'd said the words aloud.

'It's a dreadful thing when one group becomes *other*. But that's what we were. And once that shift happened – once the legal framework was in place and the heads turned away, once violence became *our* reality but not *theirs* – we lived every day in fear.'

'I'm sorry if this sounds clumsy, but I was raised in the DDR where there was a very particular slant on the war. You said your family was wealthy, and I thought there was a window, wasn't there, when Jewish people with means could request permission to emigrate to America or Britain, or some-where else in Europe? Do you mind me asking why you didn't get out when you could?'

Adam asked the question into the gap Alice had left after *fear*. If she did mind, she didn't show it.

'There was a moment, yes, and we missed it. It's a prosaic answer, but it's true. And perhaps the picture you were offered has been oversimplified. I assume most of your lessons focused on the strength of the Russian resistance to the Nazi beast, rather than the nuances of Hitler's domestic policies?'

She nodded as Adam blushed. 'History shifts, depending on who's doing the telling; that much never changes. The window to leave was very narrow, and far too many people were shoving at it with nowhere to go. And we were overconfident about our own standing, or blind to the danger – you can pick your own description. The quotas – which were shamefully small – for emigration filled before we could find a place, our assets were seized so we didn't have the means to go and then my parents...'

She took a sip of water but refused when Lucy suggested she might want a break.

'They took my father first, in 1939, just before the war broke out. He'd rented a room and carried on teaching Jewish students who'd been stripped of their university places in the same way he'd been stripped of his professorship. Someone denounced him, of course, and he was sent to the camp at Sach-senhausen. He died there about a year later – I don't know the cause; his body wasn't sent back.'

She wasn't looking at Lucy and Adam anymore – her gaze had gone past them.

'I lost my mother next, sometime in 1941; I never knew the exact date of her death either. She went to Theresienstadt with my grandparents, to settle them in to their new home there, or so she thought. She didn't know Theresienstadt was a ghetto and a holding stage for the killing camps; how could she? She believed she was doing them a kindness; she believed she would be able to return to Berlin. The propaganda surrounding that place was masterful.'

Alice was tiring. Her voice had developed a shake; one of her hands had developed a tremor. Lucy was afraid she would run out of steam before she got to her meeting with Lili, but Alice's whole story deserved the respect of a hearing, and neither she nor Adam were going to cut across that. She refilled the old lady's water glass as Alice continued.

'None of them came back from Theresienstadt, but we didn't know to expect that ending then. We still had hope. We hadn't heard of Auschwitz; we hadn't heard about ovens or gas. And people try hard to find ways to live, especially when they're young and in love. I had Jashel. We had work in a factory; we had a room to live in and a child on—'

Alice stopped. Her body curled in on itself. Her skin turned to paper; her voice shrank to a whisper. For a moment, Lucy wasn't sure if Alice knew she and Adam were there.

'No, don't do that. Don't walk that way. There's places nobody should go, stories that don't get easier with the retelling.' She shook herself, coughed; looked in Lucy's direction again but not at her. 'I lost them both, husband and child – that's all that needs saying. But I survived, which seems like a better thing now than it did then. Jashel had a friend who smuggled Jews to safety and kept them alive. And that's what he did for me.'

She was wearing all her years now, in her face and her body. But when Adam and Lucy both said, 'That's enough – you don't need to carry on,' she shook her head.

'Oh but I do. After all my talk about unnecessary chatter, I've talked too long about the wrong things. I can hardly stop now I've finally brought you to Lili.'

The renewed warmth in Alice's voice delivered Lili instantly into the room. When Alice described the two nights she'd spent hiding in the Edel and the depths of Lili's kindness towards her, Lili came as alive as Jashel and Alice's parents had been. And – a few moments into the telling – she became, once again, another woman.

'Lili was Jewish – that's why she helped us. Her husband knew, but I don't think anyone else did, except perhaps André the wine waiter, who was helping her. Anyway, she'd been hiding in plain sight the whole time, which was quite something given that she was in such close contact with Hitler. Oh my goodness, you didn't know that about her, did you? You didn't know about her background?' Alice was suddenly upright again and nothing about her was shaking. 'Dear Lord, if you could only see your faces.'

She turned to Adam, who was gaping at her, open-mouthed.

'Your grandmother was Jewish, and riddled with guilt about the safe life she'd found for herself by cutting herself off from her past and keeping that a secret. That's why she used the Edel as a safe haven for Jewish refugees: it was a kind of atonement, a refusal to turn away and be silent. That's why she acted as a spy.'

Now it was Lucy whose tongue was so tied she could barely speak. 'What do you mean, *she acted as a spy?*'

Alice wasn't only sitting upright; she was sparkling. Telling a tale nobody else knew had run a charge through her.

'You sound exactly like I did when she told me. Lili Rodenberg – who remains the most elegant and composed woman I've ever met to this day – not only had a secret life; she had a secret room where she listened in on Hitler's private conversations with his ministers when he came to the hotel for lunch. She relayed what she heard there to the man in charge of the smuggling network. I was speechless when she told me – I won't pretend I wasn't. I thought it was madness, and the bravest thing I'd ever heard. And, well, I've no proof of this, but I had a feeling that night there was more she wanted to do. We talked about how close she could get to them; I asked her outright if she'd ever considered...' Alice paused and frowned as if some memory was pulling at her. 'Well, she said she was a mother, not an assassin, but I wonder sometimes.'

Adam was no longer gaping. To Lucy's utter surprise, he burst out laughing instead.

'I'm sorry, I really am. It's not that I don't believe you, but the twists in this tale are too much to keep hold of. A year ago, I had a grandmother who was a leading light in the Nazi Party and my family's nasty secret. Now my grandmother was apparently a people-smuggler and a spy against Hitler, and possibly even imagining murder. Not a hate figure but a heroine. It's a lot.'

He stopped talking and visibly pulled himself up. The laughter – which had clearly been born out of shock – drained from him.

'I'm sorry. I do believe you, Alice. Apart from anything else, everything you've said ties in with the journal entries and the conclusions we'd started to come to. But it makes absolutely no sense when you match this version of her to the official story.'

He looked over at Lucy, who nodded.

'I believe it all too, and the stakes – and her bravery – seem to be getting higher with each new revelation. But, like Adam said, it doesn't make sense and it still leaves us with one unanswered question.'

The room fell silent as Adam and Lucy and Alice stared at each other, that same question swirling round all three heads.

If Lili was a heroine and she hated the Nazis, then who in God's name killed her?

'The answer might be in here. I got it out again when I read your advert, but it's a long time since I've properly looked through it. My plans for it slipped me by. I can steer you a little before you go, but I think it's time you took over the puzzle now. Maybe you'll be able to make the connections I can't quite make sense of. And even if you can't join every dot, maybe it will bring you closer to the real Lili.'

We'll bring the real Lili home.

Alice's words had been an echo of Lucy's determination to start the search for Lili's contacts, which made the scrapbook Alice had entrusted to her and Adam in Hannover all the more precious. She'd given them a brief introduction to its contents before they left, but she was exhausted by then and that had grown rather rambling. Now they were alone in Adam's flat and suddenly reluctant to open it. Lucy had made the mistake of saying, 'This could be the last clue – what if we can't make sense of it any more than Alice could?' and they'd got stuck.

Which can't continue or we'll be still sat here none the wiser in the morning.

Lucy reached over and picked up the book. 'This is daft. We're making it too big. We don't need to solve the whole thing tonight; I'm not even sure we can. And we can go back to Alice if we end up with more questions.'

Not trying to solve all the connections in one go made the scrapbook more approachable. But as for going back to Alice? Adam nodded at the suggestion, but Lucy knew he was as reluctant as she was to disturb the old lady again. Alice had been worn out when they left her. She didn't need another session spent digging through old memories.

'We're acting like this will be filled with more bombshells, but so what if it is?' Lucy opened the first page with more confidence than she felt. 'Nothing we discover about Lili now can be worse than the story we believed in a few months ago.'

'That's not the problem.' Adam moved closer to her, so the scrapbook lay across both their laps. 'I'm not worried about finding more secrets; I'm worried there won't be anything new in here. That we'll never get a definitive answer to who Lili was and what she was doing. That we won't be able to give her a proper end.'

Lili ran her finger down the categories Alice had carefully noted inside the front cover. She'd had exactly the same thought on the train back from Hannover to Berlin. And she'd decided then not to build that very reasonable doubt into a barrier.

'Maybe we won't. Maybe Alice is right and it's never possible to fully understand a past you haven't lived through, not when it comes to people's decisions and thought processes anyway.' She slipped her hand inside Adam's as she continued. 'Think about our situations. You feel very differently about your life in the DDR from the way Gabi would describe it; I feel very differently about how Emily's birth was handled than my parents must have done. We could all tell our own versions and – in their own way – all those versions would be true. And maybe there'll always be guesswork with Lili, but everything we learn adds more substance to the woman we now believe in, and the one we want to present to the world. Whatever else happened to her, she won't be remembered as a Nazi anymore. Isn't that a good thing, whether we can round off her ending or not?'

Adam nodded, but his face remained folded into deep lines. Lucy could see he was struggling with the idea of loose ends and uncertainty. She couldn't solve that problem for him, but she could do her best to lighten his mood.

'Besides, there's too much work gone into this to let it become a museum piece.' She smiled at the scrapbook's neat divisions and at him. 'I kept a scrapbook when I was about twelve. It was an absolute hotchpotch of pictures of ponies and David Cassidy and glitter, and enough glue to stick Noah's Ark together. I'd never have included anything as sensible as an index.'

Adam's laugh broke the tension exactly as she'd hoped and allowed them to start properly exploring the pages.

The first ones contained snapshots of Alice's life. The liberation of the concentration camp at Bergen-Belsen in April

1945, where she'd been held after her capture when a safe house turned out to be anything but. A photograph from the late 1950s of a group of women sitting on the steps of an apartment block, smoking and laughing. Another from 1962 showing Alice waving a shovel at the ground-breaking celebrations for the Haeckelstraβe synagogue. There were plenty of photographs showing Alice surrounded by smiling faces. But there were no wedding pictures, no babies. Alice's body had survived the war in one piece, but her heart had never outgrown its scars.

'Here's the first mention of the Edel, look.'

Lucy closed the pages on Alice's personal life with *We had such full lives* looping through her head. It was hard to look at the scrapbook and not see *empty* coming too close after *full*. It was a relief to switch to more familiar waters.

The first reference to the Edel was a yellowing postcard from the 1930s depicting a Christmas party in the ballroom. The second was an article from a 1985 edition of *Das Bild*, examining the history of Hitler's lost hotels. It was a lurid piece, focusing mainly on the numerous murders and affairs which had taken place throughout the 1920s and '30s at the Hotel Adlon, but there was a small mention of the Edel which Alice had underlined.

'*One of the Führer's favourite watering holes in Berlin, run by the notorious Nazi beauty Lili Rodenberg.*' Adam grimaced as he read out the sentence. 'Alice said the impossibility of that was what set her on the trail for Lili and led her to this.'

He gestured to the copy of Goebbels' eulogy which Alice had also included, but Lucy was still reading the *Das Bild* article.

'Look at what this says lower down. "*Attempts to contact members of the Edel's staff who worked there in the war have proved unsuccessful. An unconfirmed source suggests most were arrested and removed in 1944.*"'

'Does it say which month?'

Lucy shook her head. 'No, that's all there is. But surely it had to be in the April when Lili was murdered? The arrests have to be connected.'

That seemed like a reasonable conclusion, but there was nothing in the scrapbook to join the two. And there was nothing else specifically about Lili.

'But that doesn't mean there's no more to find. Things might be easier now the Wall's down. We could go to *Das Bild* and ask about the source – they might be less afraid to come forward. We could do a more detailed search of any DDR archives that have opened.' Lucy grabbed a notebook and pen off the coffee table. 'We could make a list of what we need to do next.'

Making a list helped: it stopped them seeing dead ends and kept them turning the pages without getting caught up in connections they couldn't yet make.

'We should look at the other section she told us was important. The one that lists the assassination attempts on Hitler. She said there was something about the plots that connected and could be a clue, but she couldn't remember what it was, which was hardly surprising. We really did wear her out.'

Lucy checked the index and found the page numbers Adam meant. She was surprised how many there were.

'It's an interesting idea, cataloguing the attempts to kill Hitler and looking for links between them. It's a shame she never got to write the book she was planning.'

'She'd certainly done a lot of the work – look at these notes.' Adam had begun leafing through the pages which Alice had annotated in red pen, reading through the questions she'd presumably intended as pointers for future research. 'Was it the initials – was that it? When you said FK, she was convinced it rang a bell, but she couldn't remember where she'd seen it written down. Or what the connection was between them and Lili or the Edel.'

'*I had a feeling that night there was more she wanted to do.*'

Lucy stared at the heavily inked pages as Alice's words came back to her.

'*I'm a mother, not an assassin.*' Lucy shook her head as Adam frowned. 'That's what Lili said, remember. But what if that changed? What if... No. That's crazy. I know Alice was obsessed with murder plots, but she can't possibly have thought Lili...'

Lucy stopped talking. There was only one way to finish that sentence, and she wasn't willing to do it. Neither, it seemed, was Adam.

'Let's take a step back, shall we, and not jump to wild conclusions. Let's look at the evidence Alice has left us. She's listed over thirty attempts on Hitler's life, going back to 1932. Why don't we read through them – see if we can spot anything significant?'

It was a sensible idea, more sensible than anything Lucy was currently imagining. She let Adam take the lead and turn slowly through the pages.

'I never knew so many people tried to kill him. I've only heard of one attempt before. The one with a bomb in a briefcase under a desk that someone accidentally moved, which meant Hitler survived the blast.' She ran back through her memories, but the details were hazy. 'I saw a film about it once, with my dad. Something about a wolf? And I think the operation itself had a name that was to do with the gods.'

'Is this it?' Adam was pointing to one of Alice's longer entries. 'Operation Valkyrie: von Stauffenberg's plot to murder Hitler at the Wolf's Lair, his military headquarters, and take over the army and then the country in July 1944.'

'July 1944?' Lucy started to say, 'Well that's not relevant then, it's too late,' but Adam had jumped ahead of her.

'There's a note next to the Valkyrie entry, look. Alice has

cross-referenced it to a line in another article. Here it is, and there's a note.'

The line Alice had highlighted read: *Florian Graf von Krailling, executed for high treason, April 1944; no surviving heirs.* Beside that she'd written, *Is this the von Krailling who was at the Edel the same night as me? Who knew Lili? Could this be an earlier attempt?*

That was it. One short sentence in a piece about the fates of noble German families in the Second World War and an annotation Alice didn't appear to have followed up. If there was a connection, it was a loose one, although Adam was determined to make it stick.

'Surely that's our man. *Graf* is German for count, so the initials fit. An FK who knew Lili.'

Lucy wasn't as ready as him to be convinced. 'Except we know our FK is a woman. And the Valkyrie plot was three months after this von Krailling – and Lili – died. The timeline, never mind him being the wrong gender, doesn't work.'

She was doing her best to go steadily and rein in expectations; Adam wasn't trying to do that at all. He was determined to power through to the ending he needed.

'Okay, but what if Lili's contact was Florian's wife? Maybe she was called Frida or Femke, I don't know, but we can check. And, yes, the Stauffenberg assassination plot was later, but that doesn't mean that an April attempt didn't happen too. Some of the failed methods seem to have got repeated.' He turned the scrapbook's pages again, jumping from one entry to another. 'See, there were attempts to plant a bomb in the Wolf's Lair before Stauffenberg tried it, in November 1943 and again in February 1944. What if the basic idea of a bomb rather than say a shooting was considered to be a good one and different conspirators kept trying it out? And what if somebody decided that an attack inside a military bunker was too risky and a hotel—'

'Where Hitler regularly had lunch would be an easier target.'

They stared at each other as Lucy finished Adam's sentence. There was more and more logic to what he'd said, but she still wasn't ready to embrace it.

'None of this means that – if there was a bomb plot involving the Edel, which is a big if – Lili was directly involved. It's a hell of a jump from smuggler to spy to murdering the Führer.'

Adam still wouldn't slow down and meet her.

'Is it though? Maybe once you're over a line, it's easier to keep going. She was already a traitor from the minute she helped the first refugee. And I bet nobody suspected her the way they might suspect a man.' He held up his hands as Lucy started to pick holes again. 'Or maybe you're right and it was none of her doing. Perhaps the whole thing – if, like you say, it even happened at all – was orchestrated by Florian. And it must have failed because he was executed for treason. And Lili was' – he stopped; shook his head – 'caught up in it somehow and was executed as well. What else do you call it when someone's been shot and dumped on a pavement?'

He stopped again and groaned as the explanations – as they kept doing – refused to add up.

'Oh God, there's another *except*. Why is there always an *except*? How do we get from Lili trying to kill Hitler to she died as his *dear friend*?'

Lucy sat back on the sofa, trying – like Adam – to slot pieces together which refused to fit. Which kept bouncing off *Lili Rodenberg's loyalty to the Reich knew no bounds. Her murder is a stain on the city.* When the answer suddenly hit her, she couldn't stay still.

'Because the truth didn't suit everyone.'

She got up. She'd had enough of being careful and slow. She

needed to move and let her brain go wandering. She shook her head as Adam asked what she meant.

'I don't know yet. I don't know how to go looking for proof, or if that's even possible. But there's a lie at the heart of this story, not a secret, and I think that comes back to one man. The Third Reich's master of propaganda, who was also a regular visitor to the Edel, whose job it was to look after Hitler's image. I think what happened to Lili comes back to Goebbels. I think he's where her story ends.'

CHAPTER 24

APRIL 1944

The flowers lay ripped to pieces on the floor. The silver dish was upturned and empty. And the bomb sat on the table with its two component parts – the block of explosives and the thin brass tube which contained liquid detonator in its copper tip – placed at a safe distance from each other.

Harmless when separate, lethal when combined. Very unlikely to fail once you've primed them.

Lili pushed Florian and his empty promises out of her head. The two men in dark coats hadn't identified themselves; they hadn't needed to, and they were waiting for her to speak first which was terrifying. Lili had no idea how much they knew. She had seconds to fly her hands to her face and assemble a suitably outraged defence.

'What in God's name is this? Tell me it's not a bomb? Tell me someone wasn't planning to—'

'Stop.'

The instruction wasn't offered with any particular menace, but Lili knew better than to disobey. The wider of the two men nodded as she fell silent.

'That's a much better idea than standing there making up a

story we all know is nonsense. It's never a good move to start by wasting our time.'

That was a clear instruction too, but – although she had no desire to provoke either man and no idea what she could say that would save her – Lili wasn't ready to give up and fold.

'I appreciate that this is a very troubling situation, but have you spoken to our hotel detective? I'm sure he could be of more—'

The slap came from nowhere. The second man was back in position beside the table before Lili understood that he'd moved. The blow's force made her stumble and grab on to a chair; it shot a pain from her jaw to her temple.

'Didn't I just warn you about time wasting? And your detective – who I doubt would leap to your defence – is already in custody, Frau Rodenberg. Someone attempted to plant a bomb in this room on his watch – where else would he be?'

Even if he'd wanted an answer, Lili couldn't have offered him one – her rapidly swelling mouth made it too hard to speak.

The Gestapo officer nodded as if she'd stayed silent this time by choice.

'And this is your hotel, Frau Rodenberg, not his. What happens under its roof is your responsibility. Although this *troubling situation* as you put it goes rather beyond poor management, wouldn't you say?'

His face was too chilling to focus on. Lili kept her eyes down as he continued.

'That, however, will all come later. As for now...' He waited until she was forced to look up. 'I have to inform you that you are under arrest on suspicion of conspiring to murder the Führer. That is a charge of high treason and carries the death penalty if proven. Do you understand?'

Lili licked her sore lips and managed a, 'Yes.' There was no point in adding *but*, or trying to use her now presumably very flimsy position to deny the charges or bargain for the information she needed. She couldn't ignore the reality of *they know I'm in this up to my neck* or the sense in *co-operate – it might at least buy you some time.*

'Good. Come with us.'

The man who'd done all the talking moved towards the door; the other one closed in behind her. Lili tried to move, but her legs were liquid. She saw the look that passed between the two officers as she hesitated; she saw fingers crack and stretch. She tried again, clenching her jaw with the effort of walking, refusing to gasp at the pain which instantly flooded her face. They didn't wait for her to steady herself. They marched her faster than her shaking legs could bear along the corridor towards the guest lift. There was no one in sight; the hotel was horribly silent. Lili managed to hold on to *please God André and the others have got out,* until they ushered her into the lift and the officer who she assumed was the senior one pressed the wrong button.

'Why are we going to the basement instead of the ground floor?'

The pain and the effort of talking was wasted; neither of them replied. When the lift stopped, they pushed her in front of them and in through the kitchen doors first.

'No. No, this isn't right.'

Lili whirled round, away from the sight of her staff bundled between the stoves and the counter tops and surrounded by a ring of heavily armed soldiers.

'They've got nothing to do with what was planned for upstairs. They don't know anything about it.'

What was planned was as good as a confession, but Lili didn't care. The senior officer looked over her head.

'Somebody does. This was a conspiracy. There were players inside the hotel and out. And we can take them all to headquarters and spend even more hours asking even more questions than we already have, or' – he nodded to the terrified group –

'we can keep shooting them one by one until you give the real target up.'

He wasn't bluffing. The repetition of *even more* told Lili what she'd already guessed – that she wasn't the only one of Florian's circle under arrest, that the whole plan had collapsed. And the slap had been a warning, a taster of what could follow. Lili didn't know how long she would be able to hold out once the blows grew harder. She also didn't want any of her innocent staff members to die because she'd over-reached herself. But she still couldn't say André's name. She couldn't stand there like a puppet and offer him up.

Her silence ran on too long.

The Gestapo officer sighed. 'Take the first one out.'

The first one was a young boy. Lili recognised him as one of the newest porters. He couldn't have been more than sixteen; he'd only been recruited because all the more suitable candidates had been lost to the war. And he tried to be brave – squaring his shoulders and holding up his head as he was forced to kneel on the hard floor – but the tears started pouring the second the rifle butt bit into his neck.

'It was me. I carried the bomb up to the suite. I knew exactly what I was doing, and my only regret is that the plan failed and Hitler is still alive. But Frau Rodenberg is telling the truth: nobody else on the staff was involved.'

André had stepped to the side, where the Gestapo men had a clear view of him, and he had a clear view of Lili.

'Is this true?'

The officer signalled to the soldier standing over the young boy to hold fire as he addressed Lili. It was an impossible question to answer; it was an impossible one to ignore.

If I give him up, the others will live. If I don't...

The kitchens and the soldiers and the frightened huddle disappeared. There was only the two of them left, her and André, joined by their bravery or madness. Whichever it was, there was no walking away. André smiled at Lili; Lili smiled back. She hoped he could read *thank you* in that; she hoped he knew those tiny words weren't big enough to contain everything he'd done for her. She kept her eyes locked on his as she did what she had to do to save the rest and nodded.

'Shoot them both.'

The bullets flew, and the bodies fell before Lili had a chance to protest or scream. But she did scream. She shouted André's name and she shouted *no* as she rounded on the officer who'd given the order to kill with no more thought than as if he was swatting a fly. And she dug deep welts in his face before he knocked her senseless to the ground.

There was no stylish arrival this time at Prinz-Albrecht-Straβe.

Lili didn't arrive in a Daimler. She wasn't ushered in through the main entrance or led straight to Himmler's office by a smiling secretary. No one offered her tea; no one waved her into a comfy chair. She was dragged semi-conscious from a police car instead and hauled through a dimly lit corridor in the basement. She was photographed and fingerprinted, pushed this way and that. She was ordered to give her place of birth, her address and her name, which clearly no longer counted for anything. She was thrown into a dark cell and left alone in the damp until she could no longer count the hours.

Lili curled into a corner. There was no blanket or bed, and the air was as cold as December. She gave up the struggle to sleep. She wept for André and the boy instead. When she'd cried herself out, she wrapped memories of Marius around her shaking body and tried to lose herself inside those. And she gave thanks over and over again that she'd managed to get Gabi to safety. That Gabi was out of reach became her sole thought, and the crutch which got her to her feet when they finally came for her.

The room she was marched into was as windowless as her cell. There were two soldiers guarding the door and a man waiting for her who – like the Gestapo officers who'd carried her limp body out of the Edel – didn't volunteer his name or his rank. But there was a chair for her to sit on, and none of the men were brandishing weapons. Lili took the small victories and kept breathing.

'How many of these people can you identify?'

The man sitting opposite her wasn't Gestapo; he was wearing an SS officer's uniform. Lili drew no comfort from that – both organisations were aligned in their cruelty. She glanced at the photographs he'd spread across the table. Florian was there, and Freya, and the rest of the men and women she'd met at the Spreewald estate. But there wasn't a picture of Aaron. Lili took that as another win.

'And before you deny knowing any of them, be aware that they have all named you as playing a central role in their assassination plot.'

Lili was tempted to say, 'Then you don't need me to tell you who they are.' She didn't. She needed to get the measure of the man she was dealing with, and he needed to get the measure of her. She forced herself to sit up straight, although her whole body was cramped from the hours spent sitting on the cell's stone floor. She forced herself to be Lili Rodenberg.

'I only have your word for that. And their words are lies. I saw the bomb in the suite. I'll grant you that there's clearly been a conspiracy of some kind and – or so I assume from this rogues' gallery you've shown me – people I counted as friends, who were visitors to my hotel, have trespassed on my hospitality. That is shocking. But what is even more shocking is the way I've been treated. Can I remind you that I've been a friend to the Führer for years, that he has described the Edel as his home from home in Berlin? Given that, why on earth would I want to kill him?'

She stopped talking as her bruised mouth started to throb and sat back. She'd done what she'd decided in the long hours of waiting to do: she'd stood up for herself, not for her own sake but to keep any potential spotlight off Gabi and the hotel. Which would have felt like a brave thing to do if her interrogator hadn't responded with a slow clap.

'Well done. I'm glad that's over and done with. And that is a very good question, Frau Rodenberg: why indeed? We've all been wondering the same thing, and I'm sure we'll get to the answer. But now it's my turn to do the talking and yours to be quiet.'

He leaned forward and rested his hands on the photographs. His fingers were long and slim. Lili had a sudden image of them wrapped round her neck and instinctively shrank back.

The man nodded. 'That's better. It's a lot easier if you accept who's in charge. And, to be clear, I have no interest in listening to you play the innocent, as entertaining as that is. We know that you are anything but. We have detailed testimony from your friends here which place you not only firmly in the centre of a plot which would have killed the Führer and his leading deputies, but also as the one tasked to prime the bomb. And what you presumably don't know is that the von Kraillings have been under surveillance for weeks, and so has the Edel. Ever since you went to the Bendlerblock and started throwing your weight around. That's a lot of strikes against you. Not to mention that charmingly misguided *they've got nothing to do with what was planned for upstairs* in the kitchens, which has hardly helped your case.'

I'm not leaving this place alive.

Part of Lili had known that from the moment the cell door closed, but now the certainty wiped away her fear. It distilled everything down to Gabi.

'What's happened to them?'

Lili wasn't sure he'd answer that, but he glanced down at the photographs and back at her and used his response as a threat.

'The men are dead. The women have been sent to camps they won't survive. Their children have been renamed and rehomed. Who they were and what they attempted to do has been wiped away.'

Wiped away.

Lili wanted to weep for Freya, a woman who'd charmed and infuriated her in equal measure. She wanted to weep for the children whose lives had been ruined by their parents' ambition. Except that was a weakness she couldn't allow. What she needed was knowledge. She drew herself together as if the others' fates were nothing to do with her and went on the attack.

'You have the conspirators. You've foiled the plot and saved the Führer. It appears that you've wrapped this whole business up, so – if you're as sure of my involvement as you say you are, if you're so certain I was the one who would, so to speak, pull the trigger – why aren't I already in a camp too? Why am I still alive?'

He smiled at her as if she was a toy he was about to grow bored with. She hated him for it.

'Another good question. Plenty would prefer that you weren't. But others have questions: they don't fully understand your motives yet, and they don't like loose ends. The arrests for smuggling which von Krailling helped you to quash weren't the first time suspicion has fallen on the Edel. And yours was quite the starting point, don't you think? Who switches overnight from loyal hostess to murderer?'

He paused, but Lili wasn't about to help him, so he shrugged and continued. 'We suspect there were other steps on the way. And other people involved in whatever schemes you've been hiding in your cellars. So you're alive because you're going to give us the details of those. Or the next person we pull in here will be your daughter, who will not be a candidate for rehoming.'

Lili's heart sank for a second, but only a second. She had what she wanted. She'd heard the slight pause before *or*. She'd seen his eyes flicker. They didn't have Gabi – Lili was certain of it. Only two people knew where she was, after all, and one of them was already dead.

André took that secret to the grave and so will I. But I'll give them something else to remember.

'Are my staff safe?'

The question took the SS man by surprise; his answer didn't surprise Lili.

'They're alive, if that's what you're asking. But that won't continue, not in the places they've been sent. The Edel is already under new management.'

That her staff had been held to account for her mistakes was even harder to hear than what had happened to her fellow conspirators. The Edel's staff were her family. Their suffering burned her soul. But the news was also a release – it left her with nothing else to lose or protect.

Lili took her time. She made sure he heard everything she had to say without leaving room for confusion.

'Then I have nothing to tell you about my hotel.'

She shook her head as he started to speak, and the gesture stunned him so much, he let her carry on talking.

'It doesn't matter what you threaten me with, I won't reveal the games we played with you there. But I will tell you why I wanted Hitler dead, and why I was prepared to risk my life to do it.'

Now it was her turn to pause, to watch as he blinked and suddenly looked wary.

'I'm Jewish. My birth name is Lili Krauss. My father was an elder at the Leipzig synagogue.'

The shock on his face was so perfect Lili laughed, and the sound – which was so out of place and so dangerous – danced through her ears like magic.

'That's what you can take to your bosses who don't like loose ends. Those men who thought I was their friend? They're idiots. You can tell them that too, right after you explain how Lili Rodenberg – the woman whose hand Hitler kissed, who Goebbels and Göring made eyes at – was not only Jewish, she was hiding under their noses all along. And making a fool of them all.'

She wasn't taken back to the Ordenspalais. She didn't get to wear velvet and fur. But she did get a second interview with Goebbels.

'Stand up properly – show some respect.'

Lili did her best to uncurl and straighten her shoulders, although she was through with any more pretence of respect. It wasn't easy to get her body to co-operate. Her interrogation had stopped as soon as she'd declared who she was; she'd been returned to her cell and left alone there again for hours. But when the SS man came back, his instructions for dealing with her didn't include more questions. Lili's back and legs were badly bruised from that encounter. She assumed from the pain and the way it was bent that her right arm was broken. She'd left two teeth on the floor of the cell, and one eye was so bloodied, it would only half open. She was sick and dizzy with the punishment they'd doled out, but she'd retained enough vision to see Goebbels' disgust. He entered the detention room as if he'd been asked to walk through a sewer.

'Lili Rodenberg, a Jew. Well that revelation was certainly a surprise, I'll grant you that much.'

He looked her up and down, but he kept his distance.

'And you're right about one thing: you played us for fools, although perhaps not as cleverly as you think.'

His sneer as Lili frowned, and then cried out as her battered skin protested at the movement, twisted her stomach.

'*He always ushered you into the room first.* Do you honestly think I fell for that? Flattery is my weapon; I've never trusted anyone who tries to wield it against me. Oh, you silly girl. You thought you were above suspicion, didn't you? Pretty women always do. Well you were wrong. We already had our doubts about von Krailling – he was another one who was too quick to act the toady – and then in you waltzed, tricked out like a show-girl and oh so eager to *celebrate* the Führer. You handed us the last piece on a platter.'

Lili wanted to shout, 'That's not true. We nearly had you; we nearly won.' It would have been a waste of breath, and she had little enough of that. She shifted her weight onto her less crippled leg instead and glared back at him.

'I don't care that the plot failed. There'll be another one. And I don't care that you caught me. You've hidden your beloved leader behind your smokescreens for too long. Now everyone will see him for who he truly is: a weak old man who can be fooled by a woman, by one of the Jews you're all supposed to have the skills to *sniff out*. Who was almost killed by the people he's done everything he can to break.'

She heaved to a stop, her bruised chest exhausted by the effort of such a long speech. She waited for another blow or a volley of curses. For proof of how much damage she'd inflicted. Instead, Goebbels laughed, and her knees gave way.

'Dear Lord, you really are deluded. Would you like to explain to me exactly how that's going to happen? Who's going to tell this oh so unbelievable story? The *people* you denied you were one of for years? Your little Jewish friends? Will they pop up from their hiding places and start cheering for dear brave Lili?'

One of the soldiers aimed a kick at her back and barked at her to get up.

Goebbels waved him away. 'Leave her be. She'll be easier to shoot if she's already lying down. Because that's what's going to happen next, make no mistake about that.'

He came a step or two closer and leaned over so that Lili could see his face.

'You are nothing. Your so-called people are nothing. And the way this story will be told? That's not yours to dictate – that pleasure is mine. I've already written it. It's a wonderful piece, a poem to your loyalty. It will be published in every newspaper within hours of your body being dumped outside your precious hotel. And it's what everyone will read and remember. Lili Rodenberg, the Führer's dearest friend, murdered by a group of fanatics who we've pledged to hunt down and destroy. No bombs, no plots; no plucky Jewish heroine inspiring revolts in her name. Just a fool.'

It took her a moment or two, and the pain searing through her broken body almost blinded her, but Lili pulled herself back onto her feet. She wasn't going to die on the floor.

'You're wrong.'

He laughed again, but she kept on talking. She was going to keep on talking until they made her stop.

'History won't be yours. You're going to lose this war. Then the truth will come out, and the people you've silenced will find their voices and speak. They know me. They will remember me for the woman I was. A woman who almost destroyed you.'

She saw his nod. She heard the soft slide of a gun slipping out of its holster. She sensed the arm raise. She didn't want to die, but she wasn't afraid. They could print whatever lies they liked. Aaron and Alice and the others she'd helped might survive. Perhaps one day Marius would come back and take care of her memory. She hoped he would, and that he'd remember the advice he'd given her about the Stiefels and know where to find Gabi.

Gabi.

Her name was a light in the dark room. Gabi was safe. Once Lili was dead and that death was efficiently explained, nobody would waste their time looking for her daughter. And once the Stiefels read Goebbels' lies, they'd hide her well away. Nothing else mattered but that.

And one day these men will be gone and the world will come right.

Hope surged through Lili with all the joy of flowers opening their petals on a sunny morning.

One day the world would come right. And Gabi – who'd never known anything but love – would remember.

CHAPTER 25

MAY 1991

'Everything we've uncovered is in here, sir. I'll be on hand for the rest of the day if you have questions.'

Marius gestured for the private detective – the latest in a long line of men who were increasingly far younger than him – to drop the slim beige folder onto his desk. There was only one question to ask, and it was the same one he asked every time.

'Do you really think it could be her?'

His heart skipped a beat when the detective nodded.

'Yes, sir, I do. The dates and what we could discover about Gabi Wendl fit with the few details we had. And as for the advert asking for information about you? I think it's exactly what it seems: a straightforward request. The Edel's been bought by the Compton Hotels chain – I've included those details too – so there's no purpose to be had from a money-making scam. We think this one is genuine.'

Marius – as he still thought of himself, although neither Marius nor Rodenberg had ever been his public name in America – thanked the man for his work and let him go. Then he sat staring at the folder for the best part of an hour, exactly as he'd sat staring at the advertisement which had triggered its preparation in March, trying to summon up the courage to look inside.

We think this one is genuine.

He'd been waiting to hear those words through fifty years filled with dead ends or alleyways where conmen eager to prey on the vulnerable lurked. He hadn't fallen victim to them, but he'd stopped expecting good news a long time ago. Now that good news had potentially come, and Marius was paralysed.

I could be one turn of a page away from my daughter. Who I thought was dead. Who most probably believes I'm dead and might have been told the same kind of lies about me that were told about Lili.

His heart stopped skipping and began fluttering at a speed that would have horrified his doctor.

The few details we had. Few was a generous way to describe the black hole his daughter had fallen into. Marius took a deep breath and closed his eyes, looking for the image that calmed him, smiling when it came. Lili in her blue dress, with her hair curling over her shoulder. Standing at the top of the Edel's stairs with her arms stretched out to greet him. His Lili. Not the twisted version of her he'd been greeted with when he'd finally stumbled his way out of Russia.

Stop. Don't chase that one. She was never real.

Marius blinked himself back and shook the gathering shadows away. He couldn't live without his dreams of Lili, but he hated the way one memory came too often hand in hand with the other. He couldn't manage darkness today.

My Lili wasn't who they made her into. My Lili was brave and beautiful and fearless, and she was betrayed.

He repeated the words until his racing pulse calmed. It didn't matter that years of searching for the truth about his wife had got swamped in the mire of the Goebbels eulogy, or that no one had ever been able to shine a light on what *betrayal* could mean. Years of searching had done very little to uncover the truth about his broken family, although Marius had never resented the holes the effort had dug in his ample pockets. But now?

He got up from his desk and poured himself a large whisky from the decanter his doctor wanted banned. Then he took the folder over to his armchair by the window, where the view over Central Park's treetops always lifted his spirits, and opened it with an exaggerated care that suddenly made him feel foolish. If Gabi really was alive, there couldn't be anything worse in the folder than the despair he'd been living with.

'Thank you.'

The room was empty, but he lifted his glass in a toast anyway. Some moments needed that kind of a pause. Because this time it might not be pain that was waiting; it might be his daughter – and his hotel.

The first item inside the folder was a brochure. Marius held that up to the light and studied the photograph on the cover. It was definitely the Edel, but – and he wanted to say *thank you* again – not as he'd last seen her. That memory came back so sharp, the image in front of him wobbled and turned battered and grey. On that awful day in 1950 – when he'd found his way home after years of fearing he'd never see home again, only to be escorted away as if he was the trespasser – the Edel had looked as lost as he was. What was in front of him now was the old friend he'd gone looking for, newly restored and made beautiful for what the headline said was her upcoming relaunch in July.

It's as if the war never happened.

Whoever had taken charge of the restoration project had done a wonderful job. The exterior was pristine. The old metal flower boxes under the windows had been straightened and polished and bloomed in a riot of pansies Lili would have loved. The steps leading up to what looked like the original front door had been retiled with deep-red squares which made the stairway look like a carpet. The door itself still had the engraved fanlight in place. And as for the interior...

Marius gazed at the artist's impression of how the finished foyer would look and couldn't stop smiling. The drab lino and brown paint which had smothered the hotel and horrified him had been stripped away, and all the touches which had given the Edel her pre-war elegance were back. Black and white floor tiles and a teardrop chandelier. A palette rich with jewel colours and cream. Pageboys in silver and plum. All that was missing from the scene was a sketch of Lili in place at the bottom of the renovated double staircase, waiting to greet her new guests.

Whoever's done this has done it with love.

The comfort in that was better than medicine. It spurred him on through the folder.

A report about the hotel's chequered history which he scanned through came next. There was nothing about the war or the years before it that he didn't already know, but the rest helped fill in some of the gaps he'd been unable to plug. The hotel had been transferred into government hands after 1945, which explained its drab state in 1950. After the division of the city into East and West, it had become a venue for use by politicians and their guests and a watching point for the Stasi. The photographs of that period were cheerless.

Marius put those aside and turned to the details of the Edel's purchase by Charlie Compton. That was a name he knew well. Nobody who'd worked in the hotel industry as long as Marius – who'd continued to sit on the boards of the Waldorf Astoria and Hilton Hotels after he'd retired – had could afford to ignore Charlie Compton and the waves he was making. Although this wasn't how Marius had expected the two of them to overlap. And he couldn't shake the irritation of *he pipped me to the post*. The Edel had reappeared from behind the Iron

Curtain, and Marius had missed its return. That was a bitter pill to swallow.

I'm getting too slow for this game. I'm not half as up to speed with the world's turns as I pretend to be.

His doctor would have sighed at that and told him to stop expecting that he could keep charging about at full throttle at the age of eighty-one. Marius knew that was a reasonable response – everybody else in his peer group took the generous board salaries they were given but played no active part in business anymore. Marius wasn't ready for that step, for the slow death of the golf course; he wasn't sure he ever would be. He'd lost too much of his life to accept being old.

'Are you all right, sir? You called out – is something wrong?'

He didn't know he'd done that. He couldn't understand why his secretary was standing in the doorway with her brow all furrowed and her hand to her throat. Until he looked down at the folder again.

'I'm fine. It's nothing; I'm fine.'

He waved her away as he stared at the photograph. There would be questions enough later. This moment had to be just her and him.

It's not nothing. It's anything but. It's my daughter.

The face staring back at his couldn't be anyone but Gabi. She was older, of course she was – she'd been a child when he'd last seen her. How old, and how tired she looked, was a shock and suggested that she'd lived a harder life than he'd wanted for her. But the eyes were Lili's and the mouth was his mother's. And the whole of her was Gabi.

'Where have you been? Why could I never find you?'

Marius had been asking that with no luck for fifty years. He'd asked it in Berlin and in Hamburg. He'd carried on asking it when he'd arrived in New York, remade as plain Mark Roden, having left the rest of his name behind in the immigration offices on Ellis Island in a determined effort to remake himself and fit in. Marius had come to his new world promising himself a fresh start. He'd achieved that. He'd achieved more success than he'd imagined was possible when the ship he'd boarded in tears in Hamburg had sailed up the Ambrose Channel and under the Statue of Liberty. Only a handful of people who he paid to know had ever been party to who he'd once been. From the moment Marius stepped onto dry land, he'd become a shining example of the great American dream.

And that dream was a hollow one, despite all its glitter. Until now.

Gabi was alive. She still lived in Berlin. She'd been hidden from him behind the Iron Curtain too, but Marius wasn't going to be left behind in the slow lane this time. Nothing mattered more now than being reunited with his daughter.

Or with meeting you.

Seeing the photograph of Gabi had made Marius cry out. Seeing the photograph of Adam made him cry. A grandson. His dreams had never dared carry him that far – a daughter would have been more than enough. But now there was another face stamped through with Lili's. Another link to the hope of a family he'd long given up on. And, to his shock and delight, someone else who knew the Edel. Adam, he read, was a key player in the restoration team, an unexpected piece of information which made Marius's expanding heart glow.

He might have had more luck with its history than me. He might know what really happened to his grandmother.

The publicity brochure had included Lili's name, and his, in the list of past owners but no more than that. It hadn't repeated the Goebbels slur, which was hardly a surprise, but it had hinted at more stories to come. That suggested that someone, possibly Adam, had also been digging.

Marius checked his watch. It was 12.30 p.m. in New York which meant that it was 6.30 p.m. in Berlin. He didn't want to waste time on an exchange of letters via the address on the advert. He was a fit and healthy man, and a wealthy one, but he couldn't turn back the clock, and he couldn't buy himself more years. He checked through the notes again, looking for phone numbers. There was nothing listed for Gabi. There was a number for Adam's architects' firm, but it was out of hours and Marius didn't want to wait. The frustration of even a day's delay itched across his skin as he flicked through the folder. And then he found it. A contact name and number for the Edel Hotel on the bottom of the publicity brochure.

Marius stopped worrying about *after hours*. Charlie Compton was known to be a hard taskmaster – so close to a launch date, this Lucy Stretton would very likely be still hard at work. She might not be family, but she was a starting point. He went back to his desk and reached for the phone, then paused as the sunlight glanced off the wedding band he'd never removed.

These carry our vows; these join us.

He'd lost them all. His wife, his daughter, his home. He'd been adrift from the people and the place he'd loved more than he could ever love anyone or anywhere else for more than half his life. He wore the pain of that as permanently as he wore his wedding ring.

But now there's a way to cure the longing. Now there's a way back. If Gabi will have me.

He couldn't dwell on *if Gabi will have me,* or it would paralyse him. The thought that his daughter might have given up on him, or have been so lied to that she'd stopped loving him, was too frightening to contemplate.

Don't let this go wrong; I don't have the years left to rebuild a failure.

Marius picked up the handset and – perhaps it was the warmth of the sunshine or the shiver of a breeze – but he felt her. Lili was there with him, her hand holding his. He hung on to that as he dialled.

* * *

Lucy wandered through the silent dining room, checking and rechecking every detail against the plan she'd drawn up for the evening. Only three tables would actually be in use for the night's dinner, and they were all positioned together in the centre of the room, but she'd asked for the rest to be dressed with the new linen and silverware anyway. As far as she could see – and Lucy was nothing if not eagle-eyed – the waiting staff had followed her instructions to the letter. She'd carve out time to tell them how well they'd done before service began.

We're starting to build a new family here.

Building the right team was always the highlight of any hotel opening, but building the right one for the Edel was special. Lucy had crafted those adverts with care, and she'd pored over the applications as if they were treasure maps. Now the key positions were filled and what mattered next was the atmosphere, and the food. She turned down the dimmer switches so that the chandeliers cast an even warmer glow. The maître d' would light the candles – including the ones on the unused tables – a few moments before the guests arrived at seven thirty. There were still finishing touches needed in the upper floors, but the dining room was magnificent. The cream linen tablecloths hung in starched folds. The emerald-and-amethyst napkins blended beautifully with the flowered silk brocade covering the walls. The glasses had been so highly polished, they were almost invisible. The stage was beautifully set, although Lucy couldn't help but think there was something missing. Not that she had time to work that out now, when there was a chef with his reputation at stake to keep steady.

'What is a *soft menu launch*? I've never heard of such a thing; I've never been asked to cater for one before. Normally the first night of a hotel opening is the first night for the restaurant, and I should have weeks yet to get ready.'

He was a little temperamental and a little grand in his manner, but he was worth every penny. And he was finally on board. When Lucy had explained that the evening was a show-case designed to put the Edel's name on the lips of the critics who could make or break her reputation as a fine dining establishment – that he was, in fact, the hotel's first ambassador – he'd almost bitten her hand off. She would still visit the kitchens again before the canapés came out, to make sure he was smiling.

She glanced over at the menu cards which were handwritten in silver on lilac and placed in a holder at each setting. French onion soup with golden cheese croutons. Seafood fettucine stuffed with salmon and prawns and served in an aniseed sauce. A Death by Chocolate seven-layer mousse and meringue cake with three kinds of chocolate ice cream on the side. If that didn't stop conversations and make the guests fall in love with the Edel, Lucy doubted anything would. She'd sampled all the courses at lunchtime and was still in something of a food haze.

'There you are.'

Adam was in the doorway, grinning at her and holding a huge tissue-wrapped bouquet of flowers. He gave a low whistle as he took in the silver slip dress she'd bought specially for the occasion.

'You look like a movie star. And this looks like a film set. Congratulations, Lucy, you've done the hotel proud. But – and don't take this the wrong way – I thought you'd be a lot more stressed than this. How on earth are you so calm?'

Lucy laughed. She could hardly blame his confusion. Getting the Edel in shape to face journalists in advance of the official opening had turned the last few weeks into an even bigger whirlwind than it had been since Adam's team stripped off the first layer of brown paint. She'd been living on adrenaline and too little sleep. Until this morning, she'd been a knot of nerves. She wasn't a knot of nerves now.

'Everything is as ready as I can make it. Once the guests come in, it's Chef's show, not mine. Besides...'

She stopped as she realised what he was holding. 'Are those lilies?'

Adam nodded and uncovered the top of the bouquet so she could properly see the pink-and -white petals.

'I know we've hit a bit of an impasse with Lili's story, but I've been thinking about what you said – that we might never be able to tie up the loose ends. I didn't want that to get in the way of what's been a wonderful discovery, and I wanted her here with us tonight, so the flowers seemed fitting. Is that okay? I haven't messed up your colour scheme, have I?'

Lucy shook her head, which was suddenly buzzing. 'It's more than okay; it's perfect. I want her here too. Give me a minute and I'll get one of the girls to put them in the ceramic vases I've had cleaned up and put in the foyer. And thank you – you've just solved a problem that's been niggling at me all week.' She shook her head as he asked what that was. 'It's nothing for tonight. But there is something I want to tell you before we get swamped. Wait here.'

She ran into the foyer with the flowers and thrust them at the newly hired receptionist who'd come in on trial for the night. When she came back, Adam was standing beside the window, adjusting the drape on the newly hung velvet curtains and looking as comfortable as if he'd been overseeing the Edel his whole life.

Was this what it was like for them? Did Lili stand here watching Marius as they readied the hotel for dinners and parties? Did she feel this same glow?

She had to shake herself back as Adam turned: the years had started to tumble around her.

'Come over here – there's something I want to show you.'

She shut the door so they wouldn't be disturbed and beckoned him over to the bar where she'd left her paperwork and her bag, drawing an envelope out of that as she waited.

'You were right when you came in. I do feel calm – no, I feel a whole lot better than calm, but I don't have a word big enough to describe it. Look what came this morning.'

He could read her so well, he'd already guessed what she was holding. His eyes lit up; he broke into a smile. Lucy's heart flipped at the love shining from his face, and flipped again as she opened the envelope and took out the photograph.

'It's Emily. Isn't she beautiful?'

Adam took her hand as they leaned against the bar, their heads almost touching as they stared at the picture of a young girl proudly showing off what was clearly a brand-new school uniform.

'She's lovely. God, she looks so much like you. I could have picked her out as yours anywhere.'

Yours ran through her body like honey. Lucy laughed. She felt like she'd been laughing all day.

'I know. This could have been me on my first day at secondary school, half earnest and half excited, and completely engulfed by my blazer. There's a report too, telling me how well she's been doing and that she's got a flair for languages and likes drawing and is as mad about horses as I was. And also...'

Lucy couldn't continue. Not because she didn't want to tell Adam the other part of her news, but because it was hard to do something as simple as speak when she was bubbling over and couldn't stop grinning.

Adam was almost on his toes with excitement too. 'And also what? Come on, Lucy, spill. I've never seen you this happy before – let me share it.'

She wanted to share Emily with him more than anything. The promise of family had been around her all day as she'd welcomed the new staff to the Edel. She wanted a new version of that for herself too.

'Emily knows about me, and she's happy I've been in contact.' Her heart swelled as Adam, in a very un-Adam-like gesture, shouted *yes* and punched the air. 'And she wants me to write to her, which is against the terms of the adoption, but the agency don't care because her parents have given it the go-ahead.'

There was more to say, about how loving Emily's family seemed to be and how they wanted to include her, but Lucy was tripping over her words too much to explain anything else. She was also caught in a cycle of laughing and crying and laughing again when Adam grabbed a handful of napkins from behind the bar to stop her mascara cascading and knocked a bowl of matches flying.

'The new sommelier will murder you for messing up his counter top – he's fearsome.' She smiled as he began scooping the matches up in a pretend panic. 'It's the best news. And I don't know what will happen after that. Whether she'll write back, or whether she'll want to meet me. Emily has to set the timetable, and I'm not going to push it. But she's not lost to me, Adam. She's not lost.'

Lucy was suddenly off her feet and in his arms and not caring about the state of her make-up or her hair, even though the evening's clock was ticking. They were both so wrapped up in her news, neither of them heard the ballroom door open.

'Miss Stretton?'

Lucy jumped away from Adam as if she'd been scalded as the receptionist walked in. Being caught in tears and mussed up and in a very definitely unprofessional embrace with the hotel's chief architect wasn't the image she wanted her new team to have of her.

'There's a phone call at reception for you – I believe it's a personal matter.'

The girl ignored Lucy's embarrassment. She carried on talking as if nothing she'd seen was out of the ordinary, and

Lucy made a mental note that she had instantly passed her trial period.

'I did say you were busy with an event and didn't want interruptions, like you told me to do earlier. But the gentleman was most insistent that he speak to you now. He's calling from America, and his name – which he said you would recognise – is Marius Rodenberg.'

CHAPTER 26

JUNE 1991

Marius and his daughter might have been strangers to each other, but they shared one common trait: they were both impossibly stubborn.

'There's no need for anyone to meet me at the airport – I don't require a fuss. My secretary has arranged a car and a driver to bring me to the hotel. It makes sense for everyone to meet there together, rather than to do this reunion piecemeal.'

He'd rebuffed every other offer Lucy had made – including arranging accommodation for his stay in Berlin as the Edel wasn't yet ready for guests – with the same curt response: 'My secretary has it in hand.' In the end, she'd given up trying, although she'd smiled as best as she could when Adam insisted that his grandfather was definite rather than rude and that was presumably because he was accustomed to staff running his life. In private, she didn't agree with those sentiments at all.

Lucy had found Marius overbearing and bordering on difficult from their first conversation, which had been overly focused on how he wanted events to move forward. All Adam had heard when she'd passed him the phone was that his grandfather was alive and making plans to come and meet him. He'd spent the rest of the night floating on the news. So Lucy kept her thoughts about Marius to herself.

The same couldn't be said for Gabi.

'Of course it's wonderful that he survived the war and saw the advert and wants to reconnect with me. My father's alive – of course I'm delighted.'

Her tone had made a lie of the words. From the moment Adam had told his mother about Marius's phone call, she'd been a ball of anger again.

Adam had almost called Gabi that same night; he'd wanted to, but there wasn't the room for such a complicated conversation before the journalists arrived. Instead, he'd brought her to the Edel the next morning, by which time he and Lucy had had a chance to absorb the news and to recover from the dinner which – despite the shockwave they'd both been riding – had been a tremendous success. They'd sat Gabi down together and told her Marius wasn't missing anymore. They'd given her the business profile of Mark Roden which Charlie had faxed over, describing Marius's heady ascent through the American hospitality industry and how well respected he was there. Gabi had read that without comment then pushed it away.

'He changed his name – well that tells you a lot. And he's terribly wealthy, which tells you a lot too.'

When Adam had asked her what she meant by that, Gabi's thinly held temper had snapped.

'He left Germany, so he clearly wasn't interested in the Edel or me. And a new name must surely mean that he didn't want to be found. When did he go to America – in 1951? That was years after the war, so where had he been till then, and why didn't he come looking for me before he sailed off to pastures new? Or since then, given how much money he's presumably got to spend on a search. He didn't care when he left, and he doesn't care now. There's no mention in this article of me or my mother; it's all about his brilliant business successes in America.

Well good luck to him, and good luck to them. He might as well have been dead all along for all the use he's been here.'

Discovering Marius had been alive all along had plunged Gabi back into the worst days of her childhood. And – as it'd done when she learned that her mother's past hadn't been a danger to her – the news that he had made a success of his life while she grieved over her loneliness dredged up more pain and distress than the poor woman could bear.

They'd tried to soften her fury. They'd tried to find a better story for Marius's long absence than the abandonment which was all Gabi could hear. They pointed out how chaotic the whole of Europe had been at the end of the war and for years afterwards, never mind just Berlin. They pointed out all the problems the Iron Curtain had caused and reminded her that Marius could have been searching without success for years for all any of them knew. They cared for her far too much to ask, 'Did you never think of looking for him yourself before the Wall went up?' In the end, Gabi grew so upset she made herself ill enough to need a doctor then a hospital bed. Neither Lucy nor Adam dared mention Marius's name again after that. Which had worked for the few days it took for Gabi to calm down.

Except now he's on a plane and in a few hours he'll be here.

Lucy fiddled with a flower arrangement that didn't need fiddling with. The ceramic vases she'd uncovered in the basement and had restored were filled with peonies, not lilies this time. Greeting Marius with a display of lilies had felt rather blunt. But – if she refused to get into the car with Adam and come to the hotel – greeting him without Gabi would be worse.

What will I say to him if she's not here? He's no fool – he'll read the rejection in her absence.

Lucy stood with her back to the door as if she was barricading it, staring up at the staircase for inspiration. Marius hadn't stepped inside the Edel for fifty years; he hadn't seen his daughter for as long. She didn't know if his brusque phone

manner and his determination to control what happened when
he arrived in Berlin was due to arrogance or fear.

Give me some help here. Give me some clues.

She shut her eyes, trying to conjure up Lili as she'd
conjured her up so many times before, trying to place her at the
centre of the hotel with Marius at her side. Willing the Edel to
whisper its secrets.

*You knew me when I first came – I felt it. So help me now:
tell me how to handle him.*

There was nothing but silence. There was nobody there.

It was fear, ruling them both.

'I've got her here – under duress and by convincing her she
was meeting him for my sake – but there's no guarantees she'll
stay.'

Gabi arrived at the Edel with the softness she'd been
wearing since Christmas stripped away. Her pursed mouth and
puckered forehead and her – presumably deliberately chosen
and definitely unseasonal – black dress contrasted so sharply
with the delicate lemon-and-pistachio palette in the Edel's tea
room, Lucy immediately suggested changing the setting.

Gabi refused to move. 'This will do perfectly well. He used
to bring me in here when I was little for ice cream. Let's see if
he remembers.'

'If she's determined to make every inch of this into a test, it's
going to be a disaster.'

Lucy pulled Adam to one side as he started to prowl. 'We
can't control how they react to each other, so there's no point in
trying. And I know how hard she looks, and sounds, but just
think how many times her world's been turned upside down
and rewritten. She's terrified. Have you seen the state of her
hands?'

Adam stopped pacing as he followed Lucy's nod. Gabi's

fingers were so tightly laced, her knuckles stood out like ice chips, and one of her legs was shaking.

'You do that too – the leg thing when you're nervous. And you can help her through this if anyone can.' Lucy dropped a quick kiss on his cheek and pushed him away. 'Go and sit with her and keep her calm. I'll wait for your grandfather in the foyer.'

'Miss Stretton, this is—'

'Good afternoon.'

Lucy didn't get the chance to welcome him. Marius had been serious about not wanting a fuss. He was already standing in the doorway, waving away the receptionist who'd been attempting to introduce him.

They could be doubles, the past version meeting the present.

Adam and Marius were rooted to the spot, staring at each other. Their tall slim build was identical. They shared the same eyes and jaw, and the same fall of hair across their foreheads, even if one of those falls was now silver not chocolate.

Neither man spoke. Marius took a step forward; so did Adam. For one wonderful moment, Lucy thought they were about to hug each other and set a happy note for the rest of the meeting. Instead, there was a cough and a handshake and two men unable to say, 'It's you, oh thank God.'

'Father?'

Gabi's voice was a whisper, but it turned Marius's head. And there was the fear, written across a face that instantly drained of colour as she turned away again.

He's terrified she's going to reject him. She's terrified that's all she can do.

Gabi looked as if she was ready to bolt.

'Why don't we all sit down and get everyone comfortable?'

Somebody had to hold the situation together, so Lucy switched straight into professional mode. Ushering Marius to the table where Gabi was poised on the edge of her chair.

Nodding to Adam to put a hand on his mother's arm to hold her in place. Gesturing to the receptionist to chase up the afternoon tea she'd ordered in the hopes of diverting the awkward start she'd expected. By the time that was done, nobody was comfortable, but Marius had himself under control.

'The Edel's renovation is remarkable. You've re-found her beauty. Do I have you to thank for that, Miss Stretton?'

He was talking to her, nodding when she insisted on Lucy, but his eyes never left Gabi. And he'd picked a subject which was safe ground.

'*Marius isn't me. He's been taught to smooth things over, wait problems out. He'd never dive in like I did.*'

The comment Lili had made about Marius in her journal was a perfect fit. Lucy realised she knew how to handle him after all: slowly, sticking to neutral topics until he felt safe enough to open up.

They really are doubles.

'Me and your grandson whose firm did all the heavy lifting.' She nodded to Adam. 'It's been a labour of love for us both. And I'm glad you're happy with the work we've done. We did a lot of research into the hotel's past to get the details right.'

His reaction to *research* was instant. His control slipped; he was suddenly carrying all of his years.

'Why did Goebbels say all those terrible things about her? What did my Lili do to deserve such lies?'

The question caught the three of them off guard. Marius hadn't mentioned Lili once during his brief calls, and neither Adam nor Lucy had known how to bring the subject up. Lucy glanced over at Gabi, hoping *terrible* might act as a bridge between her and her father. But Gabi had shrunk inside herself and wouldn't look at him, never mind offer an answer.

'We don't know. But we think it may have been some kind of revenge.'

Lucy found her breath again as Adam stepped in. She sat as

quietly as Marius while Adam described the journal and ran through a summary of everything they'd discovered, and everything they hadn't. When he finished, Marius nodded as if the pieces were finally falling into place.

'I remember when she met Aaron. I begged her not to get involved with his rescue network – the danger was too great. She promised she wouldn't, but...'

Marius shook his head, and so much love suddenly flooded his face, Lucy found herself reaching for Adam.

'She made that promise for me. She wouldn't have wanted me going to war and worrying about her. But I always knew she couldn't look away forever – her heart was too big for that. Nothing you've told me about the smuggling and the spying is a surprise if I'm honest, although the bomb? That's a shock. My Lili was the gentlest woman in the world, the last person I'd cast as a murderer.'

He nodded as Adam repeated what he'd said about what might have changed once the first line was crossed.

'That makes a kind of sense. And what you think Goebbels did makes sense too – he'd spin black to white to protect his beloved Führer.'

Marius suddenly took a deep breath. 'I can't thank you both enough for what you've done to rescue her good name. And I know how many threads of this can never be found, but there's one thing I...'

His certainty fell away. He stumbled, as if he was lost. As if asking the next question would rip out his soul. Lucy wanted to cry at how broken he sounded when he finally managed to speak.

'Do you know where she is, Adam? Do you know what they did with her?'

Gabi stiffened. It was a question she'd never asked. Her eyes locked on to her father, but he didn't notice – he was pinning all his hopes on Adam.

'I'm really sorry, but I don't. And so much of Berlin's been lost in the last fifty years, I doubt we ever will. There's no records of a funeral or a burial – we've looked – and no one who was at the hotel when she died has come forward. We doubt any of them survived the '44 round up.'

Adam glanced at Lucy, who knew how hard saying the next part would be. She nodded and squeezed his hand. He continued.

'But it's very probable that – if Goebbels decided to keep up with the myth that Lili was a loyal Party member – she was buried at Invalidenfriedhof. That's the graveyard where the Nazi's supporters and senior figures, including Heydrich, were interred. But there's no point in trying to find her there now – the place is a mess. The markers were removed from the Third Reich graves in 1945, at least a third of the cemetery was destroyed to make way for the Wall and the rest was allowed to fall into disrepair. If that's where she was buried, there's no way of knowing or proving it.'

Marius blinked and looked away, his eyes roaming the tea room as if he might find her sitting there instead. 'Maybe that's not a bad thing. I couldn't bear the thought of her lying in the same ground as them.'

He found a handkerchief and wiped his eyes. Then, in a gesture which was so natural he must have been doing it for years, he raised his hand to his lips and kissed the gold band on his wedding finger.

Gabi reacted as if lightning had hit her. 'The forget-me-not ring. You're still wearing it.'

The hunger on Marius's face as he turned to his child was so raw, Lucy had to look away.

'I've never taken it off. I've never remarried. As far as I'm concerned, my Lili is still my wife.'

'Where have you been all these years?'

Gabi bit her lip and shrank back again as Marius reacted to

her cry and reached for her hand. He flinched as if she'd hit him.

'And why didn't you look for me?'

Her voice was as raw as his face.

Now it was Marius's turn to shrink away. For his eyes to fill. For his mouth to open but stay empty. Lucy grabbed a water glass and pushed it towards him. She was about to suggest a break, a drink, a tour of the hotel; anything that would stop the two of them tearing each other's hearts out. She didn't get the chance. Marius found his voice before she could speak.

'But I did.' His voice dropped. 'You must have been told I was missing? You must have supposed that meant dead?'

His eyes slid away from Gabi's tortured face as she nodded.

'I might as well have been. I survived Stalingrad, but I was one of the last men to come back. I spent seven years locked away in Russian prison camps.' He waved away Adam's 'Dear God' and carried on. 'I won't talk about that – it's enough to say that I stopped imagining any kind of life beyond being a slave. I thought we'd been forgotten by the rest of the world, which is easier to say than to live through. Then one day in March 1950 – out of the blue – our captors said, "You're going home," and we did.'

'Why did they keep you so long?'

Marius closed his eyes briefly at Gabi's question and swallowed hard. 'I don't know. The Russian economy was in tatters at the end of the war – or so I was told later – so perhaps they kept us as a cheap source of labour. We didn't get paid, we barely got fed and we worked fourteen hours a day, often more, so there's a logic to that. All I know is that I couldn't get home; I didn't think I ever would. But when I did? You have to believe that searching for you was my everything.'

He stopped and waited. When Gabi said nothing in reply, Marius's shoulders slumped.

She's still stuck inside the child who thought she'd been

abandoned. She won't give him an inch; she doesn't know how. But if she doesn't hear him out, they'll both stay broken for good.

'What did you do when you got back to Berlin? Did you come here, to the hotel?'

Lucy's intervention worked on Marius as effectively as *tell me* had worked on Adam. He grabbed on to her prompt so gratefully, she almost forgot which man she was helping and took hold of his hand.

'Yes, the Edel was the first place I came. I raced here. But that was a shock in itself – I barely recognised the city, all the great palaces were gone, so much of it was a wasteland. And as for the Edel...' He shook his head. 'The state she was in – gutted and cold, and nobody knowing who Lili was, or you, Gabi. Nobody recognising my name. I couldn't make head nor tail of what had happened, and nobody could be bothered to explain, so I panicked and got angry, which was a huge mistake. You have to remember that I'd been cut off from almost all news since the start of 1943. Berlin was a mystery to me – I didn't know it was still occupied. I'd heard that Germany had spilt into two countries, but I didn't know what that meant. And when the hotel manager rang for help and Russian soldiers came... When they told me I could be sent back to a gulag...'

'Surely not? For simply trying to find your family? That would've been barbaric.'

Marius's face was as white as Adam's as he relived the worst moments of his return.

'They were deadly serious. I was hauled off to a cell for causing a disturbance. Then some Russian colonel appeared who was as fearsome as any I'd encountered in the prison camps. "You don't seem to have learned any of the lessons we tried to teach you while you were our guest, Herr Rodenberg. You still seem rather enamoured of Nazis." Those were his first words to me. Then he showed me a file on Lili with the Goebbels article in it and threatened to send me to Siberia as a

Nazi sympathiser when I threatened to kill him for spouting lies.'

This time, Marius accepted the glass of water Lucy pressed on him and drained it before he continued.

'I talked my way out of that somehow, and then asked about you...' He looked over at Gabi, but her face was a blank. 'I started to say that I thought you might have been placed with friends during the war for safekeeping. I almost mentioned the Stiefels, but I stopped myself – I was afraid he'd track them down as Nazi sympathisers too. So I tried a more general enquiry, but he wouldn't listen. He told me to forget about you. He said if you'd survived, you'd have been placed with a Russian family for re-education. And then he ordered me out of East Berlin or I'd be arrested...'

Lucy caught Marius again as his words fell away. 'So the Edel was a dead end, but I know you kept searching. Where did you go next?'

He turned to her then and kept her in his sight as he pushed on through his story.

'To Lichterfelde first, to the old family home in case Gabi was there, but that was a bombed ruin. Then to Potsdam. To find the friends who I thought Lili might have sent Gabi to if she'd known she was in danger.'

'The Stiefels. You tried to find them?'

The sudden hope in Gabi's voice pulled Marius round to face her.

'Yes, I combed the whole city for them, but there was no sign, and no welcome for a stranger asking questions. A Soviet patrol started following me, and I didn't know if you were alive or dead, or how much danger I might put you in by trying to find you...' There were tears on his cheeks now, but he made no attempt to dry them. 'I was exhausted and afraid, and I couldn't continue on my own, so I went to Hamburg, to my parents' home. But that was empty, because...'

'*A tornado of flames hit the city, a firestorm that melted the streets.*'

Lucy shuddered as she remembered the entry from Lili's journal. 'You don't have to explain – we know.'

Marius nodded, caught his breath, found a way to go on.

'I think I went a little mad then. The neighbours who found me and rallied round told me later I'd lost a week to ravings about Russia and loss they couldn't understand. But when I was finally better, in body at least?' He turned away from Lucy to finally face Gabi. 'I started the search for you again, I swear, but it was hopeless – the Red Cross and the other agencies who I went to for help were swamped with people like me and were powerless to help. Europe was full of lost children and split families. And when I mentioned that the Stiefels might have you but they were in the DDR, everyone warned me to stop before I got the whole family arrested.'

How many lives have been ruined by Germany being ripped in two? How much fear has soaked through it?

Lucy glanced at Adam, who was staring at his mother and grandfather with tears in his eyes. She slipped her hand into his as Marius carried on.

'I was broken, Gabi; I can't pretend that I wasn't. I sold my parents' house and went to America because I couldn't live like a ghost in my own life. I changed my name because every time I said Rodenberg, all I could hear were the spaces. But I tried to find you, I swear. I used all my resources to keep looking for you once I got myself established. I started search after search that ended in the same answers: she's alive in the DDR and you'll do more harm than good if you try to dig there, or she's dead and all trace is lost.' He paused as if he was weighing up every word that came next and was terrified that they'd fail him. 'The hole in my heart where you lived has never healed. But it could, if you'll only believe that I didn't abandon you, that I never could, and let it.'

Abandon brought Gabi's head up and wiped all the hard lines from her face. Her eyes finally met her father's.

She's wanted this from the moment he walked in. She turned herself into stone for fear she wouldn't get it.

Lucy held on to Adam as Gabi stared at her father and whispered, 'I believe you – I do.'

'We should go. We should leave them to mend this on their own.'

Adam nodded and got to his feet as Lucy whispered into his ear. They slipped away from the table without being noticed. When they stopped in the doorway and looked back, Gabi was crying and laughing and holding out her hands, and Marius was doing the same.

You were here all along, not silent but waiting. You've worked your magic on them.

Lucy held Adam back from closing the door for a moment. She wanted one last glimpse of Gabi and Marius sitting in the tea room where they'd once been so happy, finding that happiness again. And she wanted to feel what every sense was telling her. That Lili – the spirit of the Edel – was sitting there beside them too.

CHAPTER 27

JULY 1991

'You have a wonderful heart, Lucy Stretton, and you've breathed life back into the Edel. I want to talk to you about that.'

Lucy no longer found Marius overbearing; she found him a delight. As did Gabi now she'd brought her walls down. Once Marius had decided to extend his stay indefinitely, father and daughter had become inseparable. And – although the path wasn't always a smooth one as they adjusted their two very different lives to make room for each other – they'd forged a bond nothing, including illness, could break. Marius had already arranged appointments for Gabi with a leading cardiologist in Germany, and with another in America if it was needed. Gabi had dug her heels in at first, insisting that paying for medical care was immoral. Marius's 'I didn't find you to lose you' had quickly ended that argument.

Marius was as kind and caring as his grandson, but – as Lucy had now discovered – he wasn't used to hearing the word *no*. Not that Lucy had tried very hard to say it.

But I haven't said yes to him either.

She stood on the balcony, making sure that the curtains

covering Marius's surprise were properly drawn. The foyer below her had been polished and polished again so that every surface shone. The Edel was quiet now, but that wouldn't last long. In another two hours, the opening party would start. Tomorrow, the first guests would arrive. Lucy doubted the Edel would ever be quiet again.

Which is exactly how it should be.

She'd spent the last hour wandering from room to room, not touching or changing anything, simply admiring the beauty they'd brought back. There was nothing left to do. The champagne was on ice. The flower arrangements were suitably lavish. The canapés were, in Chef's words – which Lucy, having sampled the menu, completely agreed with – little morsels of heaven. And, best of all, Lili was everywhere.

Adam's bouquet on the night of the journalists' dinner had signposted the final touch Lucy had been looking for, and the Edel now had a new motif. There were lilies embroidered on the gauzy drapes which edged the curtains, their petals drawing the garden into the dining room. The same flowers ran in streamers and circles across the table linen and the menus and the hotel's stationery. Their scent filled the fragrance bottles lined up in the bathrooms. Marius's eyes had shone when she'd walked him round the final touches.

'You said to me the first time we spoke that I was the missing thread which held everything together, but you were wrong. That was always you, Lucy. You sparked the hotel back to life. You found the real Lili, and you brought us all together. And this is where you're meant to be. With us, with Adam. With the Edel.'

Everything Marius had said to her was true. But Lucy had a missing thread of her own. When she'd told Marius about Emily, he'd had an answer for that too.

'But that's even better – that's what the Edel needs. More family. More love at its centre.'

Lucy touched the envelope in her pocket; it contained the letter which – after more drafts than she would admit to – was finally ready for posting. A letter she'd filled with herself but also with the hotel that had changed her life. A place she hoped Emily would one day grow to love as much as she did.

Why am I keeping him waiting? Why am I pretending I don't know my answer?

Marius was in his old suite, although he insisted that he would vacate that the moment she accepted his offer because the suite was included in that too. Lucy gazed round her. The Edel had never been just a job. She didn't want to move on from it, and she didn't want to move on from Adam, which was a conversation they'd both been refusing to have. The Rodenbergs and their legacy had become part of her.

They've become home.

She checked her watch. She had time; she'd deliberately left time. She blew a kiss to the Edel, whose magic kept growing, and walked on up the stairs to find Marius.

'Is everyone ready?'

The opening party was already in full swing below them. Guests swirled round the foyer as colourful and as noisy as a flock of tropical birds. Glasses clinked; laughter rose. When Lucy rested her hand on the banister, she swore she could feel a pulse beating through it.

She mouthed a *yes* to Adam, who instantly hung himself rather dangerously over the balcony calling for everyone to charge their glasses and look up. It took a few moments for the hubbub to quieten, for the guests to notice the curtained shape behind him on the wall. Adam smiled as he gestured to it and to Gabi, who had given in and let Lucy take her shopping and was now totally transformed.

'As some of you now know, restoring the Edel has also

become a rediscovery of family. My mother lived here as a child, my grandfather Marius – the older version of me standing next to her – is the son of the man who built this glorious hotel back in 1905.' He waited for the applause to die down. 'But there's somebody missing who shouldn't be. My grandmother Lili, who was the heart of the Edel and a heroine. And a woman whose story is yet to be properly told.' He smiled at Gabi, who turned as pink as her new brocaded frock. 'I believe that my mother plans to take pen to paper to rectify that very soon, but in the meantime, we give you Lili Rodenberg. Back at the centre of the Edel, where she belongs.'

Gabi pulled the cords, and the velvet curtains fell away. The crowd gasped as the painting they'd covered was revealed. As Lili stood there smiling down on them in her sapphire-blue dress and Marius's hands flew to his heart. It took longer for the applause to die down this time. It didn't stop until – precisely as Lucy had planned it – the ballroom doors flew open and the band started to play.

'She's perfect, thank you.'

Lucy smiled as Marius stared up at the portrait which she'd commissioned from a photograph and managed to hide from him. And smiled again as he asked, 'Can I?'

'Can you what?' Adam had caught the look which passed between his grandfather and Lucy. 'What are you two cooking up?'

'Me staying here. Not moving on.'

Adam looked at her blankly, and then his face cracked into a grin which made Marius laugh.

'And she really does mean here. I've bought the hotel back from Charlie Compton, and Lucy has agreed to take care of it for me. The Edel – unless I've got something very wrong here – is back with family again.'

Adam stared at his grandfather as if he'd just given him

thirty years of Christmas presents and managed to croak out, 'You're not wrong; you're not wrong at all.'

'You don't mind then?'

Now it was Marius and Gabi slipping away and Lucy and Adam left alone with each other.

'Mind? It's all I want. *You're* all I want.'

His arms were round her, pulling her close. And the last thing Lucy saw before she closed her eyes and kissed him was Lili.

Looking down on them both. Smiling as if to say, 'Now it's you.'

A LETTER FROM CATHERINE

Dear Reader,

I want to say a huge thank you for choosing to read *The Secret Hotel in Berlin*. If you did enjoy it, and want to keep up to date with all my latest releases, just sign up at the following link. Your email address will never be shared, and you can unsubscribe at any time – and you'll get a free short story download, *The Last Casualty*, as a thank you!

www.bookouture.com/catherine-hokin

I have always loved the glamour of a grand hotel. When I was very little, my father was a sommelier, and one of the earliest pictures taken of me was at a children's party in the hotel where he was working. I remember being enraptured by the tiny jars of jam; I'm still a fan of those to this day. And according to the family stories, I was also enamoured by the Italian waiters there, who taught me some very questionable names to call my poor dad.

Pre-war Berlin had some of the most glamorous hotels in Europe, most of which were built around the turn of the twentieth century. The Excelsior, which stood opposite the now ruined Anhalter Bahnhof, was one of the biggest hotels in the world and had an underground tunnel linking it directly to the station for its most privacy-loving guests. The Kaiserhof on Wilhelmstraße was one of Hitler's favourites and was where

Herman Göring celebrated his elaborate 1935 wedding to the actress Emmy Sonnemann. But the most famous of all was the Adlon. The original (which I drew on for my fictional Edel) stood on the Unter den Linden and was an even more glamorous prospect in its heyday than the one which occupies the site today. It was also a hotbed of scandal and intrigue, including a thwarted bomb attempt during the wedding of the Kaiser's daughter Viktoria Luise in 1913 which was attended by all the crowned heads of Europe. If that had exploded, the change to the twentieth century's timeline is unimaginable.

None of these hotels are still standing now. The Excelsior and the Kaiserhof were destroyed in the war. The Adlon survived that but was then largely, and accidentally, burned down by a group of Soviet soldiers looting the wine cellars. The Edel, of course, never existed at all, although I wish that it did, and you may have met it before in *The German Child*, where it appears in its full glory in the 1940s and in its more dilapidated state in 1980. I chose to use it again as a backdrop to Lili's story, because there is nowhere like a hotel when it comes to keeping secrets. They really are places where different worlds can exist.

If you've read this, I would love to hear from you, especially if you have great hotel stories to share! There are lots of ways that you can get in touch – through my social media or my website.

Thank you again.

Best wishes,

Catherine

KEEP IN TOUCH WITH CATHERINE

www.catherinehokin.com

 facebook.com/Cathokin

 instagram.com/cathokinauthor

 x.com/catherineh66267

ACKNOWLEDGEMENTS

As always, so many books went into the writing of this one, but there are some specific sources I would like to acknowledge and recommend if you want to know more about the subjects that I've covered in *The Secret Hotel in Berlin*.

For Berlin's pre-war hotels and the hotel business, *The Lost Café Schindler* by Meriel Schindler, *The Hiltons* by J. Randy Taraborrelli and *Hotel Adlon* by Hedda Adlon, which somebody really needs to translate from the German because it's such a great read! For Stalingrad, *After Stalingrad* by Adelbert Holl and *Blood Red Snow* by Günter K. Koschorrek. For the politics, attitudes and personalities of the time, *Holocaust* by Peter Longerich and *Hitler* by Ian Kershaw. For the DDR, *Red Love* by Maxim Leo, *After the Berlin Wall* by Christopher Hilton, *Beyond the Wall* by Katja Hoyer and *The Tunnels* by Greg Mitchell. I would also highly recommend the German TV series *Das Adlon. Eine Familiensaga* which is historically all over the place but excellent fun.

And now to the thanks which are always heartfelt. To my wonderful editor Jayne Osborne for doing such an excellent job in editing my novels and supporting my work. To the Bookouture team who are detailed in the following pages and all deserve my thanks – the number of people involved in getting a book out into the world never ceases to astonish, and humble, me. To my friends, writers and not, who help me keep a sense of perspective and sometimes, maybe, even read the books. To

Robert, who listens to all the ideas which live in our house and still manages to read the books with enthusiasm. And to Claire and Daniel for all their cheerleading. Much love to you all.

PUBLISHING TEAM

Turning a manuscript into a book requires the efforts of many people. The publishing team at Bookouture would like to acknowledge everyone who contributed to this publication.

Audio
Alba Proko
Sinead O'Connor
Melissa Tran

Commercial
Lauren Morrissette
Hannah Richmond
Imogen Allport

Cover design
Eileen Carey

Data and analysis
Mark Alder
Mohamed Bussuri

Editorial
Jayne Osborne
Imogen Allport

Printed in Great Britain
by Amazon